RETURN OF EVE

Daphne Paige

EMILIA OF THE
SOLSTICE REALM

Published by Popcorn Publishing in the United States of America

Popcorn Publishing

To twelve-year-old me, who knew this story needed to be written and had the determination to do just that. Look at how far we've come.

RETURN OF EVE

Magical Definitions from the *History of Magic*

The Veiling: A curse that turns someone inhumane and Dark

Unnatural: A species that's not human

Aridam: The cursed Sword of Death

Eve: The Sword of Life

The Solstice Realm: A realm of allied kingdoms

The Banished Realm: A realm for the banished Unnaturals

Runespeaker: A mage who creates runes with magical properties

Soul Sight: An ability that allows someone to decipher the truth

Prologue

Aaron resembles nothing of his former self. His eyes, the windows to the soul, so I've heard, are dark with promises of pain. With every footstep of his boots, my pulse hitches. The sunlight filtering through the windows on either side of the ballroom reflects off the iron of his chest plate, polished to a mirror-like gleam. His usually disheveled hair is hidden underneath a matching helmet.

An infernal scratching resounds about the room as the delicate tip of Aridam's blade slides across the veined marble floor.

I watch him through the tears in my eyes, the point of a dagger flush against my throat. Tight fingers from two of his guards are looped around my wrists. My knees ache from when his guards forced me to the ground and the gentle tulle of my gown is tangled around my feet. I'm sure it's torn and dirty. I couldn't care less about my gown when my father is kneeling in front of me, head bowed in defeat. My father doesn't bow to anyone. After all, he's the king. So why is he bowing to Aaron? Surely, my father isn't afraid of Aridam. Surely, he doesn't believe the tales about Aridam, the cursed Sword of Death.

Aaron stops, and for a second, his gaze flicks toward mine. He swallows and his mouth thins into a line. A wisp of sandy brown hair slips from underneath his helmet, painting a shadow across his forehead. His eyes, the color of perfectly toasted pastries, make my heart break. I didn't think he could break it anymore; I didn't think there was a single intact piece left, not when I can feel the broken shards in the hollow of my chest.

My father mumbles, dipping his head even lower. His graying brown hair tumbles around his hunched shoulders. I don't want to see him like this. I want to see him as the king of Glaven, the man sitting on the throne with his shoulders squared and his chin held high. I want to see that confident smile he always flashes to visiting royalty. I don't want to see him so...*weak*. Kneeling before a distraught baker's son. Before a man claimed by the Veiling.

"We could have been happy, Em," Aaron whispers. His voice sounds like autumn leaves scraping the ground. Deep, pleading, and resigned to the winter that's soon to follow. His eyes flicker to mine, holding them for a long while. Finally, I realize he's waiting for me to respond. My tongue feels dry and heavy, knowing that what I say will be his verdict. I need to watch my words when he's holding a sword so close to my father. "I asked you for your hand once, and you said yes. Is that still your answer now?"

His gaze is unflinching. Unfortunately, mine's not. I look down at my tangled gown, the pink tulle rippling with shadows and sunlight. I beg my voice to behave. When I look back up, my face is stern. I will not let him see me cry. "Yes. Of course, it is."

He doesn't say anything, watching me, searching for *something*. A lie. He can always tell when I'm lying, even though he doesn't have Soul Sight—the gift I possess that allows me to see the truth in words and situations.

His shoulders relax and he straightens his posture ever-so-slightly. His fingers loosen around the spider-web thin hilt of Aridam. The sword appears as fragile as spun sugar, but if the tales are true, it's anything but. As soon as his eyes move from me, I relax. I didn't realize how tense his gaze made me, but I welcome the relief as soon as it is gone. He tilts his face down to my father, who glances up at him with eyes the color of ice. "And you? Do you give me your blessing?"

Fear wells in my chest, threatening to burst through my skin. My father denied him once, I beg

3

that he doesn't deny him again. Not when we both know what Aaron will do.

My father's voice is cracked, seeming to have aged decades in mere hours. "Aaron Baker. You're a good boy, somewhere deep down. Your father doesn't seem like the type to raise someone so evil." His tongue flickers across his dry lips. His shoulders drop even more. "But you know my answer. My daughter is not going to be doomed to live beside a man of weak nature. You can't even battle the Veiling that's spreading through you, Aaron. I don't know why it began, but you will not turn Emilia Dark too."

I'm tense in the guards' grips, unwavering. Almost as if my heart has stopped. My brilliant father, ruler of the grandest kingdom in all the realms, should've known better than to utter those words to a man clearly on the brink of losing himself.

A muscle in Aaron's jaw twitches. With a smooth flick of his wrist, Aridam's beautiful blade is arching through the air and slicing through my father's neck. Blood spatters across the white marble, splotching my gown with little crimson dots. I can feel his blood freckling my cheeks.

The sound of flesh tearing, of muscles severing, burrows into my ears. Replaying again and again, right beside the throat-ravaging sound of my scream. My father's head tumbles to the ground and rolls a few feet, his pale face staring straight at me.

Tears blur my vision, which I'm thankful for. I can't meet his glassy eyes, not when they're absent of everything that made him *him*.

Aaron sighs. "He should've said yes." I pinch my eyes shut, refusing to look at him. Tears waterfall down my cheeks and drip onto my gown, mixing with the vibrant stains of my father's blood.

Glass breaks nearby, at least, that's what it sounds like. Pain flares from the front of my thigh and something stings my cheek. I force my eyes open, just enough to discover what's causing the fire to spread through my body. A shard embeds itself in my thigh, red spreading quickly around it. I can see my reflection in it. A bloody cut across my cheek, my icy blue eyes clouded over with sorrow, and my dark brown hair matted around my shoulders.

I realize a second later what it is... *Aridam.* Aaron broke the forlorn Sword of Death. If the tales are true, then he's doomed my kingdom.

"Bring her back to the carriage. It's time we went home. And someone, keep an eye on Adriene." Aaron spins on his heel, his boots clicking on the marble.

The guards force me to my feet, ignoring my grunts and refusals. The point of the dagger falters for a second as something spins across the floor, into view. A breeze murmurs by, carrying words spoken by only one person I know. The Runespeaker. *Sky.*

A relieved smile finds its way to my face. He's going to save me from Aaron.

The guard to my left unclasps his hand from my wrist and steps forward, head cocked as he studies the faint blue stone engraved with an ancient rune. White fog creeps from the etched rune, a design of equal curves and sharp lines. The fog kisses my skin with welcoming warmth, and my eyelids start to slide closed, but the guard stomps down on the stone, chipping the surface. I can feel a panicked tug through the magic, but it's too late, I'm falling into the white void, letting it completely envelop me.

Everything is warm.

Chapter One

I spin the last dial on my locker and pull it open once I hear the satisfying click. The inside of the door is pasted with cut-outs from comics and art from my favorite movies, quotes written in cursive and taped underneath specific scenes. I have a lot of Lord of the Rings screenshots covering the blue interior. A stack of fantasy novels makes the thin upper shelf dip. I pull the first one out and slip it into my well-worn jean backpack, slinging it over one shoulder. I rummage under a pile of magazines, all containing photographs of models posed in elegant gowns. Half of them are from wedding boutiques. If someone opened my locker and took all this in, they'd assume I'm a die-hard fantasy nerd, counting down the days until I walk down the aisle in some frilly dress. Only half of that is true. I don't care about weddings or marriage, nor do I care much about dating. I like to look at the dresses, the intricate swirls of ivory fabric, and the drapes of white tulle and rose-gold embroidery. I don't have the confidence to wear something so extravagant, but I like to imagine myself in these elaborate gowns anyway.

With a dreamy sigh, I close the door of my locker, slamming it into place since that's the only way these stupid things lock. I jump back a step, hand flying to grip the strap of my backpack. "Samantha? You scared the heebie-jeebies out of me."

Samantha, my best friend since I walked into the doors of Roosevelt High, grins. Her smile is wide and unrestrained, completely *her*, and completely beautiful. Her bottom row of teeth are in braces, the metal gleaming against her pearly whites. Yellow, orange, and white bands are wrapped around the brackets.

"Candy corn?" I ask, one eyebrow raised and a laugh ready to part my lips. Samantha always has a theme for the color of the bands that go around her brackets. Since it's the beginning of our senior year in high school, and Halloween is right around the corner, it's no surprise she chose her favorite sweet.

She winks, falling into step beside me as the hall fills with the bodies of our peers. The fluorescent lights that dangle from short chains reflect off the linoleum floor.

"Who do you have now?" Samantha asks, wedging between Kevin Ross and his girlfriend,

Victoria. Victoria groans as Samantha's backpack smacks her in the midriff. It's not our fault she's scarily tall; 6'2 compared to Samantha's 5'4.

We hurry from the senior hall and finally take a breath of unobstructed air when we reach the English hall. Thankfully, I got released from my first period early so I could gather my books from my locker while the rest of the zoo animals waited in their classes to be dismissed. I'm shorter than Samantha, coming in at a scowl-worthy 5'0, so my entire high school experience is just getting shoved about by anyone taller. Which is everyone.

"Burningman. AP Literature in History," I answer, pulling the folded-up piece of paper with my class schedule from my jeans pocket. I unfold it and check the number of the class with the doors we're passing.

"Oh, that sounds like fun." Samantha runs her fingers through her sun-bleached blonde hair, smoothing her high ponytail. "I have Journalism with Brooks."

We stop in front of Burningman's, room B03, and she pulls me into a hug. She smells of cinnamon, apple cider, and something musky I can't quite place. "I'll catch you after. Lunch in the art room?"

I smile at her. "Sounds like a plan."

I don't watch her leave, returning my focus to the door in front of me. I take a steadying breath just as the first bell chimes, and push open the door, stepping into a room that smells of freshly printed paper and ink.

Burningman's room is just like any other, but also, in a way I can't quite pinpoint, it's not.

I slide into a seat at the very back of the room. The black, rectangular tables have six chairs, lined up in two rows in front of the teacher's desk and the wall-length whiteboard. A stack of textbooks rests in the center of each table.

People start to file into the room and a squirmy anxiety builds in my stomach. By the look of my classmates, none of them are like me. They're all cheerleaders, theatre kids, jocks, and members of the student council. Everyone and anyone who thinks they're better than me and acts like it too.

The chairs at my table are the last ones touched, but when the bell rings and two skyscraper-tall teens shuffle into the room, lips slightly swollen and hair ruffled, they're forced to pull out the chairs in front of me and take a seat.

Victoria and Kevin. Who would've thought they'd end up in an AP class? I certainly didn't.

Victoria pushes a wad of gum around in her mouth with her tongue and starts to chew obnoxiously loud, green eyes transfixed on me and a near-permanent snarl twisting her lips. I tug nervously on the hem of my sky-blue blouse, face flushing.

I want to sigh in relief as soon as Mr. Burningman, a middle-aged man with a pair of black-rimmed glasses resting low on his nose, starts to speak, drawing Victoria's attention away from me. I sit up a bit straighter in my seat, trying in vain to pay attention to what he's saying, but the fear of being the target of high-collar Victoria Johnson makes me feel ill.

"Oh…" Victoria drawls, crimson lips pouting. She reaches across the table and plucks the first textbook from the stack, fiery orange hair cascading down her shoulders when she leans forward to read the content guide.

Kevin does the same, so I figure I should as well. I grab a book and flip to the page listing out the chapters, not exactly sure what to do now.

"I think we should go with this one. We better choose something fun if we're going to have to study it for the next two weeks, don't you think?" Victoria says, pointing to something in her book. Kevin leans toward her and nods in agreement. Their eyes flick up to me. She scoots her book across the table, French manicured nail tapping a single sentence.

Chapter 17: History of Magic.

I raise an eyebrow. "What about it?" I ask hesitantly.

Victoria rolls her eyes, drawing her book back. "Didn't you hear a single word Mr. Burningham said?"

"It's Burning*man*," I correct automatically. My face flushes when her eyes narrow in disdain. "What about him?"

"We have to select a chapter to research and present for our first project," she explains, sounding out each word like I'm a child. She flips to chapter seventeen in her book and scans the sections. "You can take sections three and four. Kevin, you take sections five and six. I'll do the first two. Sound good?"

Protest rises on my tongue, but I swallow it down. If I'm going to survive this, I better remain compliant. "Fine." I flip to section three in my book and start to read. None of it makes sense, and I have half a mind to accuse the author of making words up. Something flickers in the back of my mind, fragments of dreams and faces. I furrow my brow and draw the book into my lap, head bent to study it, to hide my quizzical face from Victoria's dagger-like gaze.

Runespeak…

Adriene…

The Veiling…

Realms knitted in the fragile seam of the universe and tucked out of view of Earthlings.

12

A headache looms behind my eyes, throbbing and pulsating until the dull pain blossoms into something feral. I rest my forehead against the edge of the table and close my eyes. This is the worst time for another one of my debilitating headaches.

Faces blur the inside of my eyelids. A man with soft brown eyes and wind-swept hair has his hands in the pocket of his apron, the front of which is spattered with flour. Red seeps from the edges of the image, and suddenly I'm staring straight up at the same man. Though, this time he's wearing armor. Like a knight from long-ago tales. Darkness takes over, pulling me into an uneasy embrace. When light pushes away the shadows, I'm watching the knight step toward an old man kneeling on the floor. The knight raises a sword that glitters with sunlight and sweeps it through the air.

Flesh cuts, sinews tear, blood pools across marble...

I yelp and jump from my chair, sending it falling backward on the floor. My hand is over my mouth in an instant, and tears are pricking at the corners of my eyes. It's always the same vision clouding my mind, but that doesn't mean I'm always prepared for the knight's reappearance.

My classmates are staring at me, mouths open and eyebrows raised nervously. Chuckles float around the room, which soon snowballs into unrestrained laughter. Heat creeps up my neck.

Victoria throws her head back and cackles. "I'm glad we got a front-row seat for this," she says to Kevin, turning her sneer on me. "Seriously, why are you so lost in your head? It's like you're living in a completely different world."

I don't want to admit that her words sting. It *is* like I'm living in a completely different world. Though there's nothing I can do about it. I bite my lip to stop it from trembling and grab my backpack from the floor. I dart from the classroom, unable to be the center of everyone's attention any longer. Especially not when they're laughing at me. Mr. Burningman's calls follow me out into the hallway, but there's no way I'm going back in there.

By the time I make it down the hall and turn the corner, tears are cascading down my cheeks and moistening the front of my sweater. I feel stupid and embarrassed, and I have no idea what I saw. What is the significance of the knight? Who is the old man? And why do I keep getting these headaches and these strange visions? Why can't I just fit in?

The only thing I do know is that I can't show my face in there again. I push open the bathroom door and collapse on the floor, back against the wall and my face buried in my arms. Heavy sobs wrack my body. I cry until I can't anymore. Until my throat is ravaged and raw, and my eyes are puffy and red. I sit there, waiting for class to be over, running through ideas of how I'm going to make it through the rest of the year when I've already ruined my life on the first day.

"Hey," a gentle voice whispers, and suddenly a warm hand is brushing my arm. I reel back, eyes wide. I didn't hear anyone come in.

The worst part is…it's a *boy*.

The boy is squatting in front of me, his black hair is cut in a choppy manner, scraping the edge of his jaw. His bright blue eyes are the color of the ocean surrounding tropical islands, and a vertical scar runs from right above his left eye to the corner of his mouth. It's faded, leaving it a pale white against his fair skin.

I wipe my sleeve underneath my nose, trying to pull myself together even the slightest. "What are you doing in the girls' bathroom?" I ask timidly.

The boy's lips twist in a humored smile. "I should ask you what you're doing in the *boys'* bathroom."

My eyes trail across the door and land on the section in front of the stalls…*urinals*. My face drains of color.

"It's fine. Fortunately, I was the only one in here." He straightens back up and offers me his hand. I take it and he pulls me to my feet. He stands a good foot taller than me, leaving my eyes level with his chest.

I glance up at him sheepishly. "Thanks. Sorry I, uh, intruded on your…private…time…" I stutter.

He stoops down to grab my backpack. "I was just wasting time until school ended."

"You were skipping?" I ask quietly like the words alone would summon the attention of the principal.

His eyes sparkle with humor. "I'm not one for school. So, if skipping is such a horrific act, then why were you hiding out in the bathroom when you should've been in class?" He holds open the bathroom door for me and we slip into the hall.

Luckily, it's empty, save for Kennedy Barman, who gives us a conspiratorial look as he walks by. I blush and the boy behind me chuckles lightly.

"I…can't go back to class," I mutter in response, deciding it's best that I don't embarrass myself further.

The boy walks beside me down the empty hall. Our footsteps pair with the sound of the clock ticking. I notice that he doesn't have a backpack on, which is odd considering where he's at.

"So, what're you going to do now? You still have an hour before class lets out. Were you going to hide in the bathroom all that time?"

I bite my cheek. I didn't think about that. Another headache throbs behind my eyes and I shake my head somberly. "I think I'm just going to go home."

"Do you have a car?" he asks. His gait is casual and confident as if nothing in the world can hurt him, though there's a tension in his shoulders that begs to differ. I look up at him, trying to read him. He's an open book written in a language I don't understand.

"I don't even have a license," I admit.

He raises an eyebrow questioningly.

"The tests don't like me, okay?" I add further, tugging on the sleeve of my sweater.

He tilts his head to the side, considering something. "You want a ride home? I was just going to ditch anyway."

"Are you…sure?" I ask.

"Yeah, of course."

I wait for the alarm bells to go off, my conscience telling me that I shouldn't follow this strange boy to his car. But they don't. I've never taken a risk in my life, always following rules and attempting to stay off everyone's radar. I take a deep breath and nod, following him around the corner and toward the doors leading to the student parking lot. "Thanks, that's really nice of you."

He pushes open the glass doors leading outside. The autumn chill bites at my cheeks and the tip of my nose. The boy walks breezily to his car, a black

89' Mustang. The cuffs of his long-sleeved shirt are rolled up and his boots clip on the pavement. He pulls a key from his pocket and unlocks the passenger side door, holding it open for me as I climb inside. He sets my backpack by my feet and walks around to the other side, unlocking his door and sliding into the car.

A stone on a coiled rope dangles from his rearview mirror. It has a smooth, dim blue surface with an intricate carving swirled into its face. I reach a hand out and lift it the tiniest bit so I can see the sunlight reflect off the carving. The boy beside me stills, tension roiling in the air until my hand drops from the stone.

I give him a kind smile. "It's beautiful. What does the carving mean?" I ask. The dull headache rears its head, and a single thought skips to the forefront of my mind. *I should know…*

"Nothing really," he says a bit too fast. He regains his composure and shrugs his shoulder in a light-hearted manner. "Luck and all that." I can tell that there's more he's not saying.

"I think I've seen something like this before. Of course, the carving was a bit different. More jagged lines and swirls, and the blue was brighter." I watch the stone sway gently. I turn, feeling his eyes on me. "Where'd you get it?"

He draws back, brow lowered over his eyes,

shoulders tensed. His scar appears deeper from this angle, creased with ever-darkening shadows. "I made it."

"Oh," I say into the unease. I purse my lips, not knowing what else to say. Maybe I've seen his work in one of the shops downtown, or around school, or…something. None of those answers seem right.

After another moment of stillness, his hand slides up the steering wheel and he twists the key in the ignition, bringing the engine to a purr.

"Where do you live?" he asks, though his voice is gruffer than before, more distant, it hasn't lost its charm.

"Pine Avenue, 1782. The house with the blue trim and the gnomes in the front yard," I say, pointing toward a street that branches off from the main one that swerves from the school to the neighboring suburbs. He turns the wheel and dry leaves crunch under the tires. As soon as my house comes into view, he pulls toward the curb and parks in front of the yard. I could've easily walked home, knowing it would've taken me only ten minutes. But for some reason, his offer for a ride was compelling enough to accept. Doesn't hurt to save time *and* energy.

My house isn't much: a small, one-story suburban home with white paneling and light blue trim. The door is a toasty brown and an autumn-colored wreath hangs in the center. The beige curtains in my living room window shift and fall back into place. I narrow my eyes, wondering if it's my mom that's spying. I don't think anyone else is home, so it must be her.

The boy reaches over and unbuckles my seatbelt, and I note that he never bothered to put his on. He climbs out of his car and walks around to my side before I'm able to open the door myself. He opens the door to the cold. I hug my arms around myself and step onto the street, reaching down to pick up my backpack. When I straighten back up, he's staring at me with an intensity that makes my skin tingle.

"What's your name?" he asks.

I look to my front door and back to him, finger-nails digging into the strap of my backpack. "Why?"

He digs around in the pocket of his jeans for a moment, producing a crinkled flyer to Victoria Johnson's End of Summer Party. She uses any excuse for a party. "Are you going to this?"

I take the flyer from his outstretched hand and smooth the creases. It states the usual: date, time, and address, but the attire part catches me off guard. *Swimwear*? Who goes swimming when it's this cold outside? I scrunch my face. "This kind of thing isn't really for me."

"It's not my cup of tea, either." He smirks,

taking a step closer to me. "But I'd go if I had worthwhile company." He draws out the last word, chuckling as my face goes from powder pink to rose.

"It's tonight," I say, biting my cheek.

"Yeah, and?"

"A school night," I continue.

"I never intended on going to school tomorrow, anyway," the boy says plainly as if his skipping was as obvious as the sun in the sky.

"But I do." I stuff the flyer in my front pocket and step past him. I turn around when I reach the start of my driveway and sigh. "My name is Emilia. What do I call you?"

His eyes widen, twinkling a breathtaking sapphire. "A friend," he says confidently, pulling open the door to his Mustang, leaving more questions behind him than answers. I watch him with a slack jaw and narrowed eyes as he disappears into the encroaching autumn fog, the sound of his tires crunching brittle leaves and the gentle purr of his car fading as he does.

The door behind me opens and my mom's voice calls out to me. "Emilia, darling, what are you doing standing outside in the cold? Get in here."

I turn around and plaster a smile on my face, the headache pounding now.

My mom, Sandy, is bundled in a cream sweater,

her bleach-blonde hair piled in a messy bun, and her brown eyes are filled with concern. Sandy isn't my birth mom. But she's loved me like part of her family ever since she took me in. I don't remember exactly how long ago it was, nor do I remember anything of my life before her. All I recall is that I was found on a park bench in a tattered pink gown, covered in blood.

Chapter Two

My bedroom window is open, looking out on the winding street that leads to the high school. Cold wind makes the papers on my desk flutter and I tug the blanket around me tighter. My mom, after interrogating me about why I came home early, who I was with, and if I had anything to eat besides the oatmeal that morning, sent me to my room with direct instructions to rest and fill up on soup.

I gave my mom the same answer the boy gave me.

He's just a friend…

A friend without an identity, with nothing but his Mustang, a scar, and a smirk.

I lift the spoon to my mouth and sip the last drop of soup, setting the empty bowl on my nightstand. The clock across from me ticks, the minute hand moving closer and closer to noon. Samantha will wonder where I went when I don't show up for lunch. I sigh and lean over the side of my bed to grab my phone from my backpack. The flyer in my front pocket crinkles with my movement, so I draw it out too. I lay it out flat on my bed, pondering the boy's invitation. There's no way Mom will let me go, believing that I'm sick. But it might be nice to do something different for a change, with someone new. Samantha is my best friend, and I'd never replace her, but this boy intrigues me, and I can't help but want to know more about him.

The front door creaks open and I lower my eyebrows, listening for who it could be. Sandy isn't married, and the only other person who lives here is my brother, who should be at school. I climb off my bed and silently walk over to my door, opening it a crack so I can see down the hall and straight to the front door. The cold floor bites through my socks, sending shivers up my spine.

Ricky, Sandy's biological son, stands in front of the doorway, taking off his jacket and hanging it up on the coat rack. Sandy has donned an apron, dusted with flour, and splattered with droplets of soup. She claps her hands together, flour flying into the air and mixing with the dust motes highlighted by the sunlight drifting through the window.

"What are you doing home, Ricky?" Mom asks with her hands on her hips.

Ricky has the same blonde hair as Mom, and the same kind, brown eyes. He kicks off his boots. "I only had classes till noon today. I told you this."

Mom sighs and rubs the crease between her brows. "I forgot. Well, your sister is here. She came home sick with a boy."

I wince at the boy bit... Was that *really* necessary? Especially in that accusatory tone?

Ricky glances down the hall toward my room and I duck back, hoping he didn't see me. By the light-hearted laughter that resounds about the house, however, I'd have to say that he did.

He peeks into my room a second later, a pleasant though slightly worried smile on his face. "Hey. Feeling better, I assume."

I scowl at him, ignoring the hammering of my head as my migraine increases tenfold. I lay back down on my bed and hug my pillow to my chest, staring up at the ceiling. The bed dips as Ricky sits down next to me.

"How were your classes?" I ask. Ricky graduated a year ago, and since then, he's been taking classes on glass welding at the local community college.

He runs a hand through his neatly combed hair and shrugs. "They've been fine. A little harder than I was prepared for this year, but I'm sure I'll catch on in no time. How about you? How's your senior year of high school?"

I give him a withering look and he tries to suppress a smile.

"You're not sick, are you?" he guesses.

"Besides an incessant headache and the fact that I can't show my face in my Literature in History class, no, I'm not." I groan and force myself to sit up, leaning against my beechwood headboard.

"What happened? I doubt you could make a fool out of yourself when it comes to literature. Not with how many books you have," he glances around the room at my bookshelves lining the walls, save for the desk beneath the window and the door leading to the closet. Last time I counted, I was well past 200 physical books, not to mention my e-reader tucked into my desk drawer which houses another goldmine of books.

My expression says it all.

His face pales and he reaches toward me, taking my hand in his and rubbing his thumb across my knuckles. "They're back?"

Every so often, I'd have flashes of a beheaded man, a knight, and blood seeping across a marble floor. They come and go, seemingly with no trigger. And I don't know why or what they're about. Sometimes, though, I'm scared to fall asleep for fear that they'll return.

I hug my knees to my chest and shake my head. "I don't know why this happens to me. I wish I did so I could make it stop."

He drapes an arm around my shoulders. He

smells of fire and hot metal. "I don't know either, Em. Maybe you should take Mom up on her offer. A therapist might do you some good."

I glower at him. I have a hard enough time opening up to my brother about this, there's no way I'm going to tell a stranger about my nightmares.

He purses his lips to the side and nods knowingly. "It's okay. Either way, I'll help you feel better. I can start by getting you that hot chocolate you're always craving."

I gape at him. "But it's on the other side of town?"

"Then fingers crossed that it'll still be warm when I get back," he says, making his way to my door. He flashes me a loving smile before closing it behind him.

My attention returns to the flyer. If I do decide to go, how am I supposed to get in touch with him? Or do I just show up and trust that he'll be there too? I bite my lip and flip the paper over. Scrawled on the back in precise handwriting is a number and a name.

My eyes trace the curves and lines of his name. It sounds familiar as if it's left my lips hundreds of times before. Maybe we've run into each other at school; but even as the thought forms, it dissipates. That can't be right.

I unlock my phone with my fingerprint and find

the text message icon. I shoot a text off to Samantha, telling her that I had to go home because I wasn't feeling well. And then I create a new profile, typing in the boy's number and then his name. I couldn't imagine him being called anything else, it just seems too perfect, too *him*.

Sky.

If my entire body could blush, I'd assume it was happening right now. I lock my phone and toss it onto the bed beside me. Mom's not going to let me go, but if this is a day of new experiences, then what would be the harm in sneaking out?

I let the rebellious thought tumble around in my mind. It doesn't sound like something I'd do, which is precisely why I want to do it.

I crawl off my bed, surprised at the absence of my headache, and push open my closet door. Hanging in neat rows and stacked in neat piles are my clothes, all color-coordinated, with my shoes positioned at the bottom of a cubby. I find my stack of swimsuits and plop them on my bed, alongside closed-toed slip-ons and sandals. The most covering swimsuit I have is navy with a ring around my midriff, exposing my belly button and a sliver of skin. I find a lacy, black cover-up dress and toss it onto the bed beside my swimsuit. I partner them with a pair of rubber-soled, tan slip-ons.

It's only just past noon, which means I have five more hours to kill before Sky picks me up.

I can't suppress a grin at the thought. A boy… picking *me* up.

I dig out my e-reader from my desk and curl up with a couple of blankets on my bed, clicking into a fantasy novel I'm already 75% through. The sound of Mom busying herself in the kitchen and the gentle breeze drifting in from the window keeps my headache at bay, allowing me to feel relaxed for the first time today.

It's a little past one when Ricky returns and the soothing scent of melted chocolate and cinnamon drifts down the hall. I have about 10% of the novel left to finish, which I normally wouldn't be able to pull myself away from until I've reached *The End*. But with the sound of every footstep, the scent of Mo's classic hot chocolate intensifies. I set my e-reader down as my door opens. Ricky's smile instantly brings one to my lips as well. He holds the cup of hot chocolate in front of him like a prize, wrapped in an autumn-leaf-patterned cozy. When he's close enough, I practically snatch the cup from him, inhaling the sweet, syrupy scent. I haven't had a cup of hot chocolate in months—way too long for one of Mo's.

"There's another in the fridge," he says, ruffling my hair. When his eyes fall on the pile of clothes at the end of my bed, one of his eyebrows raises. "What's this?"

"I think you're trying to bribe me for my love," I tease, taking a sip of the drink. The hot chocolate explodes across my tastebuds. Hints of cinnamon, cardamom, and something I can never seem to name bring with them memories of the first time Ricky took me to Mo's: the Mom-and-Pop café on the west side of town. I set the cup down on a coaster on my nightstand. "I was invited to a pool party tonight."

"A pool party? It's like forty degrees out," Ricky says, flabbergasted. "Who would have a pool party now?"

I sigh. "Victoria Johnson."

His face twists with even more confusion. "Why are you going to a party *Victoria Johnson* is throwing? I thought you hated her?" He sits down on my bed, forearms draped over his thighs. He gives me one of his brotherly looks, meaning he's not leaving this room without an explanation.

"Because I was invited by…" my face pinches and I consider leaving it at just that, but I've heard about all of Ricky's girl problems, so I take a deep breath and mumble, "a boy."

His face lights up, rows of white teeth flashing in a proud grin. I've never dated anyone, nor have I ever even shown interest in boys. I know Mom was wondering if I ever would. "A boy? Is that the boy who dropped you off today?"

I nod, sinking my teeth into my lower lip. "Yeah. His name is Sky."

"And I'm assuming you like him," Ricky adds carefully, aware that he's treading on fragile ground. At any moment, I may duck back into my turtle shell and cower away from the mere mention of boys.

"I want to get to know more about him at least. I wouldn't say that I like him. I just met him," I admit, playing with a loose thread on my blanket. I glance up at him as he weighs my words. "Mom's not going to let me go to the party, is she?"

He grimaces, which I take as him agreeing. "I'll talk to her. I'm sure I can get her to let you go. As long as you're feeling up to it." His eyes flicker over to me, scanning my face for any creases of pain. "How's your headache?"

"Gone."

One corner of his mouth tilts up in a smirk and he stands from my bed. "I'll be right back."

I watch him leave. The floorboards beneath him groan from his weight. Mom and Ricky confer in weighted whispers. I wish I could hear what they are saying.

Ricky's head pops back into the room. He's grinning from cheek to cheek. "Mom said yes. So, do you need a ride?"

My heart jumps sporadically. Is this really happening? "He's going to pick me up at five."

Ricky waggles his eyebrows and I snort, tossing one of my pillows at him. It hits him square in the face and he staggers back into the hall, loud laughter following.

Chapter Three

I nervously run my hands down the front of my cover-up dress, smoothing invisible wrinkles. It's been a long time since I wore a bathing suit, and the amount of skin it shows is far outside my comfort range. I check my hair for the fifteenth time since I braided it. Twin pigtails of dark brown fall to right below my chest. I don't wear makeup, but I thought I might at least try out the water-proof mascara Mom bought for my birthday this past July.

There's a knock at the door that sends my heart into overdrive. Snails squirm in my stomach and I suddenly feel nauseous. My mom's pleasant voice fills the house as she lets Sky in. She calls back to me, "Darling, your *friend* is here." I don't miss her enunciation, and I'm sure Sky doesn't either.

I slowly make my way down the hall, eyes cast down at my feet, too afraid to look at him. I can see we had the same idea in footwear; he's wearing a pair of black, closed-toed slip-ons, matching his sweatpants.

I steal a breath of courage and let my eyes meet his. I'm surprised by the conflict in them.

"Party ends at nine," Sky tells my mom. His black hair is still untamed. Though, by how good it looks, I wonder if he styled it that way. I catch Mom studying his scar occasionally when she thinks he isn't paying attention. I want to elbow her and make her stop. I don't want Sky to feel uncomfortable, especially since the story behind his scar is probably one he doesn't like to reminisce on. "I'll drive her back so you don't have to worry about picking her up."

Mom nods appreciatively, one hand keeping the front door open and the other encased in my brother's calloused grip. She looks unsure, almost scared. But she's Sandy Macintosh, she's *never* scared. Sky steps down onto the narrow walkway branching off to the driveway. I stop in front of Mom, gently resting my hand on her arm. "Are you okay?"

Mom's eyes soften and she nods. "Just worried for my baby girl. You've never done something like this before."

"It's just a party, Mom," I say, shaking my head slightly. Why is she so worried about me going to a party? "I'll be safe."

There's something in Mom's expression that I

can't decipher. "I know you will, darling."

I bite my lip, wondering if I should say something more. What else is there to say? I step down onto the walkway, the door behind me creaking closed. Sky is leaning against the trunk of his Mustang, watching me in an overly observant manner. My cheeks swathe pink.

When I near, Sky pushes off of the trunk and opens the passenger door for me. He doesn't say anything, but in a way, he doesn't have to.

I sit down, tugging the door shut while Sky slides in the driver's side. He reaches up and fixes his mirror, his eyes lingering on the stone that dangles from it. It looks darker than before; more gray than blue, and the carving in it I have to squint to see.

The closer we get to Victoria's house, the tenser Sky seems. I can't place my finger on why… Maybe he hates large crowds just as much as me.

Victoria's house is huge compared to mine; three stories, wide windows, and small balconies with elegantly carved, black metal railing. Cars are parked all the way down the street and students from the high school are flooding the gate to get inside. I can't see a backyard from here, which makes me question where exactly everyone will be swimming.

Sky sighs as he parks behind a large, red Ford. His Mustang is practically hidden by the monstrosity. Before I can open the door and step out, he turns to me, more serious than I've seen him. I thought he was just a boy of coy jokes and laughter. His presence alone seems a lot darker now. "How'd you get that scar on your cheek?" He lifts his hand toward my face but stops mere inches away. He drops it back to his lap.

I flash him a quizzical look. "I'm not sure..." Why is he paying that close attention to notice a tiny, white scar on my cheek?

My answer seems to strike a chord. He sits back, face pinched. "Some of my friends are here too. I thought we could all hang out together."

He climbs out of the car, but I don't move. Humiliation claws at me. Why did I even *think* this could be a date? He opens my door, one eyebrow raised.

"What are you waiting for?" he asks in an off-hand tone.

I bite my cheek to stop from rolling my eyes and climb out of the car. The wind pushes stray strands of my hair over my shoulders and nips at my exposed legs. Sky walks a little in front of me, carving a path between the teenagers that clog the walkway. I'm grateful, pushing my way through a crowd is hardly effective considering my height. I'd more likely end up with a busted lip than at the destination I was trying to go.

Electric music buzzes from Victoria's mansion.

Heads bob and bodies sway in rhythm to the eccentric beats. I shove past someone whose elbow flies back and knocks me in the chest. Sky catches me before I fall, his calloused hands are sturdy on my waist and my cheeks turn the color of a tomato.

"I didn't know there'd be so many people," Sky admits, helping me back up, though his hand lingers longer on my waist than is strictly necessary. I find myself not minding, odd considering I've never shown even the slightest interest in anything romantic, let alone real-life *boys*.

"It's *Victoria Johnson's* party," I say matter-of-factly. "Of course it's full."

We find the front door through the mob of swarming bodies. Sky pushes through them, one hand reaching back and tugging on my sleeve so I don't get stuck behind.

Every square foot of Victoria's mansion is crowded. Light from a drop-down disco ball pulsates around the foyer, washing everyone in neon colors.

My skin turns blue under the light. Victoria is talking with two of her friends in the corner of the foyer, next to a vintage drink table. It looks like she's making her rounds. Hopefully, she never makes it over to us.

Sky must have the same thought because he tugs me toward a break in the crowd; a line of people all filing in the same direction, hands cupped around drinks tinkling with ice cubes. They flood toward a set of stairs leading down to the basement.

The stairs lead into a large room. The sound of water splashing and bubbling carries alongside bemused laughter and teenage attempts at flirting. A pool takes up the majority of the room, one side branching off to a hot tub. Steam rises from the water and drinks rest on the stone edging.

I follow Sky to the pool, where he removes his sweatpants, t-shirt, shoes, and sits down, legs in the water and fair skin tinted blue. I notice that he's wearing black swim trunks. I slip out of my cover-up dress, set my shoes next to his, and sit down next to him, concentrating on the ripples of the pool as people on the far side cannonball in, and not on the chill of his gaze sweeping over me. Goosebumps cover my body as I feel eyes besides his on me. I glance up from the pool to find a girl leaning against the opposite wall in a red one-piece, watching me with a pair of hazel eyes. Her blonde hair is cut in a bob and her lips are painted crimson to match her outfit. She looks familiar. I swear I've seen her before, though I don't remember where.

Sky follows my line of sight and his posture goes rigid. "That's my friend." He raises an arm and waves her over. She pushes off the wall, her heels clicking on the concrete floor. Seriously, who wears heels at a pool party?

"Sky," she drawls, slipping out of her heels and settling her legs in the water beside him. She draws her eyes away from Sky and toward me. I practically freeze under her scrutinizing gaze. "She looks practically the same."

What kind of a statement is that? Has Sky mentioned me to his friend before?

"This is *Emilia*," Sky answers, giving special emphasis on my name. As if my name is special, and not some god-forsaken attempt at bringing back the fifteenth century. It's always Emily these days, never Emilia. Sure, I like my name, but I don't like the sneers and side-eyes I get from my classmates, as if they truly believe I'm trying to be different when all I have ever wanted was to fit in. It's not like I can pick my name, though I do wonder what was going through my birth mom's head when she did.

The girl stretches her red-nailed hand out in front of Sky, hesitantly smiling at me. "I'm Kisha."

I take her hand, shivering at how cold it is. "That's an interesting name. Where's it from?"

Kisha's grip tightens ever-so-slightly. "A place far away."

Her tone is ominous. My mouth opens and closes like a gaping fish, unsure of what to say, when a boy sits down on my other side. His skin is dark and smooth, and his hair is pulled back from his face and twisted into thick dreads. His eyes are so dark they're almost black, and when he smiles at me, he reveals a set of bright teeth.

"And this is Quicken, another friend," Sky explains, gesturing to the boy. He seems a bit older than me and Sky, probably nineteen.

"And you must be Emilia," Quicken takes my hand in his and raises it to his lips, pressing a quick yet somehow polite kiss across my knuckles. "It's an honor to see you ag—" His lips thin and he swallows down whatever he was going to say. He has an accent that sounds remarkably British.

"Are you from the UK?" I ask him, tilting my head.

His eyes twinkle when he smiles. "I hail from there originally, yes, though I take homage in a land very different."

The way he speaks… I've never heard someone speak with such formality. It's as if he stepped right out of one of my favorite fantasy films.

"I was wondering, Miss Emilia," Quicken says, "if you would like to come with us to an after-party?"

I glance at Sky, eyebrows raised. He just nods. "I…don't know. I'd have to ask my mom if it's okay that I stay out later."

Quicken dips his chin. "I understand. We can wait while you call her."

I stand up, water dripping down my calves, and grab my cover-up. I put my phone in its pocket before I left. I unlock it, swiping past the home screen image of our beagle, Crumbs, getting his tongue stuck to a frozen pole, and click into the phone app. I hold it to my ear through the ringing and wait until my mom's voice sounds through my end.

"Is everything okay, darling?" Mom asks, worry vaguely concealed in her tone.

"Yeah, I'm fine. I was just wondering if I could go to an after-party with a few of my friends?"

Mom is silent over the line for so long that I begin to get antsy. Finally, she asks, "And what time do you think you'll get back?"

I barely stop myself from pumping my fist in the air. "Does this mean I can go?"

She sighs. "Yes, but you can't stay out past eleven. Okay?"

"Okay," I squeal, drawing Sky's attention. I swear he smirks, cheeks flush slightly, before he turns back to Kisha, listening to whatever she's saying.

I wonder what the relationship between them is… If, perhaps, she's more than just a friend. It shouldn't matter to me…and I hate that it sort of does.

After Mom hangs up, I slip my phone into my

cover-up's pocket and sit back down between Sky and Quicken.

"So, what did she say?" Quicken asks.

I grin. "She said yes, as long as I'm back home by eleven."

Quicken and Sky exchange a look. Sky says, "I'm sure we can make that happen."

Chapter Four

The term "after-party" must mean something completely different to these three. I glance around the small, two-bedroom suburban home. The faded yellow wallpaper is peeling and dust is settled on nearly every surface. The only evidence that people have been here at all are the scuff marks near the couch and leading down the hall. The only path consistently trudged.

"Do you…live here?" I ask Sky as my eyes land on a pile of blankets on the couch.

He doesn't meet my gaze, looking instead at the blankets. "I've been staying here for a while."

I can hear the strain in his voice, so I decide not to ask anything more on this topic. I nod, slipping out of my jacket and reaching toward the kitchen table to set it down, but Quicken steps in front of me before I can. His expression is scandalized. "Let me get that for you." He holds out his hand expectantly, so I let him have it.

His deep brown eyes meet mine and something

reminiscent of pain or hurt flashes across them. It's gone as quickly as it came. "We have some snacks in the fridge and some champagne."

I raise an eyebrow. "Champagne? Aren't you…a minor?" I study him more closely now. He can't be much older than me. Twenty at the most.

He scrunches his face in confusion, then it melts into understanding and he shrugs. "Habit, sorry."

I stop myself from inquiring further. Too many things seem off about these people.

I begin to kick myself. Why did I follow Sky— whom I just met—and his friends to a strange location? I'm practically begging them to kidnap me, or worse, *murder* me.

Alarm bells begin to go off in my head and I step back toward the door, eyes flicking between the three of them.

Sky must see the fear written across my features because his own face creases with worry. He steps toward me, one hand held up in the air as if I'm a spooked rabbit. "We're not going to hurt you, Emilia."

I stop with my back to the front door, panic rising in my chest. "Three strangers, an empty house, the middle of the night?" I flash him a strained smile. "I don't really like the way it sounds, do you?"

Sky tilts his head ever-so-slightly and frowns.

"We aren't going to hurt you, Emilia. We would never hurt you. You know I'm telling the truth. You can sense it."

I bite my cheek, the panic that was threatening to boil over a mere moment ago now recedes. "Then…" I take a deep breath and push away from the door. Sky's face floods with relief, though there's an edge of concern still evident. "This isn't an after-party, is it?"

"No, it's not," Quicken admits, the moonlight drifting in from the window paints half his face in a silver glow. "We need to talk to you about what happened two years ago."

Sky crosses to the couch, where a jacket is sprawled beside the blankets. He removes something from the pocket and smooths the crinkled paper between his hands. When he shows the time-worn newspaper clipping to me, my breath catches in my throat.

I take it from him with quivering hands. "Why do you have this?"

"We've been looking for you for a very long time," Sky says sullenly; his voice is deep and husky, borderline emotional. Unshed tears glisten in his eyes. My throat knots. "If you stay, we will tell you exactly what happened, exactly who you were before that day." He points to the black-and-white image of fifteen-year-old me, curled up in the center of a park in a blood-covered ball gown. He's offering to unravel the mysteries of my past... The one thing that has been plaguing me. How could I leave now? How could I say no to the very thing I want?

I sit down on the couch, staring at the newspaper clipping. My eyes catch on a list of questions brought up by the journalist: *who is she? Where did she come from? What is going to happen to her now?*

I sniffle and jerk my chin up as Sky pulls a dining room chair into the living room and sits down across from me. Quicken and Kisha stand behind him, faces grave and eyebrows drawn.

"Emilia..." Sky starts. "My name is Skylar Baker. The first time we met, you were sent to the bakery to complete a task for your father. You had to order two-dozen jam-filled pastries for your father's 42nd birthday. We were both eight. I was proving to my father that I could help out at the bakery. My first customer just happened to be Princess Emilia Strazenfield. We were fast friends, practically growing up together. Though, at the age of fourteen, you caught the eye of my eldest brother, Aaron." His voice grows cold and his lips thin, the rosy pink that his cheeks took on while he was telling his story disappears completely. I don't know what to say, so I don't say anything. "There are three of us, Baker Boys, as the village likes to call us.

I'm the youngest, and the middle child is Jaxon."

Quicken steps in, keeping Sky from straying too far from the point. "A year later, Aaron proposed to you, but everyone could sense the Veiling lingering within him. When your father refused to give Aaron his blessing, Aaron vowed to steal the Sword of Death, Aridam, and force him to." He falls silent, eyes glancing down at the dust-blanketed floor.

Kisha pitches in, "After he killed your father, he was going to take you and keep you as his own. If Sky didn't get there when he did, who knows what would have happened to you. Sky is a Runespeaker, a type of mage who specializes in teleportation. He can craft a stone and engrave it with a rune to do just about anything."

I laugh, which is an odd thing to do when being told you're a princess and mages are real. But honestly, this isn't a time to be joking.

"If you're not going to tell me the truth, then I'm going home." I stand up, wiping dust off my cover-up.

Sky doesn't move. "It's your father's blood covering you in that photo. Aaron knew that you and the king would be in the ballroom, practicing for your dance at your father's birthday a week away." He levels his eyes with mine. "You can tell if I'm lying. So…am I?"

I watch him, my eyes flicking over his face.

From his scar to his bowed lips. "Just because you believe you're telling the truth doesn't mean it *is* the truth." But even as the words leave my mouth, I can feel the uncertainty weighted in them.

Sky stands up, brushing dust off his pants. The shadows of the living room play across his stature. "You are Princess Emilia Strazenfield, first in line to the crown of Glaven, and you need to return home. When Aaron broke Aridam the day he killed your father, he cursed our kingdom to wither. The only way to save our home is to piece together Aridam's twin, Eve, the Sword of Life." He pauses, taking a quick breath before continuing, "Centuries ago, when both the swords were created, King Marcus of Nether harbored Aridam, while Eve was broken into six pieces and distributed to the rest of the kingdoms in the Solstice Realm."

"Your sister, Queen Sophia Strazenfield, cannot quell all the panicked kingdoms. We need you, Emilia," Kisha states, slipping her hand into mine. "Please, Emilia. Save our home."

Chapter Five

"So, how did it go?" Ricky asks, sitting down on the edge of my bed. I rummage around in my closet, searching for a pair of leggings and a fairly flexible shirt. I don't know exactly what I'll need, but that seems like a decent start. I twirl my finger, signaling my brother to turn around while I change. With a sigh, he complies. I grab a blanket off the end of my bed and throw it over him, earning a chuckle in response.

"It was fun. Weird. But fun," I say, slightly short of breath. Since I got home, nearly twenty minutes ago now, my mind and heart have been racing. I've never done *anything* like this before. What's wrong with me? Why am I suddenly brave, a risk-taker, and adventurous?

Ricky turns back around when I tell him I'm done, tossing the blanket to the side. He frowns at my outfit. "That's...interesting pajamas. Shouldn't you wear something a little more...warm? It's like ten degrees outside."

I roll my eyes playfully, though the constant sheen of sweat on my forehead does little to hide my anxiety. "I have a million blankets. I'll be fine."

He shrugs. "How was the party? Apparently, you made a lot of friends. That's what Mom said at least."

"Could have been better." I feign a light-hearted smile. "They don't even know how to clean up."

Ricky chuckles. "I'll let you get some sleep then. Good night, Em."

"Night Ricky." I climb onto my bed and stuff myself under the covers. Ricky kisses me on the forehead before closing the door to my bedroom and enveloping me in darkness. I left the window open a crack to make this a lot easier, but my blankets don't do much against the frigid night-time wind.

I lay there, ears perked to the sound of Mom and Ricky shuffling off to bed, an owl hooting right outside my window, and a methodical *sccccrrrttchhh* as my window opens further.

A blonde head of hair comes into view, outlined by the moon, then a pale, smirking face. Kisha climbs noiselessly into my room, eyes scanning the layout before turning to me—a lump on the bed. She rests her hand on the dip of her hip and raises an eyebrow. "You ready, sleepy head?"

I crawl out from under the covers and run a

hand through my hair. *I cannot believe I'm doing this.* But if going away with these people can finally shine a light on who I am, and why I get these constant nightmares, wouldn't that be better than staying here and never knowing?

"What should I pack?" I whisper, tip-toeing to her side. She gives me a look like I lost my marbles.

"Pack?"

"Yeah, you know, like luggage? I mean, I haven't traveled much, but I know what necessities I'd bring if this was some normal trip."

Her marble-losing-look deepens. "You don't need anything, Emilia. All your belongings are already there." She sweeps the room again and sighs. "Well, your old belongings."

Kisha opens the door to my closet and breaks into a smile, eyes glittering like she's staring at a pile of diamonds, not clothes. "Look at all these…" She pushes my shirts aside and beams at the fur-lined coats I have. I usually only wear them a couple of times during the winter, hating to draw too much attention to myself. She pulls out my black trench coat lined with faux wolf fur and presses it into my arms. "You need to take this one." She fingers the hood of the matching brown and faux fox one, a coy smile on her face.

"Take it," I say, nodding toward the coat. "You'll look amazing."

Her smile brightens. "Really?"

"Of course. What use do I have for two?"

She slides the coat off the hanger and slips her arms into it. The expression on her face is a mixture of child-like *it's-Christmas* and *I-just-had-my-first-kiss*. Rather endearing, really.

Kisha tugs the window up farther. "Let's go then. Quicken is waiting down the block with the car."

I start toward her, then stop, biting my cheek. I glance around my room. My entire life for the last two years, and I'm just leaving it behind for who knows how long. I turn back to my desk and scribble out a letter on a neon yellow index card. I hope Ricky and Mom can forgive me for this. The vision of their faces when they find this in the morning sears into my retinas, bringing tears to my eyes and palpitations to my heart.

"We have to get going," Kisha states, gesturing to the window. The cold, autumn wind tears through the trees outside, bringing a flurry of dry leaves to scatter on the ground. I swallow back my fear and follow Kisha as she ducks under the window and jumps to the ground, crunching leaves beneath her feet. I reach up on my tippy-toes and slide the window shut.

Kisha hugs her coat around herself and leads me around the corner and onto the sidewalk, where the streetlights illuminate the frost-kissed grass and the dark suburbs. The only sound, besides the unruly wind, is our shoes clicking on the sidewalk.

Sky's black Mustang comes into view, camouflaged by the blanket of night. Quicken is waiting, leaning against the driver's side, while Sky leans against the trunk. They both look up when we near, faces drawn in curiosity and alarm, only shifting to relief when they realize that it's only us and not some street urchin with a death wish.

"Ready?" Sky asks, and I realize that he genuinely wants to know if I am. It's not just one of those empty, polite questions.

I give him a small smile, which I'm sure is riddled with anxiety, as I say, "Yep."

Kisha finds Quicken. Their conversation gets swept away by the baying wind so I can't hear it, but by their intense expressions, I want to know what they're talking about.

Quicken opens the door for Kisha and she climbs into the backseat, dipping her head in gratitude. He holds it open for me to follow suit.

Quicken slides into the driver's side while Sky takes shot-gun. The car is chilly, but there's an electric sort of buzz that vibrates around the small quarters, the kind associated with close-knit friends and adventures. Of feeling welcomed, wanted, and a part of something. I've never felt this way before, and I never want to let the feeling go. I close my eyes, soaking it up, as the Mustang smoothly pulls away from the curb and purrs down the dark street.

"Where exactly are we going?" I ask, finally opening my eyes after we turn a corner, leaving my house and my family behind. I know I should be a bundle of nerves and filled with guilt, but this feels *right*, as if I'm following a path that's meant for me. I've never felt so close to figuring out who I am and who I used to be.

Sky glances at me in the rear-view mirror, the stone that dangles from it is nearly white now, save for the ice-blue glow emanating from the carving. Kisha said he's a Runespeaker... Parts start to click together.

"Is that one of the teleportation runes?" I ask, pointing to the stone.

Sky nods. "I enchanted it with a link between the Earthen Realm and the Solstice Realm. It's the only way we can get back home."

"So...what? Is it going to open a portal?" I ask, half-joking. My jeering smirk falls from my lips when Sky nods. "Actually? Portals exist?"

"Portals are the only way to travel between realms," Sky answers. "There are several other realms besides these two, but most are gatekept or locked. The Solstice Realm is the only magical realm that's composed of allied kingdoms. Well, most of them are allies, at least." His expression sours. "The Solstice Realm is also home to the most diverse species of friendly Unnaturals."

"What's…an Unnatural?" I lean back in the seat, shaking my head in bewilderment.

"Most you've probably heard of before. Were-wolves, vampires, yetis, goblins… It's a long list, one of which is kept in the queen's office," Sky explains. He situates his hand on the dash in front of him. "I'd recommend closing your eyes now."

"Why?" I ask, leaning forward in the seat. Before he can answer, the stone dangling from his mirror floods the car with blue light. I snap my eyes shut, though the backs of my eyelids are already burned white. I bite my cheek against the blinding sting. Seconds pass—or is it minutes?

"You can open them now," Kisha points out quietly, jostling my shoulder with her own.

I do as she says. As soon as the white clears from my vision, my mouth drops open. Surrounding us now, through the boxy windows of a black carriage, is a forest blanketed with golden sunlight. Sprawling grass covers the ground, and as the wheels of the carriage rattle by, rabbits and birds startle from the trees and underbrush.

"Welcome to Glaven," Sky says from the bench seat across from me. His outfit has completely changed; now he's wearing a billow-sleeved, cotton shirt, a tie of brown fabric around his forehead, keeping his hair from blocking his view, and matching brown trousers with a pair of scuffed, leather shoes. In fact, as I look around, everyone's outfit has changed. Kisha is wearing an elaborate gown made from red tulle and the jacket I gave her is now draped in her arms.

And Quicken, who somehow transported to the front of the carriage, is wearing a rust-colored tailcoat and riding pants. A top hat is shading his eyes. I stand up on wobbly feet and stick my head out the open carriage window. The wind which smells of roses and honey tugs at my hair and ruffles the puffy sleeves of my own gown, one of which I didn't realize I was wearing until now. I run my hand down the beaded corset of the pink chiffon gown. I've always liked dresses, though I've never had the courage to wear something so extravagant. Ballgowns on a daily basis would draw attention, the one thing I desperately wanted to be rid of.

A pair of mustangs lead the carriage. Muscles bulging under raven-black hide and hooves pumping on the ground, pulling patches of grass and dirt up and leaving a trail of mulch discarded behind us, along with two, parallel wheel tracks.

"Where are we going?" I ask, grinning as a pair of Stellar Jays dart from the forest, playing.

Sky rests his forearms on his knees and smiles.

"To the palace. It's about time Queen Sophia gets to see her sister again."

Chapter Six

The palace rests on the top of a hill. The valley beneath is sprawling with thatched buildings, and the scent of fried bread and fresh pastries mingles on the breeze. The streets that wind through the village are layered in mud. Wagon wheels have already carved permanent trenches along the paths.

I duck back into the carriage as soon as people come into view; if I'm truly the long-lost princess, how would they react? Would they even remember me? Would they recognize me? I don't have the answers, so I hide.

I watch the people, *my* people, supposedly…if I'm to believe what they say. Though, how could I not when I'm sitting right here?

I tuck my hair behind my ears as Quicken directs the mustangs onto a path to the right, leading up the hill toward the palace. I watch the people and the places as we pass by. The buildings are cracking and crumbling, falling apart bit by bit, but the people still smile. I feel awed by them, in the face of such impending doom, they act like nothing is wrong. I wish I could be that brave... I know I'm nothing like that. If the incident in the classroom stands for anything.

"Do you think she'll like me?" I find myself asking Sky, chewing nervously on my cheek.

Sky arcs an eyebrow. "Sophia?"

I nod, wringing my hands in my lap. "Do you think she'll even remember me?"

Sky chuckles, though it sounds strained. "It's only been two years, Emilia. Sophia has been graying with worry over you, which is saying something since she's your younger sister."

Younger sister. Not only did I have a sister, but I had a baby sister... Ricky's older than me, so I never even considered that I could be anything but the baby of the household. Now, in this far-away realm, my role is reversed. I have to be the one to look after someone else, not the other way around.

For reasons unknown to me, I want to impress my sister. I want her to feel grateful, elated that I'm back. That I can carry some of the burden of Glaven with her. "Do I look nice?" I ask Sky, smoothing a hand down my corset; the studded pearlescent beads swirl across the fabric, like a cloud at dusk. I've never asked a boy if *I look nice* before. Blush colors my cheeks.

Kisha covers half her face with the back of her hand, but her crinkled eyes give away the fact that she's grinning.

Sky fidgets with the fabric tie around his head, tucking a few loose tendrils of hair underneath. "You look…presentable," he squeaks, pivoting away from that topic as quickly as it started. "We need to get the Solstice Map from Queen Sophia. It'll help us travel between all six kingdoms with ease."

Presentable? I try not to let that insult hurt, though the sting doesn't die like a fire when being suffocated. "Is there anything else I should know before we get there?" I ask, eyes locking on the quickly approaching palace. The pearl-colored walls reflect the sunlight. A bed of white roses line the walls beside the giant jeweled doors, nearly translucent save for a sort of transcendent shimmer. I can see a maid within, holding a tray balanced in one hand. She's blurry as if I'm staring through waves of heat rising from concrete.

I don't know how that bodes for safety or privacy, though maybe those things aren't nearly as important here as they are in the Earthen Realm.

I furrow my brow. Now I'm even starting to sound like these people.

When Quicken slows the horses and pulls us to a stop parallel to the front entrance, my heart starts construction, jack-hammering against my ribcage. I press my hand against my chest, urging my heart to slow. I can't see my sister for the first time in two years—the first time since I can remember—with sweat slicking my skin.

"It'll be fine, Emilia. Forget about trying to make an impression. She's your sister, all she wants is to have you back," Sky says, taking my hand in his and rubbing his thumb across my palm. Ricky does that to me on occasion, when I'm getting worked up over something. It never fails to calm me.

I purse my lips, nod, and mouth *thank you*. Sky pushes open the carriage door, holding it for me and Kisha as we step out into the crisp, sun-warmed air. The roses are particularly fragrant, making the gentle breeze floral and sweet. If I didn't know better, I would have guessed that it's spring. But how could that be when we just left a dreary, cold autumn?

"What season is it?" I ask Sky as we make our way up the few marble steps to the entrance. He smooths the creases of his shirt and Kisha runs a hand down her skirt. With a sturdy *ha-ya*, Quicken brings the mustangs to a steady gait. I assume he's taking the carriage to a stable somewhere to the left of the palace.

"Autumn," Sky responds as the door opens quietly. A maid blinks up at us with doe-brown eyes. She has matching brown hair piled underneath a white mobcap and her fingernails are painted over with clear gloss. Every inch of her is primed to perfection.

The maid, without uttering a word, steps aside and sweeps her arm to the foyer. A large white staircase breaks the room in half, forking elegantly at the top to two balconies, each leading to numerous rooms.

A man sweeps by, a black tailcoat form-fitted, all the way to the white bow tie perfectly situated at the base of his neck. His hair is sleek and black and his brown eyes have an unnatural gleam to them. I can't place my finger on it, but I know when I'm being deceived. It's a gift I've had for as long as I can remember. Something is off about his eyes...but what? And why does that matter?

"May I assist you?" the butler asks, taking my and Kisha's coats. He blinks at them, slightly perplexed by the uncommon design. His voice even sounds like lies itself. Completely *wrong*. His voice is silky smooth, lacking anything even remotely human.

"Queen Sophia has requested to see us," Sky says, eyes falling to the staircase. My sister must be up there.

The butler hesitates momentarily, before falling into step and leading us up the stairs. No one says anything until we reach a door on the opposite side of the landing. The door is as precise as everything else. Cut from a gleaming stone and carved with shapes and patterns. I trace my finger over one, wondering what they could possibly mean. "Is this a language?" I ask Sky.

Sky watches me as my finger plays with the indents. "They're runes, warding this room from various things."

The door opens with a flourish, making me jump back a step, straight into Sky. Sky catches me, biting back a chuckle. He pushes me forward and into the luxurious room.

The outside wall is completely see-through, made of something close to glass, but I suspect much more precious. It curves like an expanding balloon, letting the golden sunlight fall onto the lush carpeted floor and modern-esque, birch desk. An armoire, a settee, and a round, crystalline side table are the only items inside, leaving a large section of the floor for pacing, I assume. If I was a queen of a distraught kingdom, I'd do a lot of pacing.

My eyes land on the girl who's sitting at the desk, back straight in the matching chair. I would've expected a monarch to be sitting in something richer, but somehow the plain wooden chair still makes her look powerful.

The maid whisks around us and to the girl's side; the same maid that opened the door downstairs.

The eerie butler followed us in, now standing before us, our coats deposited in the armoire. He moves as quietly as the dead, which brings goose-bumps to my skin quicker than his unsettling appearance does.

"Queen Sophia," the butler begins, gesturing to us.

"Garamond," Sophia says, standing up with an unnatural grace. "You're my Emilia."

I take a step toward her, drawn to my long-lost sister. "Soph." The nickname rolls off my tongue as if I've said it a million times before.

She sweeps around the desk, tugging me into a hug. She's only a few inches shorter than me, and besides our similarly angled faces and matching blue eyes, she seems to be my opposite. I can tell that she feels confident in the gowns she wears, in the ice-colored crown adorning her head, melting into the snow-white color of her hair. I fold my arms around her. I can feel the truth of the moment. I can feel the connection between us as if it's a living, roiling thing. And now, I know without a shadow of a doubt, that this is where I belong.

When Sophia pulls from my embrace, her cheeks are sticky with tears. She wipes them away bashfully, turning to Sky and Kisha. "Good job. You've exceeded my expectations." She touches her crown as if out of habit and plasters a polite smile on her face. "How may I repay you? Jewels, coins, residence?"

Sky furrows his brow. "There's no need to repay us, Your Majesty. Emilia is a dear friend. I would've found her without your insistence anyway."

Sophia takes my hand and leads me to the settee. She sits down beside me, giving me her full, undivided attention. "Sister. I am so incredibly relieved that you've finally returned. I wish I could get sentimental, but your return is more beneficial to the kingdom than it is to me." She touches the crown again—it looks like thin, spiraling icicles dripping upwards. "You are the rightful heiress to the crown, Emilia, so I won't resist when it's donned on you. I'll begin the preparations for your coronation ceremony promptly, but first, I need to request that you—"

"I don't want the crown," I interrupt, thrown completely off guard. I came here to save people, not rule them. All I want to do is help them and discover who I am and who I used to be. And what my nightmares mean. "I just want to help. Sky told me all about Aridam and Eve. We need to see the Solstice Map so we can start locating the fragments."

Sophia scrunches her face. "You…don't want the crown? Can one deny the crown?" She turns to Garamond, one thin, blonde eyebrow raised.

"If my readings are correct, Your Majesty, an

heir *can* deny the crown, thus passing it down to the next in line. Which would be you." He shrugs one shoulder lightly.

She presses her lips into a line and focuses back on me. "Both Bakers and Miss Tailor will accompany you on your journey to restore Eve. But unfortunately, I don't have the Solstice Map."

"Since when did the Solstice Map leave the palace?" Sky asks, tone reprimanding. His cheeks flush when the queen returns an icy, unappreciative glare.

"My father moved the Solstice Map to a secure location when the threat of Mr. Aaron Baker grew," she explains. "I'll look back in the records to see where he had it transferred. Until then, please follow Mr. Garamond to your rooms."

"Your Majesty, we can't stay," Kisha interjects, dropping into a courtesy. Sophia's calculating look wrings her to the bone. "If we're to get a head start on restoring Eve, than we need to leave right away."

Sophia forcefully takes my hand. "I just got my sister back, you're not taking her away until we've had time to catch up. So you'll follow Mr. Garamond to your rooms, where you'll be staying until I see fit. Am I understood?"

Sky and Kisha exchange a nervous glance, but both dutifully nod. I catch Garamond smirking with pride out of the corner of my eye.

When Sky and Kisha trail after Garamond,

Sophia turns to me, a giddy smile brightening her soft features. "Now, tell me all about the past two years."

Chapter Seven

The maid sets down a tray of steaming tea on the ornate garden table, the base of which is made from glossy white metal and twisted like the trunk of a willow, the tabletop spreading out like leaves from the center.

The maid, whose name is Trelia, according to my sister, pours us each a cup. The scent pairs with that of the greenhouse surrounding us.

"I thought we should have somewhere private to talk," Sophia explains, gesturing to the labyrinth of plants. After Sky, Quicken, and Kisha left us in her study, she took me to the very back of the palace, where a greenhouse branches out from the kitchens. I spy petunias, gardenias, and dandelions—technically not a flower, though as beautiful as one—in the closest corner. Sunlight dapples down from the tinted roof. A wall-length flower bed is directly behind me, brimming with green roses: a favorite of mine because of their rarity and extraordinary beauty. They were the original roses, before the white ones outside took over, not to mention the pricey reds.

Dangling from the translucent beam crossing lengthwise above us is a row of hellebores, flowers that have a naturally darker pigment, some even going as far as black. Another favorite. There are only a couple of careers I've considered pursuing, one of which is becoming a botanist.

"Not all these plants are in season," I comment, bringing my focus back to my sister, who is watching me like the Discovery Channel. "How do you keep them alive?"

Sophia flourishes her hand, a bashful smirk forming on her face. "I wouldn't know. I only come here for the view and privacy, not to learn about gardening." She says it with a joking tone, but I can sense that she thinks gardening is beneath her. I frown.

"I'd love to talk to the gardener sometime," I respond.

Sophia picks up her teacup, pinky out, and takes a relishing sip. "I'll set you two up, then." She sets her teacup back on the matching saucer with a gentle *tink*, extending her hand toward mine. "Now, tell me everything. What was it like being stuck in the Earthen Realm, knowing you're a princess and above everyone else? Surely none of them believed you when you told them."

I don't think Sophia hears herself when she speaks. Well, maybe the problem is that she hears herself *too* much and has become engrossed with her own voice. I don't know if she's always been like this, but I certainly hope there's more to my sister than this perfect, unblemished image.

"I didn't tell anyone," I begin, crinkling my brow. Does she not know about my memory? "When I first woke up, I was on a park bench, covered in blood, with no memory of what happened. Every once in a while, I'd get flashes of a knight and a graying man, but I never knew what they meant. Until I met Sky." Did I really just meet him mere hours ago? "He explained everything. He convinced me to come back and help save Glaven." I'm too afraid to meet her eyes. I've never laid myself so bare before, without even an ounce of armor. "I've always had this...ability, I suppose." I chew nervously on my cheek, never having mentioned this before, though somehow Sky knew. I guess I must have told him. "I can tell when I'm being lied to, and when someone is telling me the truth. I've always thought it was just really strong intuition or something."

Sophia takes my hand in hers. Her grip is warm and comforting, and her ice-blue eyes are mellow and calming. "Our mother had that same gift. It's called Soul Sight."

"Soul Sight?" I test the words on my tongue. They feel familiar. "Does that mean I'm like Sky? A mage?"

"Not exactly," Sophia chuckles. "People with Soul Sight are still humans, it's just a rare, unlocked gene that gives them the ability to decipher the truth in words."

Soul Sight…

At least I'm human. I don't think I could handle leaving my family, discovering I'm a long-lost princess, and that I'm possibly a mage all in one day. *Human* was safe. I like being human.

"Are you human?" I ask her, genuinely curious. Can I trust anything these days?

She barks out a laugh, smothers her mouth with the back of her hand then shares a conspiratorial look with Trelia. "Yes, I'm human. So, you're really telling me you don't remember anything about your life before Mr. Aaron's attack?"

I nod sheepishly. I feel guilty for not remembering, like I took something from all these people here. "Yeah. I didn't even know I had a sister until Sky told me." I wince at the momentary hurt that flickers across her face. "I'm sorry. I wish I did."

She shakes her head. "It's not your fault, Emilia. We'll just have to figure out how to get your memories back. I'll talk to Mr. Garamond about it later."

What would a butler know about returning memories? I think back to his expression in the study and his uneasy appearance, the lies I could sense radiating off of him. There's more to him than just being a butler, and I want to know what. What has him setting off all the alarm bells in my head? I'm tempted to ask Sophia, but a part of me suspects that they're in it together. Whatever *it* is.

I drink my tea and set the intricate cup back on the saucer. "Do you have a library here?" If I'm to find out more about the Solstice Realm and all the magical creatures in it, and what I will possibly be running into, I want to be prepared. Though I'm not the biggest fan of school, I've always excelled at my studies. There's a certain comfort in note-taking, knowing that, at that moment, everything is in my control.

"Oh, yes, there is," Sophia pipes up, turning to Trelia who is standing beside her. "Do you mind showing her the way? I have to get back to my study and search through Father's archives."

"Of course, Your Majesty." Trelia curtseys before leading me out of the greenhouse and through the bustling kitchens. I wave to Sophia, flashing my most appreciative, not-at-all-suspicious smile.

"Trelia, have you been here a while?" I ask as we pass through the kitchens. The smell of herbs and baked bread make my mouth water.

Trelia seems taken off guard by my sudden question. "Five years, Your Highness."

"Emilia is fine," I insist, getting to my main point. "What was my sister like before Aaron's attack?"

Trelia considers this with a speculative tilt of her head. "She wasn't always this mature. She used to skip through the halls and sing at the top of her lungs. She'd paint the walls in the foyer, irritating the other maids of course, but not your father. She had an artist's soul. Ever since the king's death, she's stopped singing, painting, and dancing. She's a great ruler, but I just wish she could have retained the shadow of her childhood."

"She's only, what? Fifteen?"

Our footsteps are the only sound in the hallway. Trelia points to a door to our left, hidden in the shadows of the main staircase. A potted fern towers beside the door, half blocking it from view. How many people come in here? By the dust settling along the doorframe, I'd have to guess that no one has in a long time.

"Her sixteenth birthday is this Saturday." Trelia opens the door to the library, exposing the dust-riddled, abandoned room. "She hasn't planned a birthday party since she became queen. It would be nice if Queen Sophia could let her hair down once in a while. Now, I hope I'm not stepping out of line, but it would mean the world to her if you could stay until then."

"I don't know how much Glaven can endure," I zip my mouth shut as Trelia's hopeful expression starts to fall, "but I'd be happy to stay. Maybe you and I could arrange some kind of surprise party."

Trelia beams. "I'll come back in a couple of hours when lunch is ready."

"Thank you," I say, dipping my head.

Trelia closes the door, leaving me alone with the shadows, cobwebs, and books offering to widen my horizons. I find a candelabra on the cabinet next to me, and a box of surprisingly modern-looking matches. Is the Solstice Realm really just a conglomeration of different centuries? By the look of the furniture, I'd have to say so. I strike a match and light the three, white candles cupped by the ornate candelabra. I move through the library, gaping at the ceiling-tall shelves, each jam-packed with books written throughout the centuries. I'm surprised to find a dust-covered first edition copy of my favorite fantasy book, *The Lord of The Rings*, sitting between a pair of illegible tomes. I lift up the first layer of my skirts to wipe the sign on the end of the aisle clean of dust, leaving the pink tulle gray and dirty. The sign reads *Fantasy, 1930-1960*.

I continue down the aisles, dusting the signs away and further staining my dress. But in the face of what I need to find out, a dress is nothing. I stop when I reach an aisle near the back of the library labeled *Solstice Realm, History*. I lift the candelabra up to the sign, noting the flaky, golden paint pressed into the divots of the letters.

When I move into the aisle, the books here are nothing like I've seen before; thick with golden covers, the paper edges are deckled and carved into the spines in loopy letters are the names of places I've never heard of before. *Aquartia, Nether, Dwarvenshire, Olympus*. The only one I recognize is *Glaven*, right in the middle of the shelf. I scan the shelves above it, realizing that the farther it goes up, the more niche the subject in that particular kingdom becomes.

I pull out a book generically labeled as *Solstice Realm, Foe or Friend*. Figuring out what species are our enemies seems like a good place to start. With two hours to kill and tons of research to do, I heft the thirty-pound book to the back of the library, where a circle of armchairs face a short glass coffee table. I set the book down and turn to the windows behind the chairs. The black-out curtains are drawn, pitching the room into utter darkness. I stumble my way around the chairs and stand on my tippy-toes, barely reaching the cord to open the curtains. With a hearty tug, the curtains part like clouds before the sun, letting the golden light spill into the library.

I gape as the sunlight touches the shelves, sparkling off the diamond-like material the shelves are carved from. The entire room sparkles, even under all the layers of neglect. It's kind of hard to look at, for fear of going blind. It's also impossible to imagine why this library was abandoned in the first place.

The door to the library opens and my attention snaps to the boy blinking in disbelief at the sight. Sky cups his hands around his mouth and calls back to me, "I like what you've done with the place!"

I shake my head with laughter and wave him over, settling onto the floor beside the coffee table and flipping open the strangely heavy cover.

Sky sits down on the armchair behind me. "Trelia told me you were in here." He scans the shelves, something unnamed twinkling in his eyes. "I'd always find you in here. This was kind of your place. I guess that's why Sophia had it closed off, why no one ever used it anymore."

His voice sounds choked and sullen, and since I refuse to have my own voice sound that emotional—considering my sister basically associated this dazzling library with me—I move onto a less depressing topic. "I decided I should learn about the different species and kingdoms. It seems like a good use of time while Soph is searching for where the king—our *father*—moved the Solstice Map." It'll never not be weird referring to a king as my father, not when I thought my entire life revolved around a mystery, Sandy, and Ricky.

"Oh, I could answer any questions you have," Sky offers, leaning forward to examine the book. "Probably starting with why that book is so heavy."

I lift the cover back up for dramatic effect. "That is a good one."

"It's made of gold," Sky explains nonchalantly. "Every book about the Solstice Realm is made of gold, in fact."

I stare slack-jawed at him, waiting for the punchline. It doesn't come. "You're serious?"

"As serious as your amnesia."

I break into a smirk, he's the first one to bring light to that particular situation, and I find it rather pleasing. Much better than tip-toeing around it. "What's the point of having them made of gold?"

"I don't know exactly. I'm sure your father had some reason, but he never told me," Sky shrugs.

I run my finger over the textured pages, chewing on my cheek. "My sister's birthday is on Saturday. Do you think we can stay until then?" I ask, already having a vague sense of what he's going to say.

"I don't know how much longer Glaven can hold on, Emilia," Sky sighs. "The buildings are crumbling more and more each day." He drags a hand through his hair, leaving a clump half-hiding his scar. "I'm surprised this kingdom has even lasted as long as two years." He catches my disappointment and reaches over to lightly squeeze my shoulder. His touch is comforting, and I wonder if I've always thought it was. "I'll talk to the others. With it being three days away, we could possibly jaunt over to wherever your father is hiding the Solstice Map, acquire it, come back, and strategize while celebrating Sophia's sixteenth."

"That's as good of a plan as any," I respond. "Now shush so I can study."

Sky chuckles, muttering something about me not changing.

Sometime after page twenty, Sky gets up and leaves, ruffling my hair. I'm so transfixed by the book that I don't realize how much time has passed until Trelia is tapping me on the shoulder.

"Your High—*Emilia*. Lunch is served in the dining hall. May I take you there now?"

I rub my eyes and close the book. I only got to chapter five, but from what I've read, I think I have a pretty good grasp on our apparent *foes*. "Yes, please." I follow her out the door and to the other side of the main floor. She opens a pair of tall, double doors and announces like I'm a boxer in the ring, "Please welcome, Princess Emilia Strazenfield."

The *Strazenfield* part is going to take some

getting used to as well. It's been Macintosh for as long as I can remember, though I've always known I had a last name prior to my adoption.

There are five heads at the long dining table that turn to stare at me, self-consciously reminding me of my dust-smudged gown. I grab my skirts and hold them in a way to hide most of the stains, though by Kisha's appalled expression, I'd bet everyone noticed them.

I sit down beside Sophia who's at the head of the table, across from Sky, and on my left is Kisha. The center of the table is covered in golden trays of steaming food: potatoes, cubed meat, fresh pastries, an assortment of different types of salad, cooked vegetables, and some kind of buttery bread that smells reminiscent of Italian restaurants. I wonder if the trays here are made of real gold as well, by the king's—*my father's*— lavishness, I'm scared to know the answer.

Sophia passes me a pair of matching tongs, grinning at me like I'm being handed the Nobel Prize. With a sheepish smile, I start to fill my plate— going straight for the pastries on demand of my sweet tooth.

"Did you find the library accommodating?" Sophia asks, spearing a potato with her fork.

I swallow the bite of pastry in my mouth and pray that nothing is noticeably stuck in my teeth while I speak. "Yeah. I found exactly what I was looking for. I learned some pretty interesting things too." My eyes shift over to Garamond, the ever-present butler who's standing by Trelia near the doors.

"Oh? And what's that?" Sophia asks, not noticing my suspicious stare. She chews delicately on a cube of meat. What kind of meat? I can't be sure.

"I was reading about the Unnatural species that were banished from the Solstice Realm." I take a sip from the glass of water that was already waiting for me at my place. "I thought the kingdoms in this realm welcomed all species?"

"Well," Sophia swallows, resting her hands on the fabric napkin in her lap, "our grandfather banished the species that defied him during the Great War; an ironically named war since it only lasted two weeks." She takes a drink and I catch her eyes shift over to Garamond. I *knew* something was weird with them. "The species, in my opinion, shouldn't be banished. I've brought it up with the other monarchs before, but they all still hold the same belief as our grandfather did: that those particular species can't be trusted, that they're dangerous and uncivilized." There's venom in her words, which she quickly suppresses with a forced chuckle. "Why are you so curious about that, anyway?" I catch the accusation, and by the warning glance Sky shoots at me, he does too.

I raise my glass into the air and shake my head. "Thought I should at least learn about the place I used to live."

Sophia's eyes flicker between mine as she chews methodically on a speared cube of pastry. Who cuts their pastries, anyway? "Curiosity killed the cat, as the saying goes."

It's not hard to unmask her central meaning: *drop it*. What is my sister hiding, and what does it have to do with the banished species?

"I think a curious princess is a valuable asset," the boy sitting next to Quicken on the opposite side of the table chimes in. He lifts his water glass in a salute. "Emilia, it's wonderful to see you again."

I raise an eyebrow, instinctually turning to Sky. His expression dims and he frowns, and that's when I catch the likeness between the two. *Brothers*. He's obviously not Aaron, since inviting the worst-guy-in-the-world over for lunch seemed improbable, he must be Jaxon.

"Jaxon?" I ask, cutting into a cube of meat. It smells vaguely like chicken with a rubberier texture. It reminds me of the mystery meat they served at lunch in Roosevelt High. A pang of guilt shoots through my chest, remembering everyone I ran away from. Have they discovered I'm missing yet? If they did, how devastated were they?

"I'd be bouncing off the walls, believing that out of all your friends, I was the one you remembered, if the unlikelihood of that didn't occur to me. So, dear baby brother must have been spewing on about the family." He shoots Sky a teasing smirk. His voice is light and jeering, and I have a feeling that past me liked him very much.

"You said we were friends?"

Jaxon's smirk shifts into a genuine smile. "We were. Hopefully, we can still be."

I match his smile. "I'd like that."

The rest of lunch passes with light banter and inside jokes that bounce right off me. Even though I don't understand most of them, it doesn't make this any less enjoyable. The sense of belonging I felt in the Mustang washes over me again.

These people are my home.

This is where I belong.

Chapter Eight

$\mathcal{I}$ run my hand over the smooth, birch desk pushed against the wall of my bedroom. Surrounding me is the feeling of familiarity; every inch of this space was *past* Emilia's. Could it become mine again?

Next door is Sophia's room. I was told she decided to stay in her childhood bedroom instead of switching over to the queen's suite. If I suddenly had the entire kingdom relying on me, I'd keep the only space that was ever truly my own too.

All the royal bedrooms are located in the palace's tower, giving the outermost wall a certain, soft curvature. On the floor above mine are the guest rooms that Quicken, Sky, Kisha, and Jaxon will be staying in. Trelia told me that those rooms were once used for the ladies in waiting, but have been vacant for several years now, ever since my mother died. I knew she wasn't in the picture, it just never occurred to me that something tragic must have happened. I wanted to ask more, but Trelia whisked away before I could get another word out. Did she know my mom? If she did, maybe I should ask her about it. Finding out about my mother is just another fragment of my identity I'm trying to uncover.

I pull out the chair to the desk and sit down, the sunlight sliding through the glass balcony doors to my left illuminate the contents of the desk. There's a light blue journal resting in the center with a peacock feather quill lying across it, and a bottle of black ink waiting to be used. Trelia informed me that Sky left something in my room earlier, so I guess this must be it.

I flip open the cover and pick up a loose scrap of paper with writing on it.

To Emilia, for your notes. -Sky

I lift the quill and dunk it in the ink. It feels natural in my grip. I guess it's like riding a bike, a skill retained in the muscles, not in the memory.

With the floral scent drifting from under the balcony doors and the nostalgic atmosphere surrounding me, I set to work, recalling everything I've learned. I even go as far as to write down my suspicions, my questions, and my goals.

Day 1:

Went to the library today, after meeting my sister. She's great! Although, I suspect she's hiding something. She's oddly sensitive about the banished Unnaturals.

And Garamond, the butler, seems off to me. There's something wrong with his eyes. And his voice.

   o *Figure out what's going on between Soph and Garamond.*

I also met Jaxon at lunch. It's strange when I didn't even go to bed and it's a completely different day. I wonder what the time difference is between the Solstice Realm and the Earthen Realm.

   o *Ask Sky about the time difference.*

What I learned:

Vampires, shapeshifters, and trolls were banned from the Solstice Realm following the Great War by my grandfather (that's weird to think about) and Soph is trying to welcome them back, but the other monarchs aren't for it.

Vampires can control people by hypnotizing them. They have pale skin and can turn into mist to fit through narrow places. A stake to the heart can kill them, but garlic doesn't do much besides making them sneeze. The most effective way to ward off vampires is crushed rose petals. Is that why there's a ton of roses at the palace?

Shapeshifters can turn into anything or anyone, so once they started masquerading as an ally in the Great War, my grandfather knew they weren't safe. The only way to tell if someone is a shapeshifter is their aversion to unnatural light. For example: modern devices, lamps, chandeliers, etc. They stay out in the open and rarely go inside. Most shapeshifters live in caves.

Trolls are three times bigger than a full-grown man. They reside in dark forests and near swamps. They eat small prey and rarely venture out of the protection of trees. Trolls are rarely seen these days since most of them were killed during the Great War. The remaining trolls were banished to various unconnected realms.

I set the quill down and close the journal, scooting it to the back of my desk. I need to figure out what's going on between Sophia and Garamond before I leave with the others to save our kingdom. Which means I'm going to have to double task; I need to plan a party and uncover a mystery, all while being aware of the invisible clock counting down the demise of our home.

Our home.

I glance around my bedroom, from the curving, white metal bedframe that reminds me of birch trees, to the far corner full of bookshelves. Without a doubt, this is my home. But what about Sandy and Ricky? I can't just forget about them so quickly. I bite my lip, promising myself that once I've discovered who I used to be and Glaven is safe, I'll go back to them to tie up loose ends. They're still my family so I can't replace them with another.

There's a knock on the door that pulls me from my thoughts. I turn just in time for Sky to poke his head in.

"Sorry for barging in, Em," he starts, using a

nickname that rolls naturally off his tongue. He must've called me that all the time before I lost my memory. I like it, it's just another reminder of where I belong, and another piece to the puzzle of my past. "Your sister found where the Solstice Map is located. We can head over there now and be back by nightfall."

I grab the journal, the quill, and the bottle of ink and head to the armoire. I dig around until I come back with a drawstring pouch, a quail painted on the canvas, and set the contents of my arms inside it, cinching it closed. Sky's face lights up when he notices my fast attachment to his gifts. I also grab the faux wolf fur coat that Trelia retrieved from Sophia's study. I don't know how cold it'll get, so it's better to be safe than sorry.

"Let's go, then." I push past him, taking the lead this time as I turn down the spiral staircase and beeline for the doors leading into the foyer and out of the tower.

"Quicken and Kisha are bringing the carriage around," Sky says from behind me. He points to the front doors, where we can see the hazy form of the black carriage waiting for us.

"Emilia," Sophia calls from the staircase. She's holding her skirts up while attempting to hurry down the steps. "Emilia." She crashes into me, nearly murdering me with the strength of her hug. "Trelia told me you'd be here for my birthday." She holds me at arms-length and I can finally see the child still in her; her eyes are bright and wonderous. "Thank you. This will be the best birthday ever, I know it." She's beaming.

No pressure or anything. "I hope so, Soph."

"Enough of this heart-to-heart. Time to get going if we're going to make it back while everyone is still awake," Jaxon says, loosening the collar of his sleeveless beige shirt, and exposing a sliver of his skin. The drawstrings of his shirt dangle halfway down his chest, bouncing off him with every step he takes. His black hair is shorter than Sky's, cropped close in the back and longer in the front. He winks as he walks by me. "Greetings, Em."

"Hi," I reply, watching him saunter by, pull open the front doors, and wave to Quicken. He acts like he doesn't have a care in the world. Admiration grows within me, wishing I could be like that too.

Sky clears his throat and I glance back at him. His brother's presence alone seems to have perturbed him. "He's not wrong." He bows to Sophia. "Your Majesty, thank you for allowing us to stay. We'll see you again tonight."

Sophia straightens him back up by tugging on his collar. She smooths the wrinkles from his shirt and smiles. "We grew up together, Mr. Sky. I may be your queen, but first I am your friend. Sophia will do." She wraps her arms around his shoulders and hugs him. "I hope you're back by dinner time; the cook has a wonderful meal planned." She seems excited.

"We'll try," Sky promises, widening my sister's smile ten-fold.

I watch her for a minute more, as her smile falters for a second, then I shake my head in confusion and pull open the front door, slipping into the warm autumn breeze.

I reach out and pluck a few petals from the white roses that are growing beside the palace, sticking them in my drawstring bag. I'll need them to enact my plan, to finally find out if my suspicions are justified.

Chapter Nine

*J*inx Moore's mansion takes up a clearing tucked in the forest surrounding Glaven. Three stories high and nearly windowless, the mansion is overrun with nature. Ivy crawls across the dark oak siding and weeds grow unchecked in the sprawling garden, even more vast and varied than the greenhouse at the palace.

Quicken pulls the carriage to a stop outside the mansion's doors. The curtains in the window above the doors shift, and a bald man disappears and reappears on the tiny porch nearly instantly. He looks to be about thirty, with coal-black eyes and sun-kissed skin. He's wearing a brick-red tunic with wooden toggles, and his gaze makes goosebumps rise on my skin.

"Is that Jinx?" I ask Sky, lowering my voice for only him to hear—as if the spooky man outside has the ears of a bat.

Sky shakes his head, and by his slightly disconcerted expression, I'd go out on a limb and say the man unsettles him just as much. "No. Jinx is a woman. A gypsy, so Sophia says."

"You haven't heard of ol' Gypsy Jinx? The Woman of the Woods?" Jaxon asks from his seat beside his brother. He was silent for the entire ride over, which was approximately an hour, though time seems to flow differently here.

"You've heard of her?" I raise an eyebrow.

Jaxon leans toward me, one side of his mouth quirked in a mischievous smile. "When I went to the Solstice Academy for Unnaturals, over near Aquartia, there were stories about a former student named Jinx Moore. Affectionately known as The Woman of the Woods. Anyway, the story says she went mad, disappeared into the forest somewhere in the Solstice Realm, and only appears to offer elixirs and potions to passersby." He shrugs. "Thought the entire thing was make-believe." He turns to gesture to the mansion, offering me a conspirative wink. "Until now."

I roll my eyes at him. "Yeah, right." Even if I don't believe his story, it doesn't make my goose-bumps disappear.

Quicken opens the carriage door and lets us file out, each step more hesitant the closer it takes us to the front doors. And the man studying us.

I stop, letting the others trudge ahead. Sky turns back, and offers me a supporting smile, before tugging on my elbow, pulling me back into position beside him.

"I'm Skylar Baker. This is Princess Emilia Strazenfield, Kisha Tailor, Jaxon Baker, and Quicken Hackman. We've been sent to retrieve the Solstice Map for Queen Sophia Strazenfield of Glaven," Sky announces. Even with all the powerful titles thrown about, the man doesn't move an inch, his hawk-like gaze fixated squarely on *me*. "May we please seek a meeting with the lady of the house, Miss Jinx Moore?"

The man finally moves, turning to his side as the doors swing open, revealing a small woman with moon-white hair. Red and green paint stripes her cheeks, and her sheer-white dress drags on the ground behind her. She stops walking when she reaches Sky, inspecting him with a speculative tilt of her head. "The queen sent you?" Her accent is clipped and concise.

"Yes, she did. May we please go inside?" Sky inquires, dipping his head in respect for the woman.

She's not the haggard, old person I was expecting to be this so-called mad woman. She appears to be twenty, twenty-five at the most. Tan skin stretched over high cheekbones and a jutted chin, a long sharp nose evening out her features. She's rather breathtaking, in an unusual way.

With a simple nod toward the mansion, she

92

turns around and disappears back into the foyer.

The man trails her like a lost puppy.

"That's Jinx?" I whisper to Sky, a little awestruck and entirely self-conscious of my dust-stained gown I didn't bother to change out of. Usually, you dress up to impress people. I have a feeling that Jinx doesn't care about that sort of thing and that the only person she wants to impress is herself.

Sky blushes, ducking his face. I'd elbow him, maybe tease him not-so-lightly about his pink cheeks if the bald man wasn't watching us, half-hidden behind a potted plant in the foyer. The doors are still wide open, giving us a full view of him acting like a statue.

The foyer smells of nutmeg and cloves. It's small, barely ten feet wide, with potted plants and woven rugs everywhere. A beige settee is pushed against the wall to my right, and underneath it lies a sleeping tabby, one eye open.

The tiled floor reminds me of traditional Spanish-style houses. I've always had a sort of fondness for their use of colors and design of construction.

The bald man watches us, shifting around the plant to stay "hidden" as we push open the foyer doors and take a step into the elaborate inner workings of the Moore mansion. If I didn't know better, I would have said this entire house was built around a large, golden tree—because that's what takes up the center of the mansion, spiraling upward, golden leaves spreading across the ceiling. Though, the mansion on the inside is impossibly tall, accommodating such a ginormous tree, one that would battle the Red Woods in the Earthen Realm. It must be…eleven stories high at least.

I start to count the balconies that look out on the center, rich red wood railing keeping the guests—since I assume there has to be more than just Jinx and the bald man—from falling.

"How is this possible?" I gape. Jaxon and Sky stop next to me, their eyes sparkling with wonder.

"It's bigger on the inside," Jaxon mutters, grinning like a fool.

I turn to him, shaking my head in wonder. "But how?"

Jaxon shrugs one shoulder, his teasing smirk reappearing ten-fold. "Magic." With that, he follows after Jinx, who's stopped in front of the base of the tree. And that's when I notice the lack of stairs or ladders. Dread crawls up my spine.

Jinx doesn't turn around when we near, she just extends her hands, pressing them flush to the coiling bark of the golden tree. And then—like something out of my nightmares—she starts to climb the tree. Feet and palms propelling her upward at an alarming speed. When she reaches the second balcony, she pushes off from the tree and pounces cougar-like over the railing.

She didn't even look human when she did that, and I have a feeling that she's anything but.

"Are we supposed to...?" I gesture to the tree, mimicking the animalistic movements Jinx made.

Jaxon snorts back a laugh, while Sky scolds me with his eyes. "I assume there's some kind of magic emanating from this tree that makes it possible," Sky tries to explain, pressing a hand to the bark.

"Or she's...a witch," I say under my breath. Jaxon snorts again.

"Let me just try it," Sky insists. He readies himself in the same position Jinx started out in, pressing into the tree with his palms, and then he does a half-jump, half-grapple-for-something-to-hang-onto while trying to get his feet to grip onto the tree.

I glance up at the second balcony, where Jinx is peering over the railing at us. She runs her hands through the air, clearly trying to tell me something. I squint my eyes until it finally *clicks*.

I step in front of Sky, examining the tree. The coils that make up the trunk are thick and intricate like rope, and trickling between the coils is an amber-colored liquid, as slow as sap. I run my finger through the sap, which glows like blood under a blue light on my skin. I rub it across my arms and ankles. Then, I press my hands and feet to the tree. I can feel the gravity shift for me, as my hands and feet suction to the tree, pulled there by a sort of magnet, which pulses through my bones. It's strong, and if I didn't just watch Jinx do this, I'd be afraid the magnet would break my bones.

Kisha and Sky gasp behind me as I begin to climb, foot after hand, foot after hand, until I'm level with the second floor. It's almost as if the tree is telling me what to do, because I plant my feet and curve my body, pushing off of the trunk and pouncing through the air, over the railing, and land in a prowl beside Jinx.

When I straighten back up, I gasp for breath. Who knew scaling a million-foot tree would require so much exertion?

Jinx meets my eyes and nods. She turns around, not bothering to wait for the others to scale the tree, before whisking me away to her study that's centered directly behind the massive tree trunk.

She closes the doors to her study, the light from the flickering fireplace casts our shadows against the wall. Her small study is absent of any windows. There's a desk situated in front of the fireplace and a beige settee behind it, flush against the wall that's painted as black as night. A Venus fly-trap is in a pot on the far right of her desk. A desk with no drawers, so where could the Solstice Map possibly be?

She clicks her tongue and the Venus fly-trap opens its mouth. A thick, silver liquid is cupped in the plant's maw. I don't even know if plants *have* maws, but that's precisely what it looks like to me. She dips her fingers in the liquid and rubs it across her palms, turning to face the black wall.

I step toward the wall, curious as to what's going to happen, when the door to the study opens and Kisha, Quicken, Sky, and Jaxon file in.

Chapter Ten

inx ignores the interruption, raising her silver-painted hands in front of her. She shuts her eyes. The air charges with tension, making my skin crawl. The feeling is comparable to the magnetic force the tree created.

Kisha groans from behind me. I wonder if she's trying to elude the magic's grip. By the following grunt, I'd say she failed.

The force reminds me of one of the carnival rides at the county fair: you're pushed flat against a mat by gravity as the ride spins and spins and spins. It's always been my favorite ride, getting off and back on for a solid hour with Samantha. Guilt trails after my unease. *I miss her.* And I just left her…with no explanation and no promise of my return. I frown, spiraling into a dark, cruel place when the wall opens into a void.

The void swirls with colors, reminiscent of a constellation in the galaxy above us. Miniscule flecks of color dart and twirl around the inky void, and

Jinx turns toward us. Her expression hasn't changed throughout all of this, as if opening a *portal* in the middle of her study is a usual occurrence. I bite my tongue. *It probably is.*

"Come," Jinx demands, hand outstretched toward me. She completely ignores the others. I slip my hand hesitantly into hers, and take a breath of courage, fighting against the wormy, squiggly feelings crawling in my gut.

Hand in hand, we step into the void. It's cold and slick, running over my skin like water. I glance around, suddenly alone in a dark chasm, stars dancing above me, flashes of vibrant colors spilling across the midnight canvas.

Just as I'm about to panic, I blink and I'm standing in a library. Unlike any library I've ever seen before. The room is tall like a tower, ivy crawling along the rough stone walls and between the soft-oak shelves. Books and books and books cover nearly every surface... The shelves are full with even more stacked on tables and in corners. Upon closer inspection, I notice that the legs of the armchairs in the sitting area of the library are made of books too; old, dusty leatherbound tomes with ancient silver writing etched into the spines.

"What is this place?" I ask, my voice full of awe.

I swear Jinx chuckles—a strange, slightly unnerving sound coming from the stoic woman.

"This is the Royal Glaven Library. I was asked to construct it and have it hidden by the king, your father. It was made to keep the Solstice Map away from the hands of Aaron, Wielder of Aridam," she explains, holding her hands out to her sides to encompass the entire library. "There are fifteen floors to the tower, and at the very top is an observatory. Best view of the stars above, in this realm or not."

Her tone shifts between sentences, like the bow of a cello being pulled back and thrust forward again. It's melodic. I wonder if it's magical.

"Where's the Solstice Map, then?" Jaxon asks, hands in the pockets of his trousers and a frown plastered on his face. He scans the room as if it doesn't impress him. I hope he doesn't catch me staring, but I can't seem to look away. I want to catch him with his guard down, to see the awe-inspired twinkle in his eye. This detached, jeering boy can't be all there is to my long-ago friend, can it?

"Follow me." Jinx summons us over to a section at the very back of the library. At first, I think I'm missing something.

"There's nothing here..." I say, raising an eyebrow at the empty wall. The blank wall space is only a four-by-four-foot square with bookshelves framing it. Knots line the wood and ancient worm trails are carved in patterns.

Jinx presses her palm to the largest knot and a humming fills the air. It sounds like a swarm of a thousand bees drilling into my skull. The wall fades away, revealing a half-moon-shaped room. Wooden railing wraps around it and an oddly modern-looking keypad is on the wall to the right of the entry. We file in, squeezing against each other as Jinx presses a sequence of buttons.

Jaxon is pressed against my back. His hands grab my waist as the room shakes. I don't know if it's to steady him or me. But I find the warmth from his hands comforting—and the fact that he's not going to let me fall.

Jinx turns to us. "Don't touch the walls."

"Why not—" Jaxon insists, cut off by the elevator zooming upward. The walls, I realize with horror, aren't part of the room. They're part of the shaft we're accelerating up. Which means, if someone were to fall or reach out, they'd lose skin—or worse. Jaxon's hands on my waist tighten. Over his shoulder, I catch a sliver of Sky's face as his eyes take in his brother's current position. His jaw ticks and he bites his cheek, turning to where he's hidden by Kisha.

"The king and I decided to house the Solstice Map on the fifteenth floor. If anyone were to somehow get into the library, they wouldn't be able to find the lift. We figured it'd be most protected up here."

The elevator slams to a stop. The sudden lack of wind pulling at my hair and the absence of the dizzying sight of wood grain zooming in a seemingly endless stream upward disorients me. We all sway forward, catching ourselves on the railing or other people.

Jaxon curses under his breath behind me, which I find kind of funny. It's interesting to see Jaxon lose some of his *I'm-too-cool* demeanor.

Then I see the room… The fifteenth floor. And it's *gorgeous*. Plants grow everywhere, the wallpaper is painted like stars, and sunshine leaks into the room from the ceiling. I don't know where the observatory is hiding since the ceiling is glass and all we can see is a blinding golden light—let's just blame magic.

I reach my hand out and the rays of light make my skin appear ethereal—like I, myself, am a walking goddess.

I turn to Jinx, about to ask *how is this possible* when she pins me with a knowing smirk.

We follow her deeper into the room, each step sending a tingling sensation through my veins, comparable to my legs falling asleep right out from underneath me.

"Resist it. It's a spell to keep people at bay. The only ones immune to it were the king and I," Jinx

explains. She stops in front of a quartz podium…
with nothing on it. It's completely empty, but Jinx is
staring down at it like she's finally laying eyes on an
old friend after years apart.

The rest of us collectively hold our breath,
watching as Jinx runs her hands across the empty
surface of the podium. She steps back as the air
around it illuminates with golden sparks. I blink,
then blink again. Sitting with pages spread and
golden ink tracing the intricate curves of nearby
kingdoms, is the Solstice Map—a thick tome made
from ancient, worn paper.

"It's a book?" I ask, crinkling my brow. It looks
heavy. How are we supposed to bring it back to the
palace? I imagined the map would just be that, a thin
piece of paper…a proper *map*.

"The Solstice Map is a book containing maps to
every single known realm," Jinx explains, entranced
by the book's reappearance. "It's more than just a
map. It's a secret key to over a hundred kingdoms. It
contains everything you need to know." She takes a
steadying breath and her eyes flit over to me. "And
now you may take it. I know the king would want
his daughter to use it to save Glaven. Holding onto
it would be unjust."

I step up to the podium and try to pick it up, but
the book doesn't even budge—it must be made of
gold! What's with this dang kingdom making

everything out of gold? "I…I can't lift it."

Sky steps up next, face scrunched. "Impossible." He tries to pick it up, huffing as the book refuses to move. "Why isn't it moving?"

Jinx crosses her arms behind her back, stepping through the group and studying everyone's faces. A smirk lingers on her lips like she knows something we don't. *Which she probably does.* The all-wise Woman of the Woods. "This must be your father's final touch. He must have cursed the book to only be lifted by someone worthy. Someone necessary to your mission." She eyes the group again. "I suggest you all try."

With a sigh, Kisha steps up. I study her intently as she hesitantly reaches toward the book, trying to lift it to no avail. She steps back with a shrug. Next, Quicken tries. But even he fails.

We all swivel to look at the only person left, mouths fallen agape and eyes wide. *No offense, Jaxon, but I didn't think it'd be you.*

Jaxon narrows his eyes at the book, frowning. "Me?" He shakes his head. "No way. It can't be me."

Jinx grins, which is slightly unnerving unto itself. "Just try it, Jaxon. I'm sure the king had his reasons."

Jaxon looks doubtful as he steps up to the book. He runs his sweaty palms down his pants before curling his fingers under the cover and lifting it off the podium. He gasps, stumbles back, and turns to look at us. The book appears light in his arms, a faint golden glow emanating from its open pages. "Why me?" Jaxon asks Jinx.

Jinx rests a hand on his arm, pinning him with an intense stare. "I'm sure we'll find out soon enough. Just know, the king must have thought you were necessary to saving his kingdom." She glances back at me. "And his family."

I can read Jaxon's expression like an open book. I've felt that before, so I know the conflict and confusion on his face, wondering how he can be so important when he never felt like it.

Chapter Eleven

On the way back, Jaxon can't stop staring down at the book in his lap. I grow bored of watching the landscape and turn to Sky, who's sitting on the seat across from me, the orange light of sunset makes his features striking. I pull the journal and quill from my bag—the tip of the quill has some ink still smeared on it. I should probably get in the habit of cleaning it off since I'm sure there are small stains on the fabric of my bag now. "What's the time difference between here and home? Well, my old home…in the Earthen Realm."

My question pulls Sky from his stupor. He glances at Jaxon out of the corner of his eye, jealousy roaring its ugly little head. He bites his cheek. "About twelve hours, I think. Why do you ask?"

"Just curious. It was a little weird to go from nighttime to the morning in less than ten minutes."

Sky nods in response, turning to look back out the window.

I know I've lost him to his wallowing again. I

flip open my journal and cross asking him about the time difference off my list of to-dos. Now all that's left is figuring out what's going on between my sister and Garamond. I dig through my bag to find the rose petals, crushing one between my fingers as my plan finishes formulating. If my suspicions are correct, everything will finally make sense.

We finally pull in front of the Glaven palace just as the stars begin to twinkle across a blanket of darkness.

"Just in time for dinner, as the queen wanted," Jaxon jeers, crawling out of the cave of shock he fell into. He pushes open the door to the carriage before Quicken has a chance to jump down and open it for us. I don't know why he's always our designated driver, or why he gets stuck with the tasks no one else seems to want. I open my journal and scribble underneath discovering my sister's secret:

   o   *Find out the relationships between my friends.*

Friends. Writing it down, confirming that I believe all this isn't some crazy dream, seems right. The same kind of rightness that calling this place *home* grants me. I snap my journal shut and drop it and the quill back into my bag, climbing from the carriage after Sky.

"I say we plan out our route to the pieces of Eve tomorrow. Tonight, let's just…eat," Sky declares. His stomach grumbles in response.

"Are you sure you'll be fine without me tomorrow?" I ask Sky, elbowing him in the side and offering him a half smile.

He returns my smile. "Yeah. You just make sure to plan your sister a birthday she'll never forget."

"I can do that," I promise. *No pressure or anything.* "But you know you have to be there. It won't be the same without you guys."

Sky's expression warms. "We'll be there."

We trail up the steps to the palace doors, the gentle wind pushes my hair away from my shoulders, carrying with it a scent of herbs I assume is coming from the kitchen. My mouth waters imagining the potatoes, rolls, and meat that's waiting for us.

A maid opens the door for us, ushering us into the foyer and out of the night. She closes the door after peeking outside. What kind of monsters lurk at nighttime, especially around the palace? I press my lips into a thoughtful line and follow her as she leads us to the formal dining room, where golden plates are being set on the table. Sophia is sitting at the head of the table, hands neatly folded in her lap, looking like anything but a teenager. If only I looked so regale when I was fifteen.

She stands up with a big grin on her face when she sees us, but I'm too distracted to return it. My eyes shift over to my right, sensing something inherently wrong. Garamond's attention flicks away from me and to Soph, pretending he wasn't just staring at me. Goosebumps flicker to life along my spine. I take a seat to the left of Soph, squeezing her hand when she offers it to me.

"So, sister, did you retrieve the map?" she asks, eagerly.

I look over at the doors where Jaxon is trying—and failing—to pawn the Solstice Map off on a maid. She scurries away, exclaiming how she can't carry such a heavy thing. With a dramatic sigh, Jaxon brings it to the table and sets it down at an empty spot. He sits next to Sky, who is across from me.

"We secured the map, but only Jaxon can lift it. Our father cursed it for some reason," I explain. Soph's eyebrows shoot into her hairline. "Jinx said we'd find out the reason soon. But, besides that, can you send Trelia to my room first thing in the morning? I have a question I want to ask her."

"I'm sure I can answer it," Sophia suggests, smiling coyly. I shut her down with a stern look, leaving her giggling as the maids whisk the golden domes off the trays and reveal the food. Just as I suspected...*potatoes*. I clench my jaw so it doesn't fall open and create a waterfall with my saliva.

As everyone piles food onto their plates, I skewer a potato and bring it to my mouth. "Soph. You know our friends much better than I do—thanks to my memory. What's the relationships between them?"

She frowns, taking a sip of her water. "Relation-ships? What do you mean?"

"I mean..." I try to think of a simple way of putting it. "Why does Quicken always drive the carriage?" I gesture with my fork toward Quicken, who is slipping through the doors just now. He bows his head in Sophia's direction and takes a seat next to Kisha.

"Oh," she squeaks, giving me an *are-you-serious* kind of look. "He's Miss Tailor's courtier. He drives the carriage, makes sure she's accommodated, etcetera. I guess that's what she deserves, being the daughter of the Solstice Realm's most prestigious fashion designer and all." She arcs an eyebrow. "You really didn't remember that?"

I glance over at Kisha, talking in hushed tones with Quicken. Both their faces erupt in smiles, cheeks tinted pink.

"Is there anything else I should know?" I ask Sophia, kicking myself for not putting that together.

Soph swallows a piece of a buttered roll and shrugs. "I can't think of anything." Then her face flushes and she leans closer. "Well, it's a bit of a sensitive subject, but Mr. Sky Baker and Miss Tailor used to have a thing going. It started about a year ago and ended almost as quickly."

My heart beats quicker. Sky and Kisha? So, I wasn't foolish for suspecting something at Victoria Johnson's pool party. Jealousy claws up my throat so I take a drink of water to force it down. While I was stuck in the Earthen Realm with no idea who I was, Sky and Kisha found the time to pursue a relationship. I know it's not my place, nor do I have any right to feel this way, but that stings. Sky was focusing on Kisha when all along I thought he was tormenting himself over my disappearance. I grab a roll and butter it, stuffing it into my mouth. It's over between them, isn't it? Why do I even *care*?

Chapter Twelve

"Queen Sophia said you requested to see me, Your Highness?" Trelia asks, standing in my doorway at literally the crack of dawn. When I said first thing in the morning, I meant a reasonable time.

I rub the sleep from my eyes and step aside, refusing to be embarrassed by the thin, lacy nightgown I wore to bed. Trelia bashfully steps into my room, looking ship-shape, as if she's been up for hours.

"Yes, it's about Soph's birthday party. I thought we could plan it out," I explain, throwing open the curtains and letting light into the room. My journal is open on my desk from last night when I checked off another item on my to-do list. I quickly close it and scoot it to the back of the desk.

"Oh, that sounds lovely! Shall I go prepare tea and sandwiches and we can arrange the whole thing?" She's grinning from ear to ear.

I wake up a bit more at the mention of food.

"Yes. That'd be spectacular. I'll get dressed while you're gone."

She claps her hands together excitedly and exits my room. Her gentle footsteps drift down the hall, toward the stairs. I pull open the armoire and pick out a pair of lightweight linen pants and a long, loose button-up. No need to go all out and wear one of these immaculate gowns, especially since I'll just be lounging in my room all day.

There's a quiet knock on the door minutes later. I hold it open for Trelia, a metal cart in tow. It's stacked with decadent, rectangular sandwiches, a pot of tea, and a familiar scented pitcher of... "Is that coffee?" I point to the dark, swirling liquid. I don't know how she got this cart up all those stairs, but I'm not going to ask.

"With honey," Trelia chirps. "I thought it might be more suitable with it being so early."

Without hesitation, I blurt, "I *love* you."

She spirals into a bout of nervous laughter, lots of hand waving, and insists that *it'll pass*. Apparently, that particular figure of speech isn't a saying here.

I pick up a tray of bite-size sandwiches and bring it over to my bed. Sitting with my legs crossed, I pat the spot across from me. As Trelia perches on the edge of the bed, cheeks still smattered pink, it takes me back to the countless sleepovers I had with Samantha. I should really see if I can get

113

cell phone connection out here so I can text her and let her know I'm okay.

"I think this is inappropriate, Your Highness," Trelia squeaks, wringing her hands on the hem of her dress. She looks down at the lacy cuffs of her socks peaking above her polished black shoes.

"It's Emilia. Or Em. Whichever you prefer," I remind her. "None of this highness stuff." I wave my hand, dismissing the notion. "Now, let's get this party planned down to the dot. I want this to be the best party she's ever had." I take a bite of a cucumber and—dandelions?—sandwich. It doesn't taste that bad, actually. "Tell me about my sister. What does she like?"

Trelia clicks her tongue, thinking. "She acts regale and proper, but I know she's still a child and wants to do childlike things. If it's not too scandalous of me to suggest, I think the party should be a small affair, including only those currently at the palace." She bites her lip, waiting for me to scold her about such a ridiculous idea—a queen should invite everyone in the kingdom!

I chuckle instead. "That sounds perfect." I climb off my bed and grab my journal, quill, and ink pot before returning. I turn to a blank page, prop the ink pot on a flat surface of the bed, praying it doesn't tip over, and dip my quill. "Alright, what about food? What's her favorite?"

Trelia brightens, knowing this is her area of expertise. "She loves seafood. We just got a fresh delivery of caviar and halibut from our connections in Aquartia."

"Is that the...uh...water kingdom?" I ask, cringing at my obvious lack of knowledge.

Trelia laughs breezily. "Yes. It's completely submerged underwater."

I scribble down *halibut and caviar* underneath *small party*. "Should we hire a band? What does she like for entertainment?"

Trelia gestures to my quill so I pass it to her. She taps the feather against her chin before writing—in far too pretty handwriting—*The Peacocks*.

"What kind of music do The Peacocks play?"

"Hm?" She smiles wistfully. "They're a tribute band to Olympus's Queen, Hera, so they mostly play classical music."

I bite my cheek, wondering how many of the stories I've heard are true. "Olympus and Hera, like from Greek mythology?"

She gives me a puzzled look. "What's Greek?"

I shake my head, a small laugh parting my lips. "An Earthen thing, sorry."

She nods in understanding. "I can start on arrangements right away. We do need to hurry with it since her birthday is in two days."

I tear the page out of my book and hand it to

her, wishing her the best of luck as she scurries from the room, clutching the paper to her chest. I glance out the window at the barely risen sun. I figured this was going to take an entire day, but since it didn't, I can help the others map out the best routes to retrieve Eve.

In a matter of seconds, I'm knocking on Sky's door with a sandwich sticking out of my mouth and a porcelain cup of coffee in my other hand, completely forgetting how disheveled I look. Sky opens the door, looking unfairly like he walked out of a fairytale. I'm half tempted to roll my eyes.

He smirks at my appearance. "Can I help you, Em?"

"Areyouguysstillplanningoutthe—"

He gestures to my mouth. "Sandwich."

I grab my sandwich with my free hand, pushing my embarrassment down for another time. "Are you guys still planning the route to retrieve Eve?"

He glances back at his bedroom window, calculating the time. "We're supposed to meet in the library in a quarter of an hour. Are you meeting up with Trelia to plan the party?"

"We just finished," I say, shaking my head at his arched eyebrow. I mutter something about *the crack of dawn*, which has him nodding in understanding. "I was hoping I could join you."

He grins, extending his arm for me to take. "It'd

be my pleasure, Your Highness."

This time I do roll my eyes. "Not you too."

He laughs, which brings a smile to my face. His laugh has the power to brighten rooms.

The library is glowing as the golden sunlight reflects off the shelves. It's like standing in a disco ball.

"Emilia, you decided to join us!" Jaxon exclaims, standing proudly over the Solstice Map, which is laid out on the center table by the armchairs. He flips through the pages until he finds a satisfactory one. "This map marks where the Solstice Realm kingdoms are located and exactly where the palaces are." He points to an inked depiction of the Glaven palace. "We need to talk to the monarchs of each kingdom."

I kneel down by the table and follow his finger as he traces a path toward Eirae, the closest kingdom. "If a piece of Eve was distributed to all the Solstice Realm kingdoms, than why doesn't Glaven have one?"

Sky growls, "Aaron took it when he left. He's holding it hostage in Nether, hoping that we're too scared of him to go retrieve it."

"Oh," I mumble. "I'm not scared." I will my

voice to sound confident. Flashes of the man in the suit of armor standing above me leaves my hands shaking. I hide them under the table before anyone takes notice.

Sky rests his hand on my shoulder. "Neither am I."

Jaxon kneels down on the opposite side of the table, hunched over the map. He starts explaining the quickest routes we can take to each kingdom, predicting how long it'll take to convince the rulers that they should hand over their fragment of the Sword of Life, but I don't hear him. Instead, I hear the shrill sound of my scream resonating in my head. I can feel the slick warmth of blood on my hands, the metallic scent stinging my nostrils. When I look up, I'm met with wild brown eyes and disheveled sandy hair. He extends his hand toward me, his soft voice proclaiming how much he loves me.

I shake my head, but my vision clouds over with white. I fall back into someone's strong arms, a scream tearing from my chest.

Sky blinks down at me, concern written plainly across his features. "Emilia? Are you okay?" He's on his knees behind me, carefully keeping me propped in his arms.

I bite my cheek, not ready to see that same concern on everyone else's face as well. I'm not crazy. At least they know that.

"I'm fine," I lie, struggling from his grip. I smile reassuringly at Jaxon, my heart splintering when he gives me an *all-too-aware* look. I'm not weak. I won't be seen as weak because of *him*. Aaron. Murderer of my father. Breaker of my heart. Tormenter of my mind.

Chapter Thirteen

*L*ater that night, I open my door to see Sky pacing a trench in the hallway. He removes his hand from his trouser pocket and runs it through his hair. "Hey."

I blink at him, opening my door wider. "Hey."

He walks in and sits down at my desk. The corner of his lip lifts as he spots my journal, open to a rendition of the map Jaxon drew, marking time frames and resting spots, taking us through the entire journey of putting Eve back together. I close the journal and scoot it to the back of the desk. "What's up, Sky?"

His smile flickers out. "Earlier… Are you sure you're fine?"

I groan, plopping down on the end of my bed. Purple tints the skin under his eyes, his posture is slumped, and his clothes are disheveled. "I'm fine. Sometimes I get these flashes of Aaron standing over me after killing my father, accompanied by a crippling migraine. I got them before you told me who I was. That's the reason I was in the school bathroom crying."

He reaches over and rests his hand on my knee. "I'm sorry. It's my fault this happened to you."

"What do you mean? I was told you saved me," I counter, sitting up a little straighter.

He deflates. "But it didn't work."

"I'd say it did," I insist, taking his hand in mine. "I'm alive, aren't I? I wouldn't be if you let Aaron's men kill me."

He hangs his head, bringing my hand up to his lips. He leaves it there, his warm breath tickling my skin. "I wish I could have done more."

I pull him over to me, wrapping my arms around him. "You did *enough*, Sky. Please trust me on that."

He rests his chin on my head, soaking in my warmth. "Are you sure you want to go with us to retrieve Eve?"

I nod against his chest. "I'm positive. I won't let Aaron scare me away from helping my sister."

"I'd understand if you did—"

"Stop."

"What?"

"Stop. I'm not weak. I'm not going to turn my back on my kingdom, not when it needs me." I pull away from his embrace, demanding that he look me in the eye. "Don't bring it up again." I hope I sound challenging.

He breaks into a smirk. "I won't. See you in the morning."

"Actually," I catch his hand before he can step back into the hallway. "Can we go to town in the morning? I want to find something perfect for Soph's birthday."

He rubs his thumb across my knuckles, leaving a tingle of lightning when he steps into the dim light from the hallway's sconces. "Sure. I'll come get you at the crack of dawn." He winks and wanders back to his room, head held higher than it was moments ago. Not for the first time, I wonder at the origin of his scar. Who would hurt Sky?

I hurry back to my desk and flip open my journal, dipping my quill before writing:

o *Find out how Sky got his scar.*

I take my journal to my bed, stashing it under my pillow as I crawl under my blankets. With the wind brushing at my window and the ghost of Sky's touch calming me, I drift into the most peaceful sleep I've had in a long time.

I try to look my best today, fluffing my hair in front of the mirror. I don't know why I want to appear pretty. Well, actually, I do. Not for the first time, my impulse to put my best cosmetic foot forward is the fault of wanting to impress one Sky Baker.

I fiddle nervously with the corset I've donned over my dress, fraying one end of the tie. I groan, step away from the mirror, and convince myself that I look good enough. It's not like Sky cares about that kind of thing anyway. Surely, he doesn't. Does he?

My face pales when someone knocks on the door. The sun is barely peaking above the village, casting a long golden glow across the sleepy kingdom. I open the door, smiling like a fool.

Sky and Jaxon greet me. They're both wearing white shirts with billowy sleeves, appearing more like twins than just brothers. Although, Sky has light brown trousers while Jaxon's are black.

Sky offers me his arm and Jaxon sidles up to my other side, draping my arm through his. With a boy on each side, we exit the palace. On our way out, I catch Trelia's attention, telling her I'll be back before lunch and that I'm going to hunt down a present for Soph.

"I didn't realize you were joining us, Jaxon," I say as we push off the last step, standing on the oddly cold Glaven street—it dips downward, looping between homes and shops, elegant trees and flowers sprouting from every available patch of grass.

Jaxon covers my hand with his. "I couldn't turn down a walk through the village, especially with the princess donned on my arm." He chuckles teasingly.

I elbow him in the ribs, which only seems to make him laugh harder.

"What did you have in mind for Sophia's present?" Sky asks. His shoes click on the cobble of the street. There's not a lot of people awake, which brings doubt to the forefront of my mind that the shops are going to be open at all. Wait—what am I supposed to pay with? Maybe I can tell them to put it on my tab? That's what people do in all the novels I've read.

"I'm not exactly sure. I'm hoping I'll know it when I see it," I admit sheepishly.

My lilac skirt brushes against my walking boots, dirtying the hem. I'm sure it'll scrub out...fingers crossed.

Sky picks up his pace as we finally reach the beginning of the village; a house with a thatched roof and broken glass windows sits to our left, drooping like a wilting flower. Is this what the effects of Aridam's curse look like? A woman stands outside the house, broom in hand, sweeping chipped pieces of her walkway into her yard. She glances up when we pass, her attention catches on me, and I swear I can see a weight lift off her. She dips her head, hazel eyes bright with newfound hope.

There's a shop to our right where the street curves. A depiction of a shoe dangles outside so I assume it has something to do with footwear. The next shop over has *Flowers* scrawled elegantly in golden paint across the front window. I slip free from the boys, pressing my hands to the window so I can see into the shop. Instead of a gorgeous array of flowers, I'm met with empty counters and dead leaves in piles on the ground. The entire shop is barren, the life sucked out of it. I swallow and step back. How beautiful did it look before the curse got to it?

"This is our father's place," Sky says, pointing to a quaint little shop on the corner of the bend. A bronze, metal cut-out in the shape of a cake dangles above the door. The window display is laden with an impressive variety of cakes and pastries, vibrant colors swathing my vision.

"Can we go in?" I ask, wanting to see if I can place the bakery into the broken remains of my memory. I may be determined to save my kingdom and help my sister, but I'm also determined to piece together my identity.

Jaxon and Sky exchange a glance. "Sure," Jaxon finally says, drawing in a slow breath. "I'm sure Father would love to see you again."

A bell jingles when Sky opens the door, and I'm

immediately hit with warm air that smells of cinnamon and nutmeg.

The shop doesn't appear to be affected by Aridam's curse. *Or* Mr. Baker has successfully repaired it. There's a counter in the back with a glass window so we can look at all the cakes they have available. On top of the counter is a stand decorated with cannoli, cupcakes, and brownies. A small sign beside the stand declares that they're *Freshly Baked Today*!

A warm light emanates from a room behind the counter—the kitchen, I assume.

"Cook'd up a perfect batch of scones—should be out of the oven in a hot minute," a loud, booming voice calls out. A man appears in the doorway to the kitchen, wiping his hands off on a towel. An apron is tied around his large waist and his soft brown eyes melt when they land on me. "Em? Is that really you?" Tears glisten in his eyes. What did I mean to him?

"I'd love to try one of those scones," I say, smiling at the kind man.

He takes a deep breath, shakes his head, and lets loose a joyful laugh. "Knew you'd be back. I'll get you a scone." He disappears into the kitchen. After something clatters to the ground, Sky excuses himself to go help his father, leaving me and Jaxon alone in the empty bakery.

"Jaxon," I say, pursing my lips to the side. "Can I ask you a question?"

Jaxon smiles at me, toying with the frayed end of my corset tie. "Of course, Em."

I slap his hand and his smile grows. "How did Sky get his scar? I'm sorry if that's too personal, but I'm really curious."

Jaxon sighs, a light flickering out in his eyes. He appears sadder, and it hits me with a sorrowful certainty that a moment between me and him got shifted to his brother when I can so clearly tell he was hoping for anything but. "Sky rushed down to stop Aaron's men as soon as they stepped on the rune that sent you to the Earthen Realm. He fought them with nothing but an old dagger in each hand." He clears his throat and his eyes shine. "He wasn't a match for men taken by the Veiling."

I stare at him in shock, knowing everything he just said is true. "He...got that scar trying to save me?"

Jaxon's expression switches to something grim. He presses his lips into a thin line and nods.

Sky enters back into the room, holding a hot tray of scones as his father wraps a towel around his hand. I study how the shadows of morning catch on his deep scar. I don't remember what he looked like without it, but it doesn't matter. This is Sky. I wouldn't change him for the world. Sky blushes when he catches me staring at him. He lifts the tray up. "Scone?"

I select one of the soft brown scones, relishing the sweet smell rising with the steam. A sudden idea occurs to me. I tug Sky to the side, his face drawn in curiosity as his brother and father engage in pleasantries.

"Sky?" I ask, grinning. "I think I know what to do for Soph."

He brightens. "And what is that?"

I gesture to the bakery, my grin transforming into a coy smile. "I want to bake her a cake. Can you teach me?"

Chapter Fourteen

*M*y apron is spattered with flour and stained with ice blue dots from when Sky attempted to dye the icing. And I thought he knew how to bake. I smirk up at him when he finally presents the bowl of icing to me, spatula half hanging out of the bowl and dripping onto the wooden floor. He has a cheesy grin plastered on his face that just makes me want to laugh.

"Would you look at that!" I jeer, elbowing him in the ribs. "You can bake after all. I thought it was all just talk."

He sticks his tongue out at me, but the light in his eyes tells me how much he's truly having fun. I wonder how long it has been since he's worked in a kitchen.

The kitchen may be small, but Sky's father has a system for getting around in it and doing everything in a timely and orderly fashion. He tried teaching us it about half an hour ago, but I think we both prefer to just ram into each other and chuckle. The marble-topped counters are flush against the wall in a sort of U pattern, along with an ice chest, fire-lit oven, and wash basin. I'm not sure if there's electricity in Glaven or any of the kingdoms, but I think it'd be quite an extraordinary thing to introduce them to.

Jaxon, who opted to stay on the sidelines, finally ties an apron around his waist and scoots up next to me and Sky. He gives Sky an *are-you-kidding-me-right-now* look and takes the bowl from him, there are still dark blue whirls throughout the icing. "You didn't even mix it in properly," Jaxon huffs, stealing the spatula from Sky and folding in the remaining color. He does it so *effortlessly*—it's hard not to be impressed when I don't know the first thing about baking. "Baking is like driving a carriage. You don't forget it after years of doing it." He flicks his gaze over to me. "I think something else is on your mind."

Sky ignores his brother's comment and swipes the bowl back. "But baking is also supposed to be *fun*, Jax, not always so serious."

They exchange a look, leaving Jaxon with his eyebrows raised and blush creeping up Sky's neck.

I attempt to diffuse...whatever is happening here. "Jax? Is that what you want to be called?" I inquire, crossing my arms over my apron and leaning against the counter.

Jaxon smirks, steps toward me, and reaches one hand behind me, resting it on the counter, where I vaguely remember a pile of flour being from when I failed at actually pouring it into a measuring cup. His hand comes back covered in white flour and he reaches up, running his thumb across my cheekbone. "If you want to call me that, go ahead, Em."

His proximity is so close, I can make out the nearly invisible freckles under his bright blue eyes. He has short sideburns that fade at the half-ear point and his smirk is paired with matching dimples.

I reach my hands behind me to scoop up flour. With a mischievous smile, I toss it into Jaxon's face. He sputters, steps back, and bursts into a surprised laugh. "What was that for?"

I grin. "Payback!"

His expression is feral and excited as he grabs a container of wheat flour, undoes the lid, and flicks some at me. It speckles my cheeks.

"Cake's done!" Sky announces from the other side, removing the red velvet cake from the oven, an orange flame flickering beneath. He sets the cake on the counter beside the oven and removes the oven mitt from his hand. He turns back just in time for icing to splatter the right side of his apron.

"What were you saying about *fun*?" Jax taunts, spatula in hand.

"Hey, we need that for the cake." Sky grabs the mixing bowl we used for the cake; batter remains still smeared on the side. With a spoon, he scrapes some off and sends it flying toward Jaxon, splatting directly in the center of his forehead.

Soon, the entire kitchen is made of obstacles and ammunition. Exclamations of surprise and laughter drift through the bakery, occasionally joined by the bell of an arriving customer or the sighs of Sky and Jax's father.

I sit back against a corner cabinet, my chest hurting from laughing so much and cake batter, icing, and flour painted across my face and clothes. Jax sits down a couple feet away, beaming, while Sky is hovering over the cake, testing the temperature with the tip of his finger.

"Looks like it's ready to be iced," he exclaims.

Jax chuckles, wiping flour from his face. He stands up, and watches me for a moment out of the corner of his eye, a half smirk curling his lips, before grabbing a towel and disappearing into the front of the bakery.

I dust my hands off and join Sky by the cake. The red velvet is vibrant and the scent of it makes my mouth water. Hopefully Soph likes it—it's not much, but it's made specifically for her. "How should we decorate it? Back in the Earthen Realm, there's this thing called fondant. It's basically like edible clay."

Sky gives me a funny look, one eyebrow arced. "Well, what would Soph like? We can ice it, let that set up, and see what other things my father has in this kitchen." He hands me the spatula while he tilts the bowl, letting rivulets of icing dribble down onto the cake. I smear the icing around, evening it out. Whenever I baked at home, I'd always snatch a bit of frosting or icing—the best part about being the cook is sampling the ingredients.

"Trelia was telling me about how sophisticated Sophia tries to act, but how this party should be an outlet for her to finally enjoy being a child," I say, scraping the long edge of the spatula around the bowl and pushing the rest of the icing onto the cake —the first layer has already begun to harden. "Since the cake is round and only a single tier—what if we made it look like a flower crown?" I suggest.

Sky narrows his eyes, chewing thoughtfully on his bottom lip. Suddenly, his head snaps up and his lips stretch into a wide smile. "We could caramelize flowers. There's this field on the outskirts of the village that's usually brimming with wildlife. For some reason, Aridam's curse doesn't seem to be affecting it."

I lean back against the counter, accidentally placing the heel of my hand in a puddle of icing run-off. I lick it off, savoring the taste—and ignoring

133

Sky's intrigue as he watches me. "That sounds awesome! We *could* leave now."

"I'll go tell Jaxon where you and I are going," Sky adds, a stray chunk of black hair flopping loose from his fabric tie.

Some small part of me catches on his words— *him and I. Just us.* I smile to myself.

Chapter Fifteen

We wander through the village, staying on the outskirts to avoid the curious eyes of early risers. Sky said that Soph should make a formal announcement of my return before people happen to spot me. It's weird, ducking behind trees and houses, avoiding the eyes of people I don't remember. Is this what it's like being a celebrity back in the Earthen Realm? If it is, I feel sort of bad for them.

Bluebirds dart from a tree to my left, circling high in the lightening sky; the orange streaks of the sun backdrop them and I can't help but feel awed at the beauty of nature. I've always loved being outside, but here...being among these trees and these creatures, I can't imagine something else that would make my heart feel as full.

Sky has his head bent, watching the eroding dirt path. From his downturned lips, I'd say this is a direct effect of Aridam. It looks like someone grabbed the path and pulled on it, stretching it like taffy. It's mishappen; rocks jut from the ground, threatening to trip us. Weeds grow along the wonky edges of the trail. A creek burbles somewhere ahead of us. And the gentle breeze brings with it floral accents.

Even with the kingdom's prophesied demise, it doesn't lack beauty.

Sky stumbles over a protruding stone, catching himself on the extended branch of a nearby tree. Bright orange and green leaves make the sunlight dapple across the ground. He mutters something mildly inappropriate under his breath and turns back to me, face flushed, biting his bottom lip. "That wasn't there before," he explains.

I chuckle, hopping over the stone. "I believe you. Now where's this flower field?" I raise an eyebrow. Sky takes my hand and I beg my body to refrain from randomly sweating.

"It's over here." He says, one hand on the trunk of the tree as he maneuvers down a sudden, three-foot drop-off. I stand on the top of the ledge, his hand still clutching mine, and gape at the scenery.

It's a clearing with thick trees that jut into the sky from the perimeters. The creek I heard earlier gurgles through the field of flowers; the vibrant petals are reflected in the water, sparkling alongside a hazy rendition of the sun. The smell overtakes my senses, it's strong, but welcoming.

Sky helps me off the ledge. I snap my mouth closed, eyes wide, still entranced by this hidden gem. "It's so beautiful," I whisper, afraid to interrupt the harmony of water, birds, and wind. Here, surrounded by nothing but nature, I can almost hear the trees speak; their whispered songs twisting through their branches, fluttering along with the falling of leaves.

"I've never brought anyone else here before," Sky admits, thumb caressing the back of my hand. He turns to me and smiles, cheeks pink and eyes bashful.

"Not even Kisha?" I ask without thinking. I zip my mouth shut and curse myself for ruining the moment.

Sky's hand slips from mine and he steps in front of me, blocking my view of the flower field. Sunlight dapples across his hair, smattering the bridge of his nose. "You know about that?" He bites his cheek and looks away.

I step closer to him, and thankfully he doesn't back away. "Soph told me. I shouldn't have brought it up. I'm really sorry."

He shrugs and nods toward the field. "Coming?"

I walk alongside him, careful to avoid directly tromping on a flower. It's hard though, they cover nearly every inch of this place.

"It was short. About a year ago," Sky starts,

hands in pockets, brow creased in thought.

"You really don't have to tell me about it," I interject, unsure if I even want to hear about his past relationship. My chest constricts just picturing them together.

"I never have. It'd be nice to finally clear some stuff up," Sky somberly adds, dropping to his knees in a bed of tulips. The creek is barely a foot away so I peek over at my reflection. I look different, bolder, stronger than I did back in the Earthen Realm. I hold my skirts aloft as I sit down beside Sky. I follow suit when he starts plucking a handful of tulips of varying colors. Once he has about seven clutched in his hand, he takes a calculating breath before continuing, "It was the one-year anniversary of your disappearance. We were at a dinner with your sister —a sort of remembrance for you, and a meeting discussing how we'll get you back. Everyone was still torn apart by what happened. Me and Kisha included." He snaps another tulip off at the base of the stem. "We had a bit too much to drink, mistook the surge of alcohol in our systems for feelings. It only lasted a week. We both regretted it and vowed not to go back there again. Clearly we both were destined for other people." He glances up at me from underneath the canopy of his eyelashes. "Just know, Kisha is nothing but a friend to me now. Do you believe me?"

I run my fingers across the smooth petals of a red tulip in my hand and nod. "I believe you." It shouldn't matter if I believe him, it's his own business. I shouldn't have brought it up. I mentally kick myself.

"Do you think this will be enough?" He holds up his fistful of tulips.

I raise the few tulips in my hand and tap their heads with his. "*Cheers!* I think it'll be perfect."

Sky beams at me, the sun catching his face and amplifying his expression one-hundred-fold. I catch my breath. The way he's looking at me…eyelashes shadowed on his cheeks, mouth quirked to one side more than the other, a single dimple on the opposite side of his scar. Eyes sparkling with a thousand untold thoughts. He moves an inch closer and my heart bellows in my ears.

"You baked an excellent cake," I blurt, cheeks reddening.

Sky draws back, eyebrows disappearing into his hairline. He suddenly throws his head back and laughs. "Thanks, Em. I kind of screwed the entire process up." He stands up, helping me to my feet. "Jax was right. I was distracted by something else."

I swear my heart just jumped onto a train, traveling a million miles an hour. I don't know what to say, so I duck my head and trudge silently toward the trail, absent-mindedly running my thumb across the petal of a tulip. What would have happened if I didn't say anything? Would he... I start to nervously sweat at the very thought.

Chapter Sixteen

Sky finishes placing the last tulip on the cake; the sugary glaze glistens in the sunlight drifting through the kitchen window. I sampled a spare bulb we had that didn't fit onto the cake after all, and it was surprisingly delicious for being a flower.

"It's absolutely perfect," I state, grinning at the cake. I hope Soph likes it—it's not tiered or fancy, but it's made from our hearts and tailored to the child still inside of her. A flower crown for a child queen.

Sky grabs a white box from on top of the ice chest. He slides the cake carefully onto a silver platter and conceals it in the box. "Ready to go back to the palace?"

I nod. I have one thing left to cross off my to-do list, and that's discovering the secret between my sister and Garamond the butler.

Sky carries the box carefully in his arms as we bid goodbye to his father. Jaxon trudges behind us on our venture back to the palace, lips pursed and eyes clouded over in thought. I'm curious to know what's ensnared him in his own mind. I let Sky gain a few good strides up the slope and wave him on when he turns back around to acknowledge that I stopped. He doesn't say anything, noticing his brother's off-putting attitude. He continues toward the palace, albeit at a slower pace than I know he's capable of.

"Jax, you okay?" I ask, walking in step with him. He doesn't register my company, so I try again. I nudge his shoulder. "Jax?"

His head snaps up and his wild eyes flick around before landing on me. There's something sad about him; his lips are tugged down at the corners and his eyes seem particularly melancholy. "What's up, Em?"

I bite my lip. "I could ask you the same thing. Are you okay?"

He looks down at his feet. For a while, I don't think he's going to answer me. Eventually, when we're almost to the palace doors where Sky is waiting, he mutters, "The flowers were a good idea. Soph's going to love the cake."

I stop, watching him walk ahead. He disappears into the palace. I know there's an underlying message to what he said. I can sense it, just like I can sense the truth from the lies. I just don't have a clue what it could be. I shake my head and huff. I guess I have another thing to add to my ever-growing to-do list: *figure out what's upsetting Jax.*

Trelia's raven black hair is knotted in a messy bun atop her head, whatever rule my sister has of appearing to put your best foot forward is clearly thrown to the wind. She tears her hands through her hair, leaving clumps to fall down her back. "I cannot do this all by myself," she groans.

I rest my hand on her shoulder, overlooking the workers carrying a round white table into the backyard. "You don't have to. Tell me what to do and I'll do it."

Trelia practically collapses against me. Her eyes are rimmed with red and a wrinkle is permanently etched between her brows. "Thank Eve. Can you oversee the banquet? Just make sure they're setting it up correctly and all the food is being put in the ice chests over by the back doors." She grimaces; I can tell that ordering a princess about makes her uncomfortable, like I'm going to suddenly snap and have her thrown in a dungeon. I smile warmly, trying to offset her nerves.

"I'm on it."

"Oh, and I asked Sky to keep Queen Sophia distracted. We don't want her coming out here and ruining her surprise," Trelia exclaims, her lips twitching with a smile. Underneath all her stress, I know she feels proud of what she's doing for my little sister.

I give her a thumbs up and head over to the section of the yard that's being converted into a quaint eating area. A large, round white table matching the one in the greenhouse with the spiraling base is situated in front of a long rectangular table, clad in a lacy cloth. A few workers —men from the village hoping to earn some extra money, so I'm told—are distancing six chairs around the table. They peek at me furtively out of the corner of their eyes, whispering to each other as I pass by. I don't know how I'm going to get used to being talked about... At school, the only rumors including me were labeling me as a geek, a homebody, or an outcast. It wasn't anything positive unless they were calling me smart when telling their friends who to cheat off of in English class.

Two women are hauling bags of fruit toward the ice chests. Trelia mentioned something about making fresh drinks for the party. The main course, the halibut, is waiting in the kitchen, ready to be whipped up in the morning.

There doesn't seem to be much I can do; everyone already has all their stations under control. A small, plain white stage is set up underneath a willow tree, ready for when The Peacocks show up tomorrow.

I smile, excitement growing within me. I just know that this party isn't going to be one easily forgotten.

Out of the corner of my eye, I can vaguely make out the hazy form of Garamond through the crystalline palace walls. I have to admit, it'll always be weird to see into the palace from the outside. I still need to figure out what Soph and Garamond are hiding, and if my suspicions are correct, then I need to head back to my room right now. I make sure no one's actively searching for me before I head into the palace. Garamond is speaking with a maid in the hallway, his hands behind his back. I sneak by him— though by the way he moves slightly in my direction, I don't think I'm very good at *sneaking*— and hurry up the stairs of the tower and to my room. I relax against the door, lines from the books I read in the library running through my head.

I hunt down the squished rose petals from my satchel and lay them down on my desk, flipping to the page in my notebook pertaining to the banned species. The most interesting section has to do with vampires:

Vampires can control people by hypnotizing them.

They have pale skin and can turn into mist to fit through narrow places. A stake to the heart can kill them, but garlic doesn't do much besides making them sneeze. The most effective way to ward off vampires is roses.

I rummage around in the closet, searching for something very specific, doubtful that it'd even be in here. I sit back on my heels when I'm proven correct. The only place I can think of that might have what I'm looking for is the maids' closet. With a huff, I slip the rose petals into my notebook and close it. If someone comes sniffing around, I don't want them to know what I'm up to. If my sister is doing what I think she is, I need to know why. If the rest of the kingdom doesn't know, then I'm sure she has a good reason for keeping it a secret. I set off on the hunt for the rest of the materials I need to enact my test.

I manage to step onto the platform above the staircase just when Sophia and Sky's voices drift up to me. For some reason, I step back against the wall and listen. They're beneath me, standing in the foyer.

"Why can't I go outside?" Soph asks, suspicion lacing her tone.

Sky sighs. "For the millionth time, Your Majesty, Em doesn't want you to see what she did—"

Soph interrupts him. "But you can't tell me what she did? I'm the queen, for crying out loud!"

"And Emilia is your sister. She's really embarrassed and doesn't want you to see—"

"Tell me, Mr. Skylar Baker, or so help me, I'm stepping out in that yard," Soph threatens.

Sky relents, groaning. I picture him dragging his hand down his face, strands of hair flopping across his eyes. "Fine, I'll tell you. Just please don't tell her I said this." He takes a deep breath and says, "She went to the hair stylist in town and got her hair dyed…well…pink. And cut. Nearly all the way off. Trelia's back there trying to get it to at least look decent before she comes in here." He sheepishly adds, "Please, just let them finish up."

"So that's where Trelia went," Soph says, trailing off into a laugh. "That's hilarious. But I'll respect her privacy. I have some personal business I need to attend to anyway. Can you send Mr. Garamond up to my study?"

"Of course," Sky says. Footsteps follow, heading toward the backyard. Another pair—lighter and genial—start for the stairs.

I squeak. Sky just put me outside with a case of bad hair day, so I definitely can't be caught up here —no pink dye in sight. I slip into one of the numerous rooms, shutting the door just as Sophia reaches the top of the stairs. I wait on the other side, carefully listening for her to retreat into her study and close the door. After a little while, another pair of footsteps follow hers. *Garamond*. A door closes and I wait a breath before stepping back into the hallway.

I nibble on my bottom lip, giving in to my curiosity; I tip-toe over to Soph's study and press my ear to the door. Their voices are quiet, but I can just make out what they're saying.

"—she knows something," Garamond argues. His voice is clipped.

"You cannot be positive," Sophia insists. Her chair legs squeak on the floor. "Has your father written back to you?"

"Not yet. I'm expecting his letter to be delivered within a day. Mail from outside the Solstice Realm isn't common, Soph."

"Yet," she adds coyly. Her chair squeaks again, followed by short, tentative footsteps.

"Happy almost birthday," Garamond says. Then silence. A silence that gives me the impression that they're hugging. Either that or—

I reel back, brow drawn low over my eyes. I trip on the hem of my dress and land on my butt, wincing with the knowledge that there's going to be a golf ball sized bruise tomorrow.

The door to her study opens and my face drains of color; not only have I blown her surprise party, but I've also heard things I probably shouldn't have.

"Em?" Soph mutters, face twisted in confusion.

Garamond is standing behind her, a head taller. He glares at me. "She knows enough now."

Soph's lips thin and she steps aside, sweeping her arm toward her study. "Emilia, I think we should have a conversation."

I push myself off the floor, refusing to be completely humiliated by this current situation, and sheepishly step into her study. She closes the door behind me, and with the too-loud thud, I know that my former plans to uncover what they're hiding (*sneakily*—though we already established I'm not very good at that) are dashed.

Chapter Seventeen

Sophia squints at my hair. "I'm getting the impression that Mr. Sky lied to me." She drums her fingers on the edge of her desk, scowling. For a nearly sixteen-year-old, and my little sister, I'm abnormally scared. "You have a few questions to answer, Em." She sits back and clicks her tongue, shaking her head in a chastising way, like I just got caught with my hand in the cookie jar.

I wring my hands in my lap, barely refraining from nervously chewing on my lip. "Ask away." Though I intended for my voice to sound strong, like I'm not hiding anything, it quivers on the last syllable. There's no getting out of this now.

"Why'd Mr. Sky lie? What's really happening outside right now?" She raises one eyebrow, challenging me to lie as well. Maybe she has my gift too—the ability to tell when someone is telling the truth. However, if that was the case, she wouldn't have fallen for Sky's terrible excuse, covering up the fact that there's a surprise birthday party being set up

150

in the backyard of the palace right now.

"He must've gotten me confused with someone else," I suggest.

She groans, rolling her eyes toward the ceiling. "What is with the secrets today?" She rests her face in her hands and promises, "I will find out what's going on, Em."

Oh, I do not doubt that.

"Now onto a more…sensitive subject," she says, glancing at Garamond, who is blocking the door behind me. Hair stands up along my spine, and my survival instincts are yelling at me to run, hide, or fight. I know the threat is Garamond in this situation, and his alluring voice and unusual eyes, but I don't know *why* he's a threat.

Unless…

"What did you hear?" Soph asks, dragging me out of my thoughts.

I purse my lips and cross my arms, feeling oddly bold. Either way, I'm finding out their secret *today*. "You're expecting a letter from Garamond's father, who apparently doesn't live in the Solstice Realm," I raise an eyebrow, "which means…"

Soph tilts her chin down, deflating in her chair. "There's no point in hiding it now. You *do* know enough." She looks over my shoulder at Garamond as she says, "We might as well tell her."

Garamond makes a disgruntled noise of disagreement but doesn't verbally dismiss the queen's idea.

Soph holds my gaze, takes a deep breath, and admits with ferocity as if she's pushing a giant bolder off her chest, "I made a deal with the king of Cyprion, a kingdom in the Banished Realm, where the exiled Unnaturals went after the war. He sent me his son as part of the agreement," she waves one hand casually to Garamond, as if mentioning that this so-called butler is actually a prince isn't worth that much explaining, "and together we've been attempting to open the borders of our realm to all those who were forced from it."

"Hold up," I insist, spinning around in my seat. "You're a vampire prince?"

Soph and Garamond both go statue-still as I play my card, admitting that I might've done my own research.

"How do you know I'm a vampire?" Garamond asks, taking one step toward me. My heart palpitates and the animalistic instinct to dart from this room right now overwhelms me.

"It's not that hard to tell," I forcefully say, battling with the prey inside of me to stay still. He's not going to hurt me, so why do I feel like I need to get as far away from him as I possibly can?

Now that he's confirmed my suspicions, there's no need for me to use the rose petals. My original idea, which I was on a mission to complete just moments ago, was to create a perfume from the rose petals and spray it on him.

"Cut it out, Garamond," Sophia hisses. "You're scaring her."

Instantly, the sense of dread leaves me and I relax into the seat. "The he—"

"Sorry about that. Happens occasionally," Garamond mumbles, returning to his post by the door.

Soph bites her cheek. "Now I guess I have some explaining to do."

I rest my elbows on her desk, receiving a tight-lipped scowl, and reply, "It certainly looks like it."

Soph slouches in her seat, massaging the spot above her left eye. She appears to be deep in thought, stringing together an explanation that might make even the tiniest bit of sense. With an aggrieved sigh, she starts, "Vampires—as I'm sure you've learned from your *research*—can control people by using their eyes. Compared to humans, vampires are predators. The very top of the food chain. Most of them have immaculate control over their Veil: a term used to describe the sense of unease they emit. It's also what we call the inhumane evil that corrupts people. Most species have Veils, of sorts. Vampires are the most prominent." She clears her throat, fixing her posture to where we're eye to eye. "Garamond has been with me for a year now. Our plan is to show the other monarchs how well they can blend with our society, in hopes of getting the ban lifted." She leans over the desk and bites her cheek, eyebrows scrunched together and leaving a crease on the ridge right above her nose. "You cannot tell a soul, Em. Please. If this gets out, not only will I be dethroned for treason, but I may face the penalties of the other kingdoms as well. Prison. Torture. *Death*. None of it is improbable."

My mouth goes dry at the cruel list. There's no way in the world I'm going to let my little sister get hurt, not when I just reunited with her. "Your secret is safe with me. I wouldn't betray you, Soph."

Her face softens and she takes my hand. "I'm so happy to finally share this with someone." She raises an eyebrow mischievously, nose crinkling. "Now are you going to tell me what's going on outside?"

I pop up from the chair, flashing her a knowing smile, before throwing open the door. Before it closes, I peek over my shoulder and say, "You can go back to kissing now."

Soph turns rose red, her mouth forming a guilty little '*o*'.

I knew they couldn't just be hugging.

Garamond chuckles, stepping toward her just as the door slams shut.

I know I should be concerned about my sister

frolicking around with a dangerous Unnatural, and I am, but I trust her. So, there's nothing I'm going to do about it.

Chapter Eighteen

The Peacocks live up to their name. The three women with bleach-blonde ringlets, high cheekbones, and natural curves are hard to look away from. I find myself tugging self-consciously on my brown hair and questioning my ability to sing when their first few warm-up notes flit into the air; I'd never sing in front of people, but I always thought I had decent enough vocals. Especially in my room when I'm home alone.

The yard behind the palace is buzzing with excited energy and last-minute preparations. The only people here right now are the palace staff, assisting Trelia with bringing the freshly cooked food out of the kitchen. Sky, Jax, and Kisha have flocked over to the singers. I can practically see the drool glinting in the corners of the boys' mouths. Kisha rubs the material of the tallest singer's long, blue dress, firing off rapid questions about the designer and material, what kind of stitch they used, the cost of such an extravagant thing, and so on.

Garamond sidles up next to me, a smirk making his ivory face brighten. Goosebumps coat my arms, the only reason I even look to my right and notice him. I squeak and stumble back, glaring at my sister's apparent beau. "*Why* are you so silent?" I'm aware it's a stupid question, but it needs to be asked.

Garamond gives me a mischievous smile and the goosebumps on my arms fade away. I've never studied him for a prolonged amount of time, too unsettled and scared by the unease that naturally succumbs to his presence. His face is long, in the shape of a diamond. His nose is slender, protruding from his profile with all the air of an aristocrat, and his dark eyelashes are unfairly full, curling upward.

His eyes flick toward me and his thin lips stretch into an even bigger smile. I never noticed before, but his amber eyes have flecks of red evenly distributed throughout. No wonder something seemed off. After all, who has *red* eyes?

"It'll last longer if you take a—" he jeers.

I hold my hand up. "Don't give me that worn-out *picture* line. Besides, I'm not admiring you." My cheeks cursedly flush. I was just…observing, putting a face to my sister's partner. I change the subject before I can make this exchange even more awkward. "Do you think she'll like it?" I nod toward the party.

Garamond's cheeks turn pink and his eyes

soften. "She'll love it."

I can tell how much he cares for my sister. The protective casing around my heart melts a bit. Maybe he'll be good for her, maybe he won't hurt her. However, something about the mere thought rings prophetically of deceit.

Trelia claps her hands together, grinning as she approaches us. Maybe she's grown used to Garamond's dangerous allure because she doesn't even falter. "Everything is ready! Is the birthday girl up and about yet?" She shuts her eyes and corrects herself, unsure of what the proper thing to say is during an occasion like this. "I meant…the uh… birthday queen? Her Majesty?" She blinks.

Garamond bites his lip to stop himself from laughing.

I pat Trelia's shoulder sympathetically. "I'll go see."

I leave the excited murmurs behind; they fade into a peaceful quiet. I cross the marble floor, drinking in the atmosphere and wondering about where all the doors lead. I've barely even scratched the surface, discovering what lurks in the palace.

I stop at the bottom of the stairs leading up to the tower, assuming Sophia is still in her bedroom, and glance at a pair of double doors to my left. They're carved from the unique, sparkling gem the rest of the palace is made of; the vague outline of the room beyond brings a sense of familiarity to the forefront of my mind, casting aside my mission to summon the queen.

I carefully push open the heavy doors, peeking my head in. The room is vast, veined floors practically glow underneath large windows, and decadent chandeliers twinkle high above.

It's a ballroom. I gasp as a headache looms behind my eyes. I haven't had a headache like this since I got here.

I stumble back, pressing my fingertips to my forehead, trying to force back the pain.

Aaron saunters toward me; the image of him is fuzzy, like TV static. He's highlighted against a black backdrop, brown eyes begging me to say *yes*. Yes to what? I crinkle my brow. Oh, *right*. I was engaged to him. The thought itself seems weird. I've never even had a romantic relationship—not that I can remember—and here I am, being told I was engaged to the Wielder of Death.

I sink to my knees; the pain is almost intolerable now.

Red washes across my vision and the metallic stench of blood fills my nose. I tangle my hands in my hair, falling back onto my butt and burying my face in between my knees. I rock back and forth, praying to whatever is out there that this *agony* ends. My headaches have never hurt this bad, never brought me to my knees, hindering any attempt at escape.

I need to get away from this ballroom. I need to stop seeing my father's blood spattered across my hands, his head rolling across the floor.

"Em?" Soph's voice sounds far away. Her warm hands snake around my shoulders, shaking me. "Em?!" Her voice raises in pitch. "Em, what's going on? Are you okay? Look at me!"

I can't look at her. I can't even open my eyes. My face is scrunched in anguish, my front teeth sinking into my bottom lip. Now I *taste* the blood.

"What's happening?" someone else demands. At first, I don't know who it is—the drilling headache playing with my senses—but then he scoops me into his arms. *Sky.* "Emilia, you're going to be okay. Let me take you to your room." He ascends the stairs, Soph pitters behind him.

I want to protest but I can't even lift my head. I allow myself to melt against Sky's chest. His slightly woodsy scent quells me.

Within minutes I'm tucked into my bed, my eyes half-open, the headache retreating into a dull hum. I'm worn out, struggling to resist falling asleep. This wasn't supposed to happen. Not today, at least. Why couldn't this entire dramatic ordeal just wait until tomorrow?

"Soph," I mumble, glancing over at her. She's

perched carefully on the edge of my bed, fabric from her light blue dress is bunched in her hands. Her bottom lip quivers. "I'm sorry I ruined your birthday."

She sniffles and shakes her head. "You did nothing of the sort. You could never ruin anything, sister. You just scared me, that's all."

"It was nothing." I struggle to push myself into a sitting position. But my muscles are weak, threatening to collapse back onto the mattress. "I'm fine now."

Sky scoffs, arms draped over the back of my desk chair. "Clearly you're not."

"Yes, I am," I insist, glaring at him.

Sky rolls his eyes, but through the playful charade, I notice the tension and concern he's suddenly carrying. "Soph," he says gently, continuing when she turns to him, "I'm going to stay here with Em. I'll keep an eye on her. How about you go out back? I think Trelia has been looking for you."

Soph starts to protest, but I kick her in the butt with my foot. She frowns at us both. "You're sure I don't need to stay?"

"Definitely," Sky reassures her. She still doesn't look like she's going to budge, so now it's my turn to jump in. There's no way I'm going to be the reason she misses her own surprise party, and although I won't be there to see her reaction, I'm hoping she eats enough cake for the both of us.

"Go, Soph. I'm fine. Nothing a nap won't fix," I insist.

Soph purses her lips, then folds. "If you're absolutely positive—"

"I am." I pretend to fall asleep right then and there just to appease her; obligatory snoring sounds included.

With a dainty chuckle, she leaves the room.

Sky fixes me with a weary look. "What was that?"

"Another vision. It happened once I looked inside the ballroom. I saw Aaron again, then blood..." I shudder just recalling it.

Sky jumps up from his seat, hovering beside my bed, unsure of what to do, but wanting to help nonetheless. "Do you need anything?"

I relax into my pillows. "I wasn't lying about the nap."

Sky sighs. "All this is happening to you because of me."

"What?" I shake my head. "That's not true, Sky."

"It *is* true," he exclaims, raking a hand through his hair. "If I didn't throw that stupid rune—"

"Then I'd be dead," I interrupt bluntly.

He grits his teeth, but any reply dies on his tongue. He knows I'm right. I'd rather live with occasional headaches than not live at all.

I grab his hand and tug him closer to me. I cup his cheek, gently caressing the length of his scar. Electricity flares in the space between us, throbbing with every stroke of my thumb. "You are not at fault, Sky. This is *not* your fault." I urge him to believe me. His face heats up and his eyes widen. I pull his face closer to mine and gently kiss his scar as it crests over his cheek. "This is not your fault. You *saved* my life."

He doesn't move for a while, stunned into a statue-esque stillness. Then he throws his arms around me and sobs against my shoulder, releasing whatever guilt and shame he's carried for the past two years.

I hug him, not wanting to let go.

Chapter Nineteen

The sun shines over the party as I stop just outside the back doors, my heart swelling as I take it all in. Soph is sitting at the round table, a ravished plate of food in front of her and a pile of gifts and wrappers taking up the rest of the table. A huge smile plays on her face, but when she notices me lurking near the doors, looking much better courtesy of an hour-long nap, she leaps from her seat and bounds over to me—her smile growing ten times the size.

"Em!" she calls, barreling into my arms. "I'm so glad you're feeling better."

I stroke the back of her head. "It was just a one-off, Soph. How's the party?"

She pulls away, eyes sparkling with child-like delight. The sweet music from The Peacocks floats through the afternoon, carried on the gentle breeze.

I'm so grateful I didn't miss her entire party. When someone calls over the din "Cake time!" I know I couldn't have arrived at a more perfect moment.

Soph wraps her arms around my waist and side-hugs me as we shuffle closer to the banquet table, where my and Sky's large, one-layer red velvet rests on an elaborate crystalline cake stand. "I'm having so much fun—even more now that you're here."

Trelia presents the knife to Soph as I step to the side to catch her reaction to the cake. She beams. "How poetic." I didn't think she'd catch onto the underlying meaning—*it's okay to embrace the child inside you*—but I'm elated, buoyed on by her reverence while sliding the knife through the cake as if it's nearly too perfect to destroy. The deep crimson winks back at us, promising a mouthful of rich, decadent red velvet.

She hands the knife back to Trelia, who divvies a thin slice onto a plate for all those in attendance.

"The cake was your idea, wasn't it?" Sophia asks, sitting down at the table and clearing a place for me to sit with her. She settles down and glances at me expectantly, taking her first bite. She holds her hand up in front of her mouth and exclaims, "That's delicious! The flowers…they add that extra…"

"Something?" I supply; I know it's the most generic, over-used, non-explanatory word *ever*… But come on, it's a saying.

Soph nods, scarfing down another forkful. "This is what you were up to yesterday." It's not a question.

"Sky knows this amazing place full of gorgeous flowers," I add, feeling inclined to supply some kind of detail about my whereabouts, though I suppose it's not strictly necessary.

Kisha, Sky, Jax, and Quicken take up the remaining seats at the table, pushing aside the queen's presents and stacking them up on the ground; mostly books and slippers I notice.

Jax steals my fork from my hand and snatches a quick bite of my cake before returning it. He leans across the table, a devilish smirk on display, and conspiratorially asks, "So, what are we all talking about?"

I bat at him and he leans back in his chair, shooting me a bemused glare.

"Thank you all for the party," Soph says, dabbing at the corners of her mouth with a little cloth napkin that she pulled out of who knows where. She drops it beside her empty plate. "I haven't felt this free in a long time."

Sky and I exchange glances, both catching onto the despair evident in her tone.

"Is everything okay?" I ask.

She gives me a discontent smile. "I know you all have to leave soon in search of Eve's remnants; I suppose I'm just a little saddened without the knowledge of when I'll see you again."

I take her hand, running my thumb across her smooth skin. "We'll be back before you even know we're gone." A lie, of course. She's on to something; I don't have a clue how long securing and repairing Eve is going to take. We could be gone for days, weeks, months… I certainly hope that it doesn't take longer than that.

Soph sighs. The melody of the music swells and a shriek resounds through the party, raising the hair on my arms. The horrific sound is followed by a hard and resolute *thud*.

All six of us jump from our seats, necks craning to find out what's happened. Bodies surge around us, all directed toward the back doors of the palace. A scent I'm far too familiar with drifts toward me, a subtle note in the suddenly humid air.

Soph pushes through the crowd, annoyed that they don't immediately part for her, and gasps when she takes in the scene. I follow quickly behind her, eager to find out who's hurt—and how.

Laying propped against the doors is Trelia, her arm is trapped underneath a boulder-sized chunk of the transparent gem the exterior of the palace is made out of. Her arm is hazy through the material, but the wrong angle and the splotches of crimson blood are unmistakable. It's broken. That much we can tell by the agony creasing her petite face if nothing else. Seeing the poor, mangled limb is particularly macabre.

I drop to her side, pushing strands of sweaty hair away from her forehead. "Trelia, we're going to get this off you. Look away." Without protest, she pinches her eyes shut and turns to me, burying her face against my chest. A group of servants from the crowd step forward, positioning their hands around the jagged edges of the gem and heaving it off her. A collective gag weaves through the onlookers. Unlike them, however, I'm not brave enough to look again.

"Someone run down to the infirmary and grab the healer," Sophia orders, pointing in the direction of the village. "Emilia, Mr. Sky, follow me to my study. You there, keep Miss Trelia distracted until the help arrives." With a swish of her skirts, she's heading toward the front doors of the palace—the closest unobstructed entrance—and Sky and I are baying on her heels like dogs.

We reach her study, a shroud of silence hanging heavy around us. I have no idea what Soph wants to talk to us about, but my gut—and the purse of her lips—is telling me that it's serious.

Soph sits down in the chair behind her desk and tents her fingers together. She appears a lot older than she is; her demeanor alone makes me feel five and ready for a lecture.

"You'll leave tonight," she says, cutting through

the silence.

"What?" I blurt, stumbling forward and catching myself on the guest chair. She studies me, the bags under her eyes are a light purple and her cheeks are sunken as if the last ten minutes aged her ten decades. I zip my mouth shut; I won't be another factor in my sister's stress.

"I was selfish, demanding you stay until my birthday when I should have been urging you on to retrieve Eve and save the kingdom from the start." She sucks in a breath and hangs her head. "Trelia wouldn't be hurt if I did the right thing. Therefore, you all—whoever is going on this journey with you —are to leave tonight. Do you have your course mapped out?" She directs this question at Sky, who blankly nods. "Then pack your bags. I'll tell Mr. Hackman to prepare your carriage. Be ready by sundown."

My little sister was one moment enjoying herself, acting like a proper sixteen-year-old on her birthday, and just like that…she's the queen again.

And now she's sending us away.

I swallow, bite my cheek, and peek over at Sky, who seems as shocked as I am. But we both know she's right; we came here to save a kingdom, not throw a party.

Chapter Twenty

The wheels of the carriage rattle along the broken roads, synchronized with the steady beating of the horses' hooves. I cross my arms on the back of the seat, watching the palace—and my sister —shrink in the distance.

Jaxon, who was curating a map with all the routes and shortcuts that would take us to the different kingdoms while I was reconnecting with my sister, exclaims, "We're going to Eirae first. Now, there are a few things we should be wary of."

I try to ignore him, sinking deeper into my sorrow; I miss my sister already, but I know that this is why I came here. Why I decided to follow these relative strangers to a completely different *realm.* Jaxon kicks my foot and I whip around, glaring at him. "*What?*"

"You're not even paying attention," he hisses, curling his fingers around the edges of the map laid out in his lap. "You're going to need to know this, Em."

I sigh and relent, knowing he's right. I slouch back against the upholstered seat, arms and ankles crossed. I chose to wear an outfit that's more flexible, selecting a pale purple dress that's cut off right below my knees. The one-layered skirt sways gently against my skin. If, for some reason, I need to make a run for it, I don't want to be tripped by my own fashion choice.

"The monarch of Eirae is a twenty-something king who inherited the throne after his father's unfortunate passing. His name is Jayden Prince, and he's hardly ever alone." Jax smirks. "I'd try to avoid direct conversations with him if I were a…uh… *female*." He snickers. "It might be best if you let me and Sky do the talking in this particular kingdom."

I furrow my brow, slightly perturbed. What was the point of coming if I was just going to stand silently by? As if Jax could read my mind, he replies, "We need you to act like a lie detector. Stand aside, do your thing, and keep him from pulling the wool over our eyes. Got it?"

I nod.

"It shouldn't be too hard to persuade him to give us Eirae's fragment of Eve. Glaven and Eirae have had excellent relations for centuries. I'm sure he'd be eager to help us." Jaxon moves his finger down farther on the map, then peeks out the window and shouts to Quicken, "Take the next left! Past the elms!"

Quicken grunts in response, rolling his shoulders. His dreadlocks tumble across his back. His top hat sits back on his head, leaving his face illuminated by the lantern perched beside him. The moon is high in the sky now, still faded from the brilliant rays trailing off the sinking sun. In only a matter of minutes, the sun will be completely gone, leaving us to pick our way across the terrain by Jaxon's directions and a single, flickering lantern. My confidence in us getting to Eirae in one piece starts to dwindle. I bring my knees up to my chest, tugging the hem of my dress toward my calves, and lean against Kisha's shoulder.

Kisha takes my hand, lacing her fingers between mine, and smiles. "I'm glad you're back, Em."

I blink up at her. "I am too. Now, how are you feeling about allowing Jax to navigate us?"

Kisha throws her head back and laughs. Wispy strands of blonde hair tickle my face. "I have absolutely no confidence in that. He once walked into the Glaven Mother's Auxiliary Meeting thinking it was a pub. He wasn't even old enough to drink. Nor was he tall enough to read the sign posted on the door, apparently."

Jax clicks his tongue. "The mothers loved me."

"Because you were ten!"

The carriage erupts in content laughter, and

stories of the past—none that I can remember—are swapped between them, reminding me just how much I've missed out on and just how much has been taken from me. I watch Sky. He's pressed into the corner across from me, one foot on the seat with his arm hooked around his knee. The tie around his head has loosened, allowing chunks of black hair to fall across his forehead. The last rays of sunlight dart through the open window, and the scent of pine needles and smoke carry on the gentle breeze. The light catches his face, brightening the ravine of his scar and making his blue eyes sparkle like the depths of the ocean. I catch my breath, utterly entranced, when he turns toward me. We watch each other for a moment, the tension between us magnifying. Everything else—the sound of the wheels and the horses, the chatter and laughter from Kisha and Jaxon, the bark of village dogs, and the shouts from playing children—all disappear. It's only us for a space of time that feels like a millennium. But then he looks away, and nothing's changed, except for the tightness in my chest and an uncertainty rattling in my mind.

Why does he make me feel like this?

I push myself toward the window farthest from him, hip to hip with Kisha, and tune myself into their conversation. I don't want to acknowledge whatever is brewing between me and Sky, and

173

maybe, if I push it aside, I won't have to.

"So I had to stitch the sleeve back to her gown right before she walked down the aisle. Life lesson? Don't commission a seamstress from another kingdom unless you can pick it up yourself. Carriage deliveries these days are *so* unreliable." Kisha rolls her eyes before starting into a tale of how she paid for a custom tea set from Aquartia but it got broken from the jarring of the carriage ride alone.

Heat swathes my cheeks. I bite my lip, knowing it's heat associated with Sky's attentive gaze, lingering on me, probably wondering what in the world just transpired.

I refuse to think about it any longer. My eyelids feel heavy and there's a dim humming lingering from my migraine earlier. I have dozens of things I need to discover, consider, or even just ponder. Stress weighs on me. Now is not the time. I let my head fall against the back of the seat, succumbing to the persistent desire to sleep.

I jolt awake, sweat clinging to my lower back from where I was pressed against the seat for several long hours. The carriage bumps into something in our path and I jolt forward, squeaking in surprise.

"What's happening?" I ask Sky, who's thrown upward when the wheels ram into what must be a boulder. He hits his head on the top of the carriage and slams back into his seat, groaning.

"I don't know," Sky says, probing the spot on the top of his head.

Jax leans out the left side window, squinting into the void of nighttime. I must've only been asleep for a few hours since it doesn't appear to be close to morning. "Hey, Quicken! What's going on? I can barely see a thing." The wheels smack into another object and Jax is thrown back into the carriage, right onto Kisha's lap. She grumbles and shoves him onto the narrow floor between the seats.

Quicken's reply comes in a hasty manner, "You're not the only one! I think we took the wrong path."

Jax reaches onto the seat and fumbles around for the copy of the map he made, deciding that it may be best just to stay on the floor for a while. He narrows his eyes at it, struggling to make anything out. "I need a light!"

Sky rolls his eyes. "And how are we going to make that happen?"

Something occurs to me, and I reach into my satchel beside me to dig out my phone. It doesn't work since the Solstice Realm doesn't have electricity, but maybe the flashlight will still work. I find my phone, turn it on, and shake it; a cone of blinding white light shoots over Jax's shoulder and onto the map. He startles. "I shouldn't even be surprised. *Mages*."

"It has nothing to do with magic," I try explaining to no avail. Jax is lost in the intricate calligraphy of his map, tuning me out. I hunch forward, keeping my phone flashlight aimed so he can put us on route again.

Jax *hmphs* to himself then crawls over to the window, rolling the map up and clenching it securely in one hand. "You went down a shortcut! It's rough driving for another half hour, but it should cut a day out of our journey!"

Quicken seems satisfied with that answer, leaning forward. Tense yet prepared for the challenge ahead. "Hang on then! And watch your heads!" He pulls on the reins and the horses jolt to the right. Tree limbs scratch the carriage as we pass under them. The cacophony of hooves pounding on hardly trodden dirt, rocks hitting the wheels, and the branches maiming the exterior of the carriage keeps me on edge. I'm not going to be able to fall asleep again. Suddenly alert, I crawl closer to the window. I watch the world pass by, the fresh smell of the forest mingles with the musky scent of something freshly dead. My skin crawls. There must be a dead deer or something just beyond the trees; a predator eating happily. I scrunch away from the windows, no longer awed by the forest at night.

Chapter Twenty-One

The morning sunlight burns. I lift my arm up to block it. My neck is stiff from sleeping curled in a ball in the corner of the carriage, and my right leg fell asleep. Pins and needles shoot through it when I move. Kisha stirs beside me; her dress has, somehow, not gained a single wrinkle. How unfair. Mine looks like a mountain lion took it to its den and used it as a blanket—a de-clawed mountain lion since there's yet to be any tears.

I rub a hand down my face and smack my lips drowsily, wanting to return to my sleep and catch up on the hours so rudely taken from me during the night. But I know I shouldn't. People are talking outside the carriage and the distinct sounds of a village envelop us.

I peek out of the window to see Quicken talking with another man. The second man has sun-kissed skin and a weathered face. His black hair is flecked with silver. I lean forward, keeping everything besides my eyes out of sight.

The older man says, gesturing to the tiny, secluded village behind him, "We don't have enough food to feed your entire party. We can't handle a single mouth more."

I wrinkle my brow and frown. My internal senses scream at me, pointing to the obvious lie the man told. It may be a small village—hardly able to even be considered a village—but there are gardens in the backyards of the houses I can see. I'm positive there's enough food to feed us, so why doesn't the man want us to stop here?

"It's just for the morning, sir. We'll be out of your hair by lunch." He steps closer, earning a glare from the older man. "We've been traveling all through the night." Quicken juts his thumb toward the carriage, where the marks from the branches and beat-up wheels are surely visible. "Please. We're just after a bit of hospitality. Food and water for us and the horses. Then we're gone." He mimes disappearing with his hands, flicking his fingers outward.

The man shifts from foot to foot. "Food, water, that's it. Don't talk to anyone either, ya hear?" He glares coldly at the carriage, then nods toward the closest house behind him; it's tucked underneath a section of tall pine trees, a battered fence sectioning off a small yard from the rest of the secluded village.

My stomach grumbles at the mere thought of a hot meal.

"Thank you, sir," Quicken says, bowing politely before hurrying back to the carriage.

I return to my seat as the carriage rattles off toward the man's house. I decide I should probably wake the others since we'll be getting out soon.

I shake Kisha by the shoulders until she groggily opens her eyes. "What?" she hisses, cowering from the sun.

"Get up. We're stopping." I move onto Jax, kicking him in the shin until he opens his eyes to glare at me. "Up, up, up."

"You're like a child," he groans, stretching and popping his back. The sound always makes me cringe.

I ignore his comment, moving onto gently shaking Sky awake. The gentle part is more to get under Jax's skin than because I have a soft spot for the youngest brother.

Sky blinks up at me, a frown on his face that quickly evaporates once he realizes who it is. "What's up?" He yawns with a hand over his mouth, retaining his dragon breath.

Before I can get a word in to explain what's happening, the carriage slams to a halt and Quicken hops down, peering through the window and sighing in relief once he finds us all awake. "Breakfast!"

Kisha and Jax dart to their feet, pushing open the

left door and excitedly jumping onto the muddy ground. Sky and I exchange a glance before we follow them.

Quicken herds us to the front door, where the unnamed man is waiting with a grim scowl. "This is Ruddy. He's *offered* to give us shelter and food for a couple of hours. I'm sure he'll be very *hospitable* while I go tend to the horses." Quicken smiles at each of us in turn, lingering a little longer on Kisha than I find strictly necessary. Maybe it's just an employee-to-boss kind of thing, though I doubt that.

Quicken pats my shoulder as he passes, and I suspect that it has something to do with me not calling him out on the lie. Hospitable, offered... Ruddy obviously wants to wash his hands clean of us as soon as possible.

Ruddy opens the door grudgingly and leads us in. His home, much like the outside, is weathered and washed in neutral colors. Boring to the eye, though very cozy. A fireplace is lit in the corner and a woman is bundled up on the couch in front of it, a paperback novel is situated on her lap and a mug of tea leaves a moist circle on the end table beside her. There's one large window on the left wall, lighting the house up and leaving little need for torches or sconces.

It's tiny, more of a shack than an actual house.

Standing from this spot on the welcome mat, I can see the dining room—a tiny two-person table pushed beneath the window—the living room, and the even smaller kitchen which is essentially just a counter and an ice chest. There's a hallway across from us that I assume leads to the bathroom and their bedroom.

The Solstice Realm might not have electrical lights or technology, but its furnishings and water systems seem to be up to date: showers and indoor bathrooms.

"Make yourself at home," Ruddy grumbles, his scowl deepening.

The woman on the couch startles, fingers curling around the edges of her book as her head whips toward us. She's pretty, probably around thirty-five to forty. Her red hair is tied in a messy bun and her face is angular and sharp. She scans us with a pair of green eyes. "Ruddy?" She shifts on the couch to face her husband. A silent question passes between them. She tugs the blanket tighter around her, avoiding looking at us completely now.

I wonder what Ruddy said in their silent exchange.

"We appreciate what you're doing for us," Sky says, sensing the unease between the couple. His lips thin when Ruddy only returns a disapproving grunt. I swear, it's like a caveman is living inside him.

"Food's right o'er here." Ruddy points to the kitchen, crossing his arms again. "Darlin', they're also partaking in some of our horse feed." He huffs, watching us with an accusatory gaze as Sky tugs open the lid to the ice chest. Inside, there's little more than meat and bottles of milk.

My hopes for a hot meal are immediately dashed. What are we supposed to eat?

"Got some oats in the cupboard, berries and such on the counter." He points to a small, wicker bowl. Raspberries add a splash of color to the dreary kitchen. "I could prepare you somethin' if you want." I sense that he only offers to get us out of his home as soon as possible, but I'm not going to deny food.

Sky smiles warmly at him. "That'd be great. Thank you, again."

"You can wait outside with your friend. Got a table out there with some chairs." Ruddy nods to the door, agitation rolling off him in waves.

Sky tries to say thank you again, but is immediately halted by the withering look on Ruddy's face. His entire demeanor screams *if you say another word, I'll murder you with my bare hands.*

I can understand being territorial to a degree; I would hate it if random strangers came insisting upon delving into my carefully preserved and collected resources as well. But I'd help people if they looked like they needed it. Wasn't our carriage enough evidence that we've been traveling in rather rough conditions?

By their unwillingness, I've also come to the conclusion that they don't know who I am. I rather like it. The stares of people passing by and the whispers about me behind raised hands make my skin crawl and my heart beat faster. Being treated as normal? As nothing? I find safety and comfort in that.

We file outside. Sunlight slants across our skin, dappling through the canopy of pine needles and tree branches. I stop with the heels of my boots an inch deep in the mud outside the house and look around. The village reminds me of a camping trip I went on once with my family back in the Earthen Realm. It was the first and last camping trip I've ever been on and I loved it. The smell of the wild, the thrill of adventure, the bond between me and my family strengthening: *we are in this together*. Though it was nowhere near the rough conditions dedicated hikers go through, we still reaped the satisfying feeling of survival from it, knitting us together and having each other's backs. I love my Earthen family, and though I was never supposed to meet them at all, I'm grateful I've gone through what I have. That they, even if it was for a short amount of time and I may never see them again, are still my family. A part of who I am.

But who am I really? With only two years of memories and a disjointed vision of my past…

That's something I'm going to have to figure out.

Chapter Twenty-Two

$\mathcal{J}$ax rests his forearms on the rickety wooden table and leans toward me. His mouth quirked to the side. "What did the mage say when he walked into a bar?"

I scrunch my face. Is he really telling a joke right now? I have to appreciate how he lightens the mood though, so I make my smirk match his and ask, "What did he say?"

"Give me a drink." Jax leans back in his chair, face thrown to the sky, a bellowing laugh resounding around the worn-down patio.

I sneer in disappointment. "That wasn't even funny." Honestly, that was the worst excuse for a joke I've ever heard in my life.

"It's so funny because it's so true," Jax scoffs, rolling his eyes playfully. He mutters something about *no sense of humor* under his breath.

"Jax, you do understand that wasn't actually a joke—" Sky states, one eyebrow lowered, the other hedging toward his hairline. He looks like he's holding back a laugh. I'm appalled that I'm traveling with people who think *that* is remotely funny.

Even Kisha has her hand raised, hiding a growing smile behind it. Who are these people?

I bite my cheek. "What did the unicorn say when he walked into a bar?" If we're telling crappy jokes now then I might as well just throw it back in their faces.

"What did he say?" Jax mirrors, his smirk growing wider by the second.

I lean in really close, glancing to my left and right like I'm going to reveal a massive secret. "Give me a drink," I whisper in a conspiratorial tone. I don't know what I expected to happen, but Jax sitting back with a perplexed expression on his face wasn't it.

"But unicorns don't drink," he says slowly, mouth pursed. Gears in his head whirring.

I drop my face into my hands. "Are you serious right now?"

Then the entire table erupts in hysterical laughter.

"Kidding, kidding," Jax insists. His blue eyes dance with mischief. "I had to say something."

"I was really starting to question the brain cells in this group," I admit, shaking my head.

"We've got at least…" Jax does a headcount then clicks his tongue. "Five."

Before we can discuss who has the most brain cells, Ruddy and his wife come over and plop a tray full of chipped, white ceramic bowls down on the table. Inside is something surprisingly familiar.

Yogurt with fresh raspberries resting half-submerged, like people resting around the border of a hot tub.

Ruddy's wife sets a fistful of spoons down on the tray, then retreats behind her husband as fast as she can.

"Dig in," Ruddy says. Then his voice hardens and he adds, "Then leave."

I swallow; being somewhere where you're un-wanted is probably one of the most uncomfortable feelings. Sky is the first to pick up a spoon, "digging in" as Ruddy demanded.

He smacks his lips and shrugs. "It's not that bad."

The rest of us pick up our bowls, eating our yogurt in awkward silence. The joyous laughter from moments ago leaves no trace that it even happened.

As soon as all of us are done eating, we pile the bowls back onto the tray and hand it to Ruddy's wife at the door, whispering our gratitude— Quicken bowing deeply—before we retreat to the welcoming privacy of the carriage. The sooner we get out of here, the better.

I sidle up next to the window, studying the tiny

village as Quicken directs the horses back onto the main path. There's something off about this place; the trees bending low over the buildings, faded burn marks scarring the weathered homes, scared eyes peeking out from drawn curtains.

Sky follows my line of sight and sighs. He rests his forearms on his knees, his hands hanging down. "This was one of the villages Aaron stormed after his tirade at the Glaven palace. One of the many villages marked by my brother's cruel hand." His usually vibrant eyes darken. I wonder how Sky and Jax took it, not only losing a friend but also a brother. "Trust is hard to come by these days. I'm surprised they even let us stay."

I watch Ruddy's humble home disappear behind a wall of trees, the cacophony of branches scratching the hull of the carriage begins again, and I know— just as I know lies from the truth—that this journey won't be as easy as I originally thought. Dread settles in my stomach, churning with the yogurt and raspberries. We settle into an uncomfortable silence as the carriage bumps along.

Short, clipped whispers dance on the breeze. Quicken is singing. My eyes slide closed as I rest my head against the door, letting the warm sunlight trickling through the leaves and pine needles and the hopeful tone of Quicken's song lull me to sleep. Though, by no means is it peaceful.

The next day passes; the carriage continues through the forest path, curving around hills lush with wildlife. The farther we get from Glaven, the more prominent Aridam's curse becomes. Out here, in the Northeast of the Solstice Realm, everything is blooming. Everything is alive, together, thriving. Houses aren't crumbling, which I notice in awe as we turn down the main street of Eirae, gaining the attention of the villagers. Eyes snag on the sleek, black carriage, out of place among the crisp, white infrastructure. Everything here is white. White houses, neatly shaped in spacious squares, create an identical grid on the hill beneath the stark palace. Unlike the sparkling walls of the Glaven palace, these walls are monotone, save for the intensity of the sun glaring down on them.

I catch my breath, eyes impossibly wide, trying to take it all in. I'm sure I resemble a little girl at an Earthen zoo, half-hanging out of the window, but I don't care. I've never seen something so...lush, flaunting the kingdom's wealth. The king must be a fantastical, male version of Victoria Johnson. *Oh, this is going to be so great.* I find that I don't have a problem with Sky taking charge this time. It may be best to stay out of the king's eye after all.

Quicken snaps the reins and the horses take off in a gallop. The palace looms in front of us, daunting yet inviting. A weird combination that makes the hair on the back of my neck stand on end.

The sooner we can get out of here, the better. Who knows what kind of damage Glaven could sustain while we're gone. The sooner Eve is repaired, the sooner we can all rest, knowing no one else is going to be hurt because of Aridam's curse.

Sky chuckles, bringing me back to the present as the carriage slows, pulling into the round courtyard in front of the palace. A thin white curtain shifts in the window directly above the entrance.

"What's so funny?" I ask, slipping back into my seat. My hair is windblown and frizzy. It probably wasn't the best idea to stick my head out of the carriage like a dog right before a very important meeting…with a *king*, nonetheless. But I don't have much self-control, apparently.

Sky tucks a few wild strands behind my ear, attempting to tame it. I flush and back away from his touch. *Don't acknowledge it. Don't think about it. These feelings will go away.* But, as my heart pitter-patters in my chest and my cheeks continue to redden, I have a sinking suspicion that my cowardice plans won't work.

"Is everyone ready?" Sky asks, facing the rest of

the carriage. He tidies his hair and smooths his shirt. We're all running on two days without a change of clothes, let alone a shower.

"Ready as we'll ever be," Kisha adds, jutting her chin toward the palace doors. She clicks her tongue. "Too late to back down now."

I turn to see a butler with blonde hair and hazel eyes approaching the carriage, white-gloved hands behind his back and a kind smile warming his rather sharp features. Just like everything else in this kingdom, he's wearing a white tailcoat that swishes with every step.

"Greetings," he calls, dropping into a short, polite bow. "How may the palace assist you today?" His bright eyes take in the battered carriage. "Travelers, I suppose?"

"Of a sort," Sky says, pushing open the carriage door and stepping down onto the stone-laden courtyard. Tall, neatly trimmed bushes conceal half the courtyard, only opening up to the palace and to the main street down into the Eirae village. "We're here to discuss something incredibly important—and time-sensitive—with King Jayden Prince." His tone commands authority. A baker's son turned into a diplomat.

The butler straightens his posture, suddenly on edge. He glances between the five of us as we all pile out in front of him. "Does His Majesty know you're coming?"

"Not exactly," Sky responds. He takes a step around the butler, closer to the palace. The butler is about half a foot taller than Sky, but that doesn't seem to phase him. I'm practically a mouse compared to the butler. "Queen Sophia Strazenfield sent us on an emergency mission. Business between us and the king, you do understand?" He raises an eyebrow, challenging the butler to question the Glaven queen.

"I'm sure His Majesty would be most pleased to welcome in our neighbors." The butler flashes a quick smile before pivoting and heading back into the palace. We're hot on his heels.

The inside of the palace is as stark as the exterior. The walls are crisp white with large box windows overlooking an elaborate garden. Flowers of every variety balance out the lack of color inside the walls.

The foyer branches off into three hallways and a massive, crystal chandelier dangles from the ceiling, refracting rainbow-colored light across the walls. I took an art class in my junior year and I remember learning that white signifies the entire spectrum of colors. Is that why the entire kingdom is white? I catch up to the butler as he leads us down the center hallway and up a flight of narrow steps, into a labyrinth of doors and archways, windows and torches. For a poised man, he certainly walks fast. Of course, his legs are practically three times longer than mine. That may be why I'm out of breath by the time I push my way to the front of the human train.

He stops in front of a door with intricate designs carved into the smooth surface. "Is everything white just to catch the rainbow?" I ask, tilting my head as the butler's eyes sparkle with a sudden observation. The door opens and I'm met with an impossibly beautiful face. My mind goes blank.

"Very smart, Princess Emilia," the man says, though the term *boy* may be more accurate. He extends his hand toward me and I take it without thinking. "It's a pleasure to have you in my kingdom. It has certainly been a long time." He steps aside, sweeping his arm out to the room. His study is dazzling; white settees are pushed against either wall, and a bleached fur rug trails from the doorway to the glass desk sitting in front of a window. A curtain swings gently, moved by his hand only moments ago. He returns to his chair behind his desk. He leans back and beams at us as we shuffle in. "I'm King Jayden Prince. So tell me," he directs his enchanting brown eyes toward me, "is it true that you don't remember anything before Aaron's unfortunate…escapade?"

I settle down onto one of the settees, struggling to keep my surprise masked. We've met before?

Why didn't anyone say anything? "It's true," I mutter, glancing wearily at the king.

He frowns, though the corners of his mouth are still tilted upward, so I figure he can't be that sad. "How devastating." He snaps his fingers and the butler hurries over to him. "Bring us some light refreshments, will you, Carson?"

Carson, the butler, nods before scurrying back into the labyrinth.

Silence settles over the room; rainbows dance across the walls as sunlight hits the perfectly poised chandeliers. Jayden rests an elbow on his desk and his chin in his hand. His fingertips graze the underside of his top lip as his mouth spreads wide in a mischievous smirk. "Emilia, Emilia, Emilia…" he chuckles. "It has certainly been too long." The accompanying wink sets my nerves on edge. Jax shifts uncomfortably on the settee beside me. His words ring through my mind: *he's never alone.*

"We have something incredibly important to ask of you," I say, forcing his attention away from admiring me and to what we came here to do in the first place.

"Ah. No need to tell me." He runs a hand through his blonde hair and pushes up from his seat, returning to the window just as Carson opens the door, a tray of drinks carefully positioned in his arms.

Only as I stare at the glittering, illuminated liquid inside the decanter, do I understand that '*light refreshments*' means precisely that.

Jayden pours all of us a glass that's half-full, sparkling like the sun.

"What…is that?" I ask, taking the glass he offers to me.

Jayden takes a sip of his own after distributing the rest. "It's nectar from a flower—the Solstice Flower—rumored to have been created a century ago after a solar flare entered the Solstice Realm's atmosphere. Who knows if it's true or just a fairytale." He takes a longer swig and sighs, tilting the glass toward the sunlight; golden rays dance across the far wall. "Delicious nonetheless."

I hesitantly take a sip of the drink, startled to find that he's right. It *is* delicious. Sweet and bitter, and increasingly warm as it slides down my throat. Comparable to lemonade in the Earthen Realm, which used to be my favorite drink—besides Mo's hot chocolate, of course. Now that pedestal just got taken over. I down the rest of the glass, my stomach blooming with a comforting heat.

Jayden tilts my chin toward him. Since when was he this close? He was over by his desk only a second ago, and I didn't even see him move. "Emilia," he whispers. His voice is a promise of both pain and desire. I rise to my shaky feet, sinking into his touch. I don't spare a glance at the rest of the group. I don't question the unusual silence blanketing the room. All I can focus on is how he bites his bottom lip with his canines, how his brown eyes turn amber in the sunlight, and how his hand on my cheek feels so good.

"Jayden," I purr. My head is foggy. I know I should be questioning *this*... My sudden need to be closer to him. I trail my fingers gently across his cheekbone. "Jayden, you remember me?"

Jayden steps closer. He smells of roses. "Of course I do, Emilia. Why don't you stay here with me? The others can continue on without you." His hand ventures toward my neck, fingertips pressing into my skin. Pain flares through my lungs, but I don't tell him to stop. I don't resist as my lungs burn for air.

"I will," I squeak. "I would want nothing more."

Jayden's grin turns feral, wild, animalistic. He leans closer, breath flush against my throat. Then he whispers something that waves away the fog clouding my mind, "Wake up."

I jump, frantically glancing around. My glass lies broken at my feet, small nicks are bleeding on my exposed calves, and there are tiny tears in my dress. I reach for my throat, scared that I'll find purple fingerprints.

"What happened?" Sky asks, already in front of

me, ignoring the glass as he kneels in front of the settee. He searches my eyes, brow furrowed. "Was it another vision?"

Confusion tears through me. What just happened? My attention snags on the glowing decanter and my stomach turns. Creatures in nature warn people of their toxicity by flaunting bright colors...I can't help but compare that to this swirling drink before me. I catch Jayden watching me out of the corner of my eye, he's chewing delicately on his bottom lip. "Yeah. Same vision as usual. Aaron, my father..." I tell Sky, wincing at the lie as it slides over my tongue. I don't want to lie to him. Friends don't lie to friends, so why did I? Jayden exhales so quietly that only an ear already trained on him could pick it up.

There's something wrong going on here, and I'm not going to leave until I figure it out.

Chapter Twenty-Three

*J*ayden tents his fingers on the desk in front of him. He's smiling, though I don't know why. What's so exciting about this situation? About me imagining him choking me? About no one else knowing what happened.

I tower over him, my palm flat against the desk. I'm channeling my inner Victoria Johnson, not letting anyone walk over me. That was Earthen Emilia. And as far as I'm concerned, she's part of the past now. I'm grateful that Jayden sent Kisha, Quicken, Sky, and Jax to help Carson dig around in the archives, searching for the location of Eirae's fragment of Eve.

"What was in that drink? What did it do to me? And—" I throw my hands out to the side, anger barely smothered under my controlled façade, "why do only you and I seem to know about it?"

Jayden sighs, as if I'm inconveniencing him. "I don't know what you're talking about." The lie is so smooth, it's almost believable. Except for my gift. I *know* he's lying. My fingers inch toward my neck. The air leaving my lungs felt too real. It couldn't have been just my imagination.

I slam both my hands down on his desk this time, rattling a cup of quills and knocking over his glass. The gold liquid spills across his desk; the sunlight bounces off the nectar, reflecting across the room. "Stop lying to me, King Jayden."

Jayden's expression is masked; lips turned up slightly in amusement, eyes feline and mischievous. He rakes his fingers through his hair before dipping one in the spilled liquid and dragging it across his desk, drawing something.

I narrow my eyes when he finally retracts his hand. "What is that?" I crinkle my brow. It looks like an honest-to-God child drew it.

"The sun, clearly," he says exasperatedly. "Don't you see the little lines representing sun rays? I thought it was pretty good, but now you're making me question my art skills." He pouts.

If he wasn't so adorable while pouting, I'd say something bitter and cynical. "Please just tell me. There's no point in lying. I can tell."

He raises a thin blonde eyebrow. "So, it's true then? I heard rumors, sure, but I didn't believe that the rightful queen of Glaven is also a mage."

"I'm not," I say, biting my lip. I would have never guessed that I'd be sitting in front of an incredibly handsome king, discussing the ins and outs of magic. I was gossiping with Samantha over what band players were cute or not only days ago. "It's called Soul Sight. It's a gene that allows me to see the truth in words." I purse my lips and gesture for him to continue. "I'd stop with the lies if I were you."

Jayden kicks back in his chair, propping his feet on his desk. His stare is intense, but I'm not backing down. I'm not going to leave without the truth. I'm done being kept in the dark. "Sit." He nods toward the settee. "I have a feeling we won't have very long. The archives are the most organized thing in this kingdom, it won't take them long to find the location of our fragment of Eve, and then they'll be back. And I'd prefer if this discussion remained between us."

"I agree," I respond, quicker than I intended. But I don't want to explain how the drink affected me to Sky and Jax. Not only would it be awkward, uncomfortable, and admit that I lied, but it'd also make them angry. I'd rather they focus on our task at hand and let me deal with the king. I take a seat on the edge of the settee, unprepared for what he's about to tell me.

"The Solstice Flower harnesses immense hallu-cinogenic powers. I have a mage in my staff, Rebecca, who can play with the flower's genetics and meld them to create a targeted fantasy for the consumer." He waves his hand toward me, completely nonchalant about the fact that he roofied me. "It was a test. If it worked on you, then you really are Princess Emilia Strazenfield. It's been too long since we've seen each other, and you've changed so much. Not to mention that Aaron is still a threat. Who knows what kind of mages he has recruited to his side?" He bats his eyelashes, clasping his hands together. "It was a safety precaution, Emilia. I'm sorry, but my kingdom, my people, come first." He narrows his eyes when I squirm in my seat; if all it was, was a test to determine my identity, then why was it so...intimate? "What did you see, Emilia?" When I don't respond, trying to force the blush that's creeping up my neck away, he admits, "It was supposed to be a memory of us the last time we were together. The Eirae library, novels spread out in front of us. I will never forget how brilliant your smile was; you were vibrant, nearly as much as the sun."

"Well, it certainly wasn't that," I blurt, biting my tongue and wishing I could retract the statement. It'll only open up a floodgate of questions that I don't want to answer.

But the king's eyes widen and he flushes, balling his hands into fists on his desk. "She...must've given you the wrong one."

Correct me if I'm wrong, but does the fabled King Jayden Prince really use a magical flower to attract companions? The idea itself is absurd, yet Jayden's reddening face seems to be answer enough. Before I can delve deeper into how completely wrong that is, Sky, Jax, Kisha, and Quicken burst through the doors.

They're covered in white dust, but they're grinning, arms full of weathered parchments and old tomes.

Sky shakes his head and dust flies everywhere. He unrolls a scroll and spreads it out on Jayden's desk, minding the spilled drink. He taps a neatly scrawled line. "It says the fragment of Eve is safely stored in Eirae's Temple. Where exactly is that?"

Jayden stands up, fingers nimbly straightening the buttons of his tailcoat. "Eirae's Temple is a storage ground for several of Eirae's most ancient artifacts, including the resting place for both my parents." He frowns down at the scroll, brown eyes tracing the curved letters. I wonder if his mother or father was the one to write it. "It's about an hour-long hike down to the swampland where the temple is hidden. Carson," Jayden waves the young man forward, "can you please see to it that all my appointments are canceled for the afternoon? I want to personally escort our neighbors there, besides, the temple has a blood seal that can only be unlocked by me. And send Rebecca."

Carson nods. "Right away, Your Majesty." He quietly exits the room; his footsteps sound no louder than a rat's.

"Follow me, please. We'll meet my resident mage at the entrance."

Rebecca, whom I've decided to hold a small grudge against since the vision slip-up, turns toward us as we push open the palace doors. Her ruby red hair falls in a straight line down to the small of her back, and her calm blue eyes shine as they meet Jayden's. The air intensifies as they near each other. Is she something more than just Jayden's personal mage?

Her face is petite, full cheeks tinged with pink, crimson-tinted lips, and a matching short stature. Shorter than me, which is saying something. She can't be more than 4'8.

She falls in step with me while Jayden and Sky walk ahead of us, immersed in conversation. The afternoon sun glints down on us, reflecting off the white buildings sprawled on the side of the hill. Everywhere I look now, I see a rainbow: reflected in a puddle on the ground, shining across the clear surface of a trough, in the gentle spray flung up from a horse's hooves as it clops down the street.

Jayden leads us around the side of the palace, toward a break in the line of hedges encircling the palace grounds. Ominous trees loom behind the gap, gnarled branches bent in low angles, shadows cast across the overgrown walkway.

"You must be Princess Emilia Strazenfield," Rebecca chirps, offering me her hand. Her voice matches her appearance; it's squeaky and mouse-like. Apparently, several of Eirae's occupants can be compared to a rodent of some kind. She fidgets with the clasp of her dark green cloak when I don't take her hand. How chipper she is just seems…wrong. Though, I instinctually know that this is her true self. My Soul Sight offers me that much, protecting me from being deceived, as in the case of Garamond. "I'm sorry about confusing the visions." She says, cutting straight into the tension shrouding me. She grits her teeth and winces, guilt conforming her expression. "By the time I realized what I did, it was too late. I'm such a scatterbrain sometimes!" She throws her hands up, offering me an apologetic smile.

"What's your ability, anyway? King Jayden said you can mess with the genetics of the Solstice Flower?" I soften my tone. Somehow, her demeanor whisks away my grudge. Most of it, at least. I won't say she's forgiven, but I'm not going to act like a complete scumbag. Everyone makes mistakes.

"Yes, I can do that, among other things," she says, grinning proudly. "I can also breed plants, animals, and the likes of such, creating mutations that wouldn't be possible without magic." She wiggles her fingers, bursting into a melodic laugh. "And you? Are you a mage, as well? I haven't heard much about Princess Emilia, save for the tragic events that unfolded two years ago. Everyone has heard about that."

"No, I'm not," I say bluntly. I'm so relieved to not have magic, to not be a mage. Though the specialty that Rebecca must feel has to be nice; only she can bring those particular animals and plants to life. Anyone can do what I can do. There's nothing about me...that makes me *special*.

She nudges me with her elbow. "That's okay. You're perfect the way you are."

I smile at her genuine words, letting the compliment smother out the self-doubt that started to bloom deep in my chest. "So, is there something between you and the king?" I gesture toward King Jayden. He's talking to Sky, wildly moving his hands to punctuate whatever point he's trying to make. The shadows of the forest blanket us, dotting across the path as the canopy above gives way to a few rays of golden sunshine. A rabbit scurries in the underbrush, darting in front of Jayden and Sky before disappearing back into the thick foliage.

Rebecca goes silent beside me, and when I peer down at her, I notice the increasing redness of her cheeks. She's staring straight at the rough ground, entirely focused on not answering my question. I'm not going to press her. Whatever it is can remain private; a secret between the two.

The breeze shifts, one moment smelling of trodden earth, nature, the fresh scent of a stream bubbling off to our right, and the next it reeks of rot and mildew. *The swamp.*

The ground beneath us gives way to mud and puddles of green water that are scattered about. The ominous croaking of toads and the buzzing of dragonflies rise in the air. An owl hoots off to our left and my head snaps there accordingly. My hair stands on end, perturbed by the ghoulish scenery.

Roughly twenty feet ahead of us, the ground gives way to an algae-ridden pool. Moss and lichen blanket the surrounding trees, hiding the roots that protrude from the wetlands.

And, in the center of it all, behind the eerie waters, is a building that appears to have been built around the time that the first king stood in front of the Glaven people; the pearlescent walls are crumbling, cracks have spread across the foundation the same as wrinkles creasing an aging face, and the archway is black. There doesn't seem to be a door, which seems off for it being a storage place for Eirae's ancient artifacts.

"How are we going to get across the swamp?" I ask, standing on the edge of the solid ground and staring at the sprawling water before us. I shiver, just imagining what kind of creatures could be lurking underneath the algae, in the darkest depths of the water. Dip one toe in and it could grab me. I give myself goosebumps, deciding it may be best to face the king and focus my wondering mind on something else.

Jayden smirks, meeting my eyes before turning to Rebecca. "Would you mind?"

He doesn't have to ask her twice. She steps forward, her face creasing with concentration. She holds her hands out in front of her and pinches her eyes closed. For a moment, everything is still, and I question if anything is even going to happen.

Then, the ground starts to shake. Birds flit from the trees, darting into the sky on frightened wings. Water splashes onto the ground at our feet. The swamp surges like an ocean. Waves beat at the sloped terrain on either side. Water drops start to rise, hovering for a single heartbeat in the center of the swamp, before dissipating, leaving behind a walkway of cracked, dry earth. I gape at it. How is this possible? Though, I should know by now that asking that question will never get me an answer. It just *is* possible.

It's *magic.*

Jayden steps onto the bridge. He turns around and flashes me a confident smile before offering me his hand. I take it and Rebecca tenses beside me. I'm hesitant to step onto the path of hardened dirt that's extended a foot above eerie, sludge-water, but Jayden tugs me forward. I stumble, waiting for the bridge to collapse right out from underneath me.

I sigh in relief when it doesn't.

We reach the entrance to the temple, the *mostly* solid ground is welcome.

Upon closer inspection, the black archway shimmers with a vague, almost unnoticeable streak of red. It pulsates across the wall of shadows. "What is that?" I ask, reaching toward it, needing to feel the magic under my fingers.

Jayden catches my hand before I can. "It's a blood seal. It'll burn whoever can't unlock it." He presses his palm flush against the seal and an ear-shattering *boom* echoes through the swamp; the red glow magnifies, traveling outward with the sound waves. Then the shadow wall falls away, revealing a marble hallway, leading into the depths of the Eirae Temple.

The temple smells of mold. The musk stings my scrunched nose. I attempt to bat it away, to no avail.

"What is that *smell?*" I hiss. Sure, you'd expect a

foul scent from a sealed temple. But this is beyond normal.

Jayden stops in front of a doorway leading into a small room to our right. The ceiling is cracked, allowing a thin stream of light to trickle across a stone box resting on a raised platform. I don't register what it is until Jayden sighs, his head hanging low, and says, "That'd be my parents."

Acidic bile climbs up my throat. I swallow and turn away from the casket.

Sky shifts uncomfortably. We lock eyes for a moment, but I pull my attention away. I won't be caught in the throes of his warm gaze. I refuse to be distracted by the tension between us. Not when we're so close to finally having our hands on the first fragment of Eve.

We shuffle further into the temple and the suffocating darkness. I'm not usually claustrophobic, but the narrow walkway and encroaching shadows make my heart stutter, sweat beading on the small of my back.

Jayden stops in front of a rectangular silhouette —a doorway, I realize with a start. "This is where we keep the artifacts." He steps into the room and takes a deep breath, as if pushing down all his memories of the place, putting his best foot forward. I don't know what's going on inside his head, but I instinctually know he's battling something. I rest my hand on his shoulder and he startles, casting a solemn look back at me. "I haven't been here since my parents passed."

"How did they die?" I ask tenderly, sensing he longs to talk about it.

He tenses, though his amber eyes shine through the shadows. "Vampires. A small group that escaped banishment. They came to the palace in a rampage, thirst controlling their actions." He scans the room, straightens his posture, and adds, "That is in the past. Now we must focus on the present."

Rebecca takes her cue. She enters the room on silent feet. With a single snap, the shadows shift into light; flecks comparable to dust float around the moderately sized room, glowing a hazy yellow.

Her modest explanation of her magic didn't do her justice. Not only can she change the genetics of plants and animals, but she can also toy with the atoms of nature.

How insignificant am I, compared to her?

I bristle as Rebecca raises an eyebrow, button-nose pointed at me. It's unnerving how she can sense what I'm thinking. How she can sense when I'm doubting myself.

I focus on the room instead, on the artifacts housed within, but when my eyes finally adjust... the room is empty.

Jax lets out an annoyed huff, crossing his arms

and shooting daggers toward the king. "Well? Where is everything?" He doesn't exactly use tact when dealing with royals. It's admirable, though I fear, one day, it'll hurt him.

Out of the corner of my eye, I catch a vague shimmer of red, darting across the walls. *A blood seal.*

Jayden presses his hand to the wall and I cover my ears in preparation for the teeth-grinding sound. Even though it's muffled, it still invites a dull headache.

Shelves are now lining the walls—the room seems to be three feet deeper than it was before. And on those shelves are silver boxes, gold etchings on the forefront of each glow ethereally.

Sky gasps, running his hand over a box on the middle shelf. When he whips his head around to take it all in, his demeanor shifts from disbelief to euphoria. "They're runes."

"The same kind you use?" I ask, curiously tracing the straight-forward angles and curves of the etchings. I conjure an image of the rune stone that dangled from Sky's Mustang's mirror, comparing it to the ones glowing all around the perimeter of the room.

He nods quickly, sliding the box off the shelf and setting it gently on the floor in the center of the room. I kneel down next to him, watching as he slips the lid off and grins at the item inside. Sitting alone in the center of the box is a piece of metal, as thin and white as ice. *Eve*. He turns to me, mouth forced into a restrained smile. "Care to do the honors?"

With slightly shaky hands, I reach into the box and gently lift the fragment. I don't realize I'm holding my breath, scared to even *breathe* around such a relic. The room around me shifts and another ear-splitting boom resounds from the temple. I grit my teeth against the onslaught of pain, my hand clenching out of instinct. I wince and draw my hand back, glaring at the line of red cut into my palm. The blood on the edge of the sword fragment fades into the ice-like blade, melding with it. And when I glance again at my cut, it's sealed back together, almost as if it never even happened, and the stinging has stopped completely.

"How?" I ask, snapping my head up to direct the question at Jayden, who must know what the sword is capable of—at least, more than me. But he looks confused, incredulous.

"Eve is the Sword of Life, Emilia," Sky says gently, his astounded voice ringing through the temple. "She's healed you because that's what she was made to do."

Hopefully, now she can heal our fragmented kingdom.

Chapter Twenty-Four

ou'll visit again?" Jayden asks, twirling a lock of my hair before gently setting it back on my shoulder.

I smile at him, my back to the carriage where the rest of my friends are waiting. "Of course I will. But after Eve is restored and my kingdom is no longer in trouble."

His hand lingers on my shoulder, affection overtakes his brown eyes. Not the affection of romance, closer to the affection between a brother and a sister. I turn to Rebecca, who's standing loyally at the king's side, cheeks tinged pink with jealousy. "Take care." I pull her into a hug, surprising us both. I'm not exactly a touchy person, so I don't know why I did that. "And go after what you want." I pull away, offering her an understanding smile. I can see the love she has for Jayden brewing in the space between them. I can only suspect that he feels the same.

Without another glance nor another word, I

scurry back to the carriage, suppressing my pride with having finally gathered the first fragment of Eve. One out of five down.

As the carriage rolls down the streets of Eirae, with Jax leaning out the window, map clutched in his hands and directing Quicken on where to turn, I pull my journal from my satchel and start to take note of today's adventure.

The silver glow of the moon trickles through the trees, stretching like bony fingers across the thatched roof of the Mirabelle Inn. We stop in a hand-constructed carriage house, lanterns dangling from the rafters, illuminating the dry hay patching the uneven ground.

The air is humid, different from the fresh breeze that seemed constant in the Northwest.

"How much farther until we arrive in Aquartia?" I ask Jax, hopping down onto the ground. Jax rolls the map up, looking out on the shadowed forest; trees sprawl as far as the eye can see, daunting, concealing whatever monsters dare to be lurking about.

"Another day at the very least," Jax says.

Quicken ties the horses up to a bar by a bag of

feed, and a trough of clean water rests beside them, untouched, almost as if it was waiting for us. With a loving pat, he joins us at the mouth of the carriage house. "Ready?" he asks, facing Kisha. His British accent still takes me off guard.

Kisha smiles warmly at him. Her cheeks appear to be tinged pink in the lantern light. "Yeah. I'm too tired. And my butt hurts. I can't sit in that carriage for another second." She pouts.

We cross into the shadows and head toward the main building. There's a crack of light that slips out from underneath the front door of the inn; it's gold and inviting, distorting every few seconds as if someone is walking in front of it on the other side.

Sky takes the last step onto the time-weathered porch, raising his fist to knock on the blush-colored door. The copper sign declaring it the *Mirabelle Inn*, squeaks above us, moved by a phantom wind. Accompanying the name is a depiction of a teapot, steam rising from the spout.

A man opens the door: his face is long, his eyes sunken into the recesses of his skull, circled by purple skin. And he's completely bald, not a hair on his head, his lip, nor his brow. He stands straight, a black suit fitted to his rectangular body.

Deceit, lies, lies, lies.

I stumble back a step, the sudden desire to turn and run pulsates through me. My heart skips a beat and my legs slightly tremble. Jax's warm hands cup my elbows, keeping me from falling down or fleeing. He's sturdy behind me, but his grip is tense. He can sense the danger as well.

"Rooms for five?" the man asks. His voice is smooth and silky. I find that I can walk again. I take a shaky step toward him, Jax's hands never leaving me.

"Sky," Jax whispers, trying to stop his brother from placing us willingly in the hands of danger.

But he's too late.

"That'd be most accommodating," Sky agrees, stepping into the picturesque inn. The gentle smell of rosemary drifts around the cozy foyer.

The walls are plastered with pink wallpaper and the floors are shining hardwood. A desk sits to our right, almost as long as the room. There's nothing behind it, and nothing on it save for a piece of parchment and a quill. There's not even an ink pot.

The foyer leads to three archways: the kitchen, a formal dining room, and a library with a stone fireplace. A staircase is almost flush against the desk, ascending to the second floor.

"Let me grab your keys." The man walks behind the desk, footsteps as silent as Carson's. Trained to not make a sound.

Run away, run away, run away. My mind and instincts are shouting at me, demanding that I turn from this inn immediately. I spin around, my heart beating so fast that I no longer have the strength to stand. I crumple to the floor, breathing erratically.

"Em, are you okay?" Sky asks, at my side in a second. He's tugging me up, holding me still against his own body. I'm cold all over, chilled to the bone by an inconceivable fear. But what am I afraid of? And why aren't the others as affected as I am?

Sky takes the keys from the man's outstretched hand, distributing them among our group, before helping me up the stairs. With each jolting step, my body aches, goosebumps peppering my skin.

I barely notice how impossibly long the hallway is, how each door looks the same, and how the scent of rosemary is stronger up here as if it's covering the stench of something else.

Sky fumbles to unlock the closest door. He stumbles through the darkness, stubbing his toes and cursing a few times. But he doesn't relent until I'm sprawled across the bed, fatigued by the pounding headache now threatening to drown out my every thought.

"Emilia, are you okay?" he asks again, urgently. The others have followed him into the room, forgoing their privacy and their exhaustion. Kisha settles onto the settee on the opposite wall of the bed. Jax and Quicken steal a quilt off the end of the bed and throw it on the floor, laying down on their backs and intently waiting for my panic to subside. I didn't even realize I was whimpering, curled into a ball, my hands clenched and my nails digging crescents into my palms.

A sheen of sticky sweat coats my forehead, but I don't wipe it away. I can feel the vision coming, just as I can sense the danger around us. I don't know who it was intended for, but I'm certain we just walked into a trap.

A lair of some kind...full of vampires.

I roll to the side, digging my fingers into the soft mattress. My teeth break the skin of my lip. The acidic taste of blood coats my tongue. Darkness overtakes me, and almost as quickly, it fades into a blinding light.

A boy is sitting beside me, looking at me with blatant love in his brown eyes. His thin lips are twisted into a grin and his sandy hair is disheveled. There's something melancholy about him as he rests his head against the bark of the tree we're propped against. "You've met my brothers, haven't you?" I can tell that it's not a question, not because I remember my past, but because my Soul Sight buds in my chest at the vaguest hint of dishonesty.

I nod, eagerly waiting for him to continue.

His eyes darken and his smile falters. "They're only my half-brothers. When my parents separated, my mother left. Gone who knows where. And then he met *their* mother, and they started their own little family. Excluding me." His irises continue to darken until they're almost pitch black. It scares me and I recoil, my fingers slipping from his forearm. He doesn't seem to notice, too lost in his own, sorrowful world. "Then their mother died, breaking my father's heart. Instead of turning to his first-born to help put him back together, he turned to *them*." The bitterness in his voice is as sharp as a knife. Peril flares around me. "One day, they'll know what it's like to not be chosen. To be outcast from their own family, from everyone that means something to them." Spit bubbles in the corners of his mouth. He takes a moment to calm himself, his eyes shift back to the chocolatey brown they used to be. "Emilia, you've entrusted me with your secret. Telling me about your Soul Sight, how you can sense when people lie. I think it's time I told you something too."

My hand returns to his arm, pulling him closer to me. His body heat mingles with my own as I burn to hear what he has to say.

"Everyone thinks that Skylar is the only Baker's Boy who is a mage. But I've been hiding my truth since I was nine and developed it." He takes a steadying breath, holding my eyes. He looks so vulnerable and open, entrusting me with something no one else knows about. "I can see the future,

Emilia. It's not always clear, and the output of each is foggy, only becoming clear the closer I get to it. But I can see what you're doing right now."

His voice is so loud as if he's speaking directly into my ear. "I'm coming for you, Emilia. I've sensed your return for a long while. And thanks to some help, I know how this is going to end."

Chapter Twenty-Five

I jolt up, my dress is plastered to my skin with sweat and my hair is matted against my scalp. I gasp for breath, scanning the room. Quicken and Jax have long ago deserted their spot on the floor, now watching over me, perched on the wooden edge of the sleigh bed.

Sky and Kisha are pacing the bedroom, so lost in thought that they don't even realize I've awoken.

Until Jax exclaims, "I thought you died!"

I lunge toward him, covering his mouth with my hand. My eyes are frantic, searching for an intruder, for a monster lurking in the corners. "Be quiet."

He furrows his brow, pressing his lips into a silent line.

Kisha and Sky snap their heads in our direction, practically lunging onto the bed, desperate pleas and questions leaving their mouths in breathless tangles.

"*Quiet,*" I insist. I must look crazy, terrified, because they all fall into a confused, startled silence.

"I had a vision. It was different this time. I was talking to Aaron about his family and about his power." Jax and Sky exchange a look, one eyebrow raised.

"What power?" Sky whispers, hesitant to interrupt my story. None of them were aware.

"He can see the future, Sky," I say, my voice coming out scared and desperate. "He knows we're here. He said he's '*coming for me*'."

Sky's face pales. "We need to leave. *Right now.*"

Footsteps thud on the stairs outside the room sending a jolt up my spine. "I think it's too late." I taste the truth in my words. The door is blown clean off its hinges, earning a shriek from Kisha. A growl tears through the inn, parting between the dripping fangs of a vampire. The man from downstairs. Saliva patterns the hardwood floor, like spit cascading from the droopy mouth of a dog.

Sky tugs me off the bed, toward the window. Moonlight shrouds us, the vampire's Veil burning our veins with the hereditary instinct to run away.

Sky stands in front of our group, hands balled into fists as if a solid punch to the vampire's jaw will leave him sprawled unconscious across the floor. This isn't a high school cafeteria fight. This is a battle to the death; a trap meant to spill our blood and leave me in the hands of our sworn enemy.

Quicken picks up an end table, clutching the

carved wooden legs in his hands and swinging it at the window like a baseball bat. He does it again. The window breaks, glass splinters embed themselves in our exposed skin, and knit themselves into the fabric of our clothes. The end table goes flying out the window, breaking on impact. Chunks of wood scatter across the illuminated grass.

Ivy and moss climb up the side of the inn, tiny blue flowers dotted throughout. Quicken helps Kisha climb out the window, fingers knotted in the ivy, his hand on the small of her back until she finds her grip. His black eyes are laden with worry as he watches her scale down the inn, dress occasionally getting snagged. Then I'm next. I'm hesitant to leave them, but the prey inside me demands I escape, especially when four more vampires emerge from the lantern-lit hall. They're skinny and frail, though the hunger in their eyes is unmistakable.

I swing out onto the ivy, my fingers clawing into the paint of the inn, terrified that I'll lose my grip and plummet to my death. Though dying among nature seems like a better ending than being drained by a vampire.

As soon as I'm halfway down the inn, Quicken is hurrying after me.

My chest constricts, needing Sky and Jax to get out of there as soon as possible. I don't know what I'd do if they got hurt, or worse, *died*. Even thinking about it makes a sob escape my lips. I hop down onto the grass, grateful for the solid ground. I'm becoming increasingly afraid of heights.

Quicken lands beside me, panting. Sweat glistens on his forehead. "I'm going to go get the carriage ready. Hide behind the trees. As soon as Sky and Jax come down, meet me on the road." He meets Kisha's eyes. His lips quiver, words forming and falling away. He steps toward her and takes her hand gently in his own. Something passes between them. And then he's running around the inn, toward the carriage house. I can only wait and hope that he makes it there and that we get out of this trap.

It seems like an eternity has passed before Jax finally emerges from the window. I want to fall to my knees in relief, ready to thank any god for not hurting my friend…until I notice the favor he gives his left side; crimson seeps through his shirt and the far too familiar metallic stench hits my nose.

I scramble to his side as soon as his feet touch the grass. At the sight of his wound, bile climbs up my throat. "What happened?" I ask, biting my cheek so I don't break into a fit of tears. Though I can't prevent the drops that balance on my bottom eyelashes.

Jax's skin is clammy. His complexion is pale, his body losing too much blood, too quickly. "One of them had a knife."

I press my hand on top of his in hopes that it'll help staunch the flow of blood. "We need to get you help." I call for Kisha, who hesitantly steps out of the safety of the shadows. Her expression goes blank when she sees Jaxon's condition. "Take him to Quicken. I'll bring Sky over. We need to get out of here. *Fast*."

Kisha nods quickly. She lets Jax lean against her, one arm slung over her shoulders. With a half-nervous, half-petrified look at me, she's disappearing behind the corner of the inn, leaving me with a feeling of dread pressing down on my chest.

Sky hasn't appeared yet, and the background of grunts and growls has died away. There's no sign of a single life in the story above me.

I fall to my knees, my dress now torn and stained a tie-dye of swamp water and blood. He's dead. He has to be dead.

My Soul Sight doesn't comfort me. It doesn't offer me a glimpse into the accuracy of my prediction. As if it's not even there.

Then someone lands in front of me. I don't even tense, fully prepared for the vampire to rip out my trachea.

The warm hand that cups my cheek startles me. I draw back, eyes wide, tears freely streaming down my cheeks. Sky's kneeling in front of me, a knowing smile curling the edges of his lips. He has a cut on his forehead that trickles into the ravine of his scar, creating a river of blood. His blue eyes are vibrant. I'm lost for words, so I don't say anything. I hug him, melting into his chest. I let myself cry, so thankful that all my friends made it out of this trap alive. He combs his hand through my tangled hair, leaving streaks of blood in its wake. "We should get out of here before they come back."

"Before they come back?" I ask as he pulls me to my feet. I'm hesitant to move, to allow time to continue, to allow the possibility of another vampire attack to happen in the future. I want to stay here with him, safe in his arms forever.

"I always carry a rune stone with me. It teleported them somewhere—I'm not exactly sure where," Sky tugs on my hand frantically, helping me to my feet. Once his eyes roam over my body and he makes sure I'm unharmed, he pulls me toward the carriage house. We round the corner of the inn, pieces of broken glass crunching under our feet. Moonlight illuminates the sleek black carriage waiting for us in the middle of the hardly traveled road; weeds grow along the dirt edges, flowers sprouting in long clumps of grass, clueless to the bloodshed and terror that took place less than thirty feet away.

Quicken strikes the reins before we're even fully into the carriage. Tension is taut between us. We don't say anything until the golden light of sunrise seeps into the forest.

"What…happened back there?" Kisha asks. She's as white as the moon, quivering. Her eyes look haunted.

Sky rests his face in his hands, purple bags hanging under his eyes. "It was a trap."

Obviously. I wait for him to continue.

"Aaron knew we'd be heading to Aquartia, that we would need a place to rest for the night. He filled that inn full of vampires—newborns, I think—in hopes that he could either catch us or kill us." Sky bites his lip and shakes his head. He lost the tie that was around his hair, so now it hangs loosely over his shoulders, dark as midnight. "I can only assume that he's going to regroup and come after us again. If we put Eve together, we would be undoing the curse he placed on Glaven. He's not going to let that happen."

"But what should we do?" I lean toward him, desperate for his answer. The wild wind outside howls, whipping our hair about.

Sky looks helpless. "He can see the future. He'll know where we are, what we plan to do."

"So you're saying we *give up*?" I can't believe what I'm hearing. "We've come too far to give up. My sister is counting on us. Our people are counting on us." Rage bubbles inside me. How could he give in so easily? Where's the resilient, determined Sky I started this journey with?

"What else would you rather us do, Emilia?" Sky shouts, an angry crease knitting itself between his brows. He gestures to the world of trees traveling on either side of us. "There is nowhere that's safe from him. *Nowhere*. What do you think we should do?"

I'm struck by his anger. "I think we should at least try to complete our mission," I insist, throwing my hands up in the air. Why is he so determined to give up? This isn't just about him, it's about everyone we know and love. "I'm not going to let everyone down."

His voice is chillingly cold. He drapes his arms over his thighs and leans closer to me, breaching the space between the seats. "Then you're going to die trying to do something impossible."

His venom makes my heart hurt. I force my eyes to stop watering, telling myself that he's only saying such nasty things because he's lost, not knowing where to go next. But I was lost once, and he's the reason I was found. "At least I won't die a coward."

We fall back into silence, neither one of us brave enough to be the first to apologize. As far as I'm concerned, I didn't do anything wrong. His cowardice, his lack of courage, appalls me. I'm not going to let my sister down. My father's death and my people's suffering won't be in vain.

Chapter Twenty-Six

*H*alfway between the Mirabelle Inn and Aquartia is a small village called Kase; the wood-paneled buildings are tall and constructed in even rows. Windows house identical brown curtains and every door is the same autumn orange.

The street leading through the main section of the village is barren. Spiky trees grow from patches of emerald green grass, while most of the ground is overtaken by hard-packed dirt. The storefronts lining either side of the street are neatly labeled with white paint across their windows.

The carriage rumbles down the street. The clack of the wheels and the clomp of the horses' hooves seem to be the only sound in the entire village, echoing awkwardly off the buildings.

Jaxon's grown worse. His skin is as white as a ghost, and I fear that in little time, he might become one. Not that I believe in ghosts, I just wanted to avoid using the word *dead* while referring to my friend.

"There!" Kisha exclaims, pointing out the window toward a building near the end of the right row. Across the window is the word '*Apothecary*'. "That may be our best option right now." She refrains from glancing at Jaxon. Her lips thin into a grave line. "We don't have enough time to make another loop." Sky and I don't respond, our shoulders most certainly cold toward each other. She rolls her eyes and leans out the window, calling up to Quicken, "On the right! Yes, there! Go there now!"

The carriage jolts to the side as Quicken snaps the reins, pulling alongside the front of the apothecary. Before the carriage even stops moving, Kisha has the door open and is hopping out onto the ground. Her dress is torn and stained, but she doesn't seem to care. There are more important things than clothes. A first for Kisha, most likely.

I open my door too, joining her in front of the store. The windows are dim. Doubt starts to spiral within me: what if no one is here? What if we can't help Jaxon in time? What if he… I swallow the thought, refusing to even put it out there. To even acknowledge it. *He'll be okay.* We all will. We have to be.

Kisha raps on the door; it curves inward, the hinges squeaking in protest. Everything about this village screams of poverty. Maybe when Glaven is repaired and my people are safe, we can reach out to the other kingdoms. We can start to help villages that lie in kingdoms besides our own.

The thin, weathered door opens. An older gentleman in an ankle-length nightgown balks at us, small, brown eyes shifting between our faces behind a pair of scratched glasses. He adjusts them higher on his nose and steps aside. His voice is deep and wise. "It must really be an emergency if you're knocking on my door this early in the morning," he exclaims. Then he catches sight of Jaxon, supported in between Sky and Quicken. "Oh dear. Come in, come in. Go through there." He points to an archway to our left; a wooden table rests in the center of the small room and thin streams of gray light drift from the dirty window, highlighting motes of dust in the air. "Set him down and tell me what happened."

I take the opportunity to look around the room while Sky and Quicken lower Jaxon onto the table. His strained grunts make my heart sting. I never want to hear those sounds again.

The room is disorganized; a tiny desk is pushed against the farthest wall, littered with papers and dog-eared books. A shelf stands beside a coatrack on the wall with the archway; the shelves bow in the center from the weight of the dusty tomes.

"He was stabbed," Sky says, out of breath. He's

clutching his brother's hand, urging him to keep his eyes open, to force himself to stay awake. If Jax drifts off to sleep... I shake my head. *No, don't even think that.*

The man pushes them out of the way, beady eyes taking in the rapidly decreasing condition of his patient. "He needs blood. Quickly." He sticks his head out the archway, calling up the narrow flight of stairs, "Morris, get down here!" He returns to Jaxon's side. "Are any of you related to him?"

"I'm his brother," Sky says; his face is gaunt with worry. I immediately feel awful about our fight. I want to comfort him, to tell him everything will be okay, even if it is a lie.

"Perfect, perfect." The man clasps his hand around Sky's wrist and shoos the rest of us out into the hallway, where a couple of chairs wait in the cramped space under the staircase. A boy with shaggy auburn hair and matching brown eyes to the elder darts down the stairs, taking them two at a time. He passes us without a single glance.

"Do you think he's going to..." Kisha swallows her question, refusing to mention the mortality of Jax. She sits down on one of the chairs, resting her head against the wall. Quicken lets me take the second chair, squatting on the floor instead.

I don't know how long it's going to take, but with each passing second, a breathless prayer leaves my lips for the well-being of our friend.

I watch the dust motes swirl in the air, and the stale scent of coffee drifts from the archway opposite the operation room. I assume it leads to a kitchen of some sort.

Minutes pass, or hours, I can't keep track. But my butt has long since gone numb, and my ears throb from the pained groans coming from the operation room. An even mix of the healer's and Sky's deep voices. I want to climb out of my skin and get away from the agony shrouding the apothecary. Go anywhere that isn't here, waiting to find out if my friend survives. The worst part is that there's nothing I can do. Nothing but sit here and chew the flesh of my cheek until it resembles ground meat. Blood coats my tongue, turning my stomach.

"Do you think they're done?" Kisha asks, interrupting the growing quiet. I'm thankful for the distraction, my mind began to wander in terrible, haunting directions.

"Soon, I hope." That's all I can say. I can't make empty promises, not even to comfort Kisha. Why isn't anyone comforting me? Why am I always comforting others?

Sky would be here, comforting me. Telling me everything is going to be okay—and I'd believe him. But he's not here. He's standing by his brother's side as he fights for his life, enduring who knows what.

The healer emerges, his face grim. He purses his lips, makes eye contact with me, and nods toward the room. I'm on my feet in a heartbeat, which is pretty impressive considering how fast mine is beating. I follow him through the archway. Sky is sitting on the edge of the table, next to the still, pale figure of his brother.

"What—" My question dies on my tongue. My heart drops into my stomach as I stare down at Jax. His face is neutrally poised, his hands resting palm-down on the table, his chest completely still. "No," I sob, crumpling to my knees. My hands brace on the edge of the table, the floor blurs beneath me as tears drip down my cheeks, uncontrollably. *He's dead*. Gone. I'll never hear his laugh or terrible jokes. I'll never see his charismatic smirk or his twinkling eyes. I'll never feel the warmth of his touch or the comfort he brings me. Ever again.

My chest heaves, sorrow wracking my body. Maybe Sky is right. Maybe there's no point in continuing, not if Aaron is going to come after us again. I won't put the rest of my friends at risk.

Then warm fingers slide over mine, an electric jolt tingling down my arm. I gasp, snapping my head up to meet his enchanting, bright ocean eyes. "Jax, you're—"

"Not dead?" he teases, his mouth stretching into

a wide grin. He's as radiant as the Solstice Flower. "The healer here wouldn't let me die." He smiles warmly at the older man, and then his attention veers over to his brother. A moment passes between them, both their features softening. I notice for the first time how blotchy and red Sky's eyes are, and how pale, nearly translucent, his skin is. "Thank you, brother. I wouldn't be here without you."

Sky takes his brother's hand, shaking his head. His raven-feather hair swishes over his shoulders. "I'd do anything for you, Jax. You know that."

Jax snorts, ducking his head. "I do now."

For the first time, I wonder what exactly Sky did to help Jax. What he's been stuck in this room for the past few hours doing. The desire to hug him washes over me again, but we're not done fighting. So I step back out of the room to break the good news to Kisha and Quicken, leaving the brothers alone.

Chapter Twenty-Seven

The sky outside the window is black with stars twinkling between the brilliant rays of the moon. The street beneath the apothecary is empty and silent, just as it was this morning.

The blankets on the matching twin bed on the opposite side of the room shuffle, a pale hand protruding into the streak of moonlight, followed by a dainty face. Kisha groans and rolls to the side, tugging the blankets around her. "What are you doing awake?" she asks, peering up at me. I'm standing in front of the window, a blanket around my shoulders and draped down to my ankles. The moonlight paints my face silver.

"I couldn't sleep," I say, not wanting to go into *why* I couldn't sleep. Not that I would have to. I doubt Sky is sleeping now either, hovering over his brother in the room they're sharing with Morris. Jax's pale face haunts my dreams, brought back to life on the underside of my eyelids.

Kisha sits up, sympathy smothering her expression. "He's going to be okay, Em. They both are. We've known them forever. They're strong and resilient. They're not going to break after one little —"

"Vampire attack?" I supply, smirking as her face drains of color.

She swats at me, scowling. "You know what I mean, Em."

I return to my bed; the chill of the floorboards pricks the bottom of my feet and I decide I've had enough. I'd rather be warm right now, snuggled into a cocoon of blankets, hidden from the unkind world around me. Maybe sleep will find me, or maybe I'll lay awake the entire night, fighting away the nightmares. Either way, I'm going to be comfortable.

Kisha lays back down, her hazel eyes are highlighted in the moonlight, turning a silvery brown. "Em?" Her gentle voice carries across the room, a question she's hesitant to ask.

"Yeah, Kisha?" I respond, rolling onto my back and staring up at the rafters; slits between the wood panels and thatching exposes slivers of speckled sky.

"You can have him, you know." Her words don't carry any weight until I realize exactly who she's talking about. "You won't be breaking some kind of girl code. I just wanted to let you know that."

"What…" My voice sounds too shrill. I take a steadying breath before trying again. "What makes you think I want him?'

She laughs, a bell-like sound tingling through the silent house. "I see the way you look at him. The desire, longing, whatever you want to call it, is obvious to anyone who can see."

I don't say anything; listening to my heart beat as fast as a horse can run.

"I see the way he looks at you too," Kisha breaks the forming quiet. "I can tell he feels the same."

Could it be true?

The moment in the flower field comes back to me: his fingers grazed my cheekbone, his breath was warm against my lips, the tension was palpable, electricity throbbed between us. *He almost kissed me.*

I roll over so my back is toward her. *No.* Sky is not mine, nor could he ever be mine. I pinch my eyes shut against the onslaught of desire, silently praying for my feelings to go somewhere deep inside me and die.

If something happens between me and Sky…

So many things could go wrong.

He could leave me. It could ruin our friendship. We could ostracize ourselves from Kisha, Jax, and Quicken. Would it be worth it? All the pain it could cause? *No.*

But the tiny, longing part of my heart begs me

to reconsider. I try to fall asleep. I know that if I do, I'd either be haunted by visions of an impossible future with Sky, or visions of the painful past.

We bid the healer and his son goodbye, leaving whatever coins we can spare in his empty hand.

The healer tries to refuse, but Sky isn't having it: "You brought my brother back to life," he says, thrusting the pouch of jingling coins toward him. "You won't be rid of us until you accept this." And with that, the healer reluctantly closes his fingers around the leather pouch. Though his gratitude shines in his sunken eyes.

Quicken snaps the reins and the carriage pulls away from the apothecary. I watch it shrink behind us as we storm down the barren streets of Kase, glad to leave it in the past.

I sigh, lean back against the seat, and try to look anywhere but at Sky. He makes it so hard, though. He found a scrap of crimson fabric in the doctor's wardrobe, which he now uses to keep his hair out of his face. It contrasts magnificently with his sapphire eyes.

"Aquartia should only be a few hours away," Jax says, fingers curled around the edges of his map. "Do you think Aaron is going to come after us again?"

The brilliant light from sunrise parts the sky, slipping through the windows of the carriage and slanting across our laps. The wind is gentle, almost humming in the silent village.

"Yes," I blurt, snapping my mouth shut. I wish I didn't say anything; I wish I let them hold onto their hope. But Sky was correct. What's the point in trying? Jax must see the resignation on my face because he elbows his brother, eyebrows knit in disappointment. "He can see the future. He'll see anything we try to do."

"We're not going to give up," Sky's tentative voice rings through the carriage, his hand slips onto my knee, warm even under the layer of my dress. My eyes meet his, holding them. Moments pass, but I don't look away. Enchanted by the magnetic pull between us.

"What changed?" the tone of my voice is cold, surprising us both. He reels back. His mouth tugs down in the corners.

"I was taught to never lose hope, to give in." He glances at Jax beside him, who looks like he wants to crawl out of his skin. "Jax is still here, which means Aaron didn't get his way. Maybe, just maybe, we can devise a plan to make sure that he *never* gets his way." He turns back to me, a maniacal grin spreading across his lips. "We've won twice now.

Let's make sure the third time is the final time."

"Twice?" I ask, raising an eyebrow.

His face softens, ever-so-slightly. "We stopped him from taking you, didn't we?"

The carriage wheels crunch over gravel and bits of loosely packed dirt, leaving Kase behind us as we venture into the forest for yet another leg of our journey.

"Do you have a plan?"

Sky chuckles, hanging his head. His hair falls wildly around him, framing his beautifully chiseled face. A gentle breeze drifts through the carriage windows, toying with our hair, carrying with it the nostalgic smell of nature: sweet berries, flower blossoms, and cut grass. I can almost picture the rabbits hopping through the underbrush, and the birds perched on the highest branches of the trees, singing a melody meant for no one but themselves. And the bees, busy with a task inherently their own —unaware that they're affecting the entire world around them.

If the Solstice Realm can defy the seasons, then why can't we defy Aaron?

Chapter Twenty-Eight

The trees end, bordering the sandy, white shoreline of a lake, separating the Aquartia kingdom from the land dwellers. From my perch, half-hanging out of the window of the carriage, I can't see any sign that the lake is more than just water and sand. The light of the afternoon sun sparkles across the lake, making it seem like a world unto itself. A dimension different from the one we're residing in now.

"See that," Jax whispers, leaning out of the window as well. He's pointing to a part of the water where the sunlight seems to ripple, fade, then disappear altogether. "You can almost make out the kingdom, can't you?"

I squint my eyes, following the line of his arm toward the section of the lake where an ethereal darkness seems to leach from the place beneath. A coral spire reaches toward the surface. To someone not expecting to find anything, it'd just look like an abnormally large spear of coral. But to us... We see the top of the Aquartia palace; twisting with sunset orange and pearl, seaweed clinging to the sharp edges.

"And how are we supposed to get down there?" I ask, fearing the answer.

Jax smirks, meeting my eyes with a sort of mischievousness that makes my stomach flip. "Have you never gone diving?"

"Not in a dress," I glower.

His smirk widens. "Then take it off."

My face flushes; exactly what he was hoping for, according to the grin that transforms his expression. I have half a mind to punch him in the shoulder, wipe that stupid smile straight off his face, but he opens the door and I tumble onto the grass, my feet crossing the line into the sand.

"Why'd you push Em out of the carriage?" Kisha demands, stepping out after Jax. She offers me a hand, scowling. "Her dress is ruined enough anyway…"

I nod toward the sprawling lake, a stone of dread settling inside me. I've never been the best at swimming. Sure, I like the feel of the water gliding over my skin, of being one with the nature around me. But the actual floating part? I'd be much better at drowning.

"Oh gracious," Kisha mutters. She looks down at her dress, now torn and stained with blood and mud from the journey. "It's not like I could get this out anyway." She lifts up her skirt, a splotch of Jax's blood has dyed it brown.

We move to the edge of the water, where a line of white foam crests the beach. Our shoes sink into the wet sand.

"Are you…positive we have to…go down *there*?" I ask, cringing as my voice wobbles. I'm not afraid of the water. I'm afraid of dying in the water. Of the beasts that may lurk beneath. There are monsters in this world, that I'm certain of, so who can promise me that there won't be one down there? Lurking, waiting, right beneath the glistening surface of the lake?

"Unfortunately," Sky mumbles, taking off his shoes. He lays them on the dry sand behind us. He stretches, cracking his back, much to my disgust.

Kisha crinkles her nose but follows suit. With a whimper, she leaves her heels behind. Hiking up her dress, she steps ankle-deep into the water.

Jax kicks his shoes off, then reaches up, peeling his sweaty shirt from his skin. He casts it aside. His pale, surprisingly chiseled stomach teases me to look at it, the sunlight defining the edges.

I bite my cheek, forcing myself to focus on the water. However, it doesn't help that his reflection is mirrored in the world beneath.

Sky takes a deep breath. Without warning, he

plunges into the water. Hands slicing through the surface as he disappears below.

Kisha weighs her skirts in her hands, then with a frustrated groan, she tears the first layer off. Stray strings hang around the uneven cut. She does the same with the second skirt, leaving nothing more than a thin cream layer and a belt of uneven fabric. I swear I can see the pain in her hazel eyes. I wonder what such a gown cost, though I'm too scared of the answer to ask aloud.

Kisha and Jax both suck in a lungful of crisp, blossom-scented air and plunge into the water. The hazy rendition of Kisha's figure is visible for a split second before the dark overtakes her.

"It'll be okay, Emilia," Quicken says, startling me from my stupor. I snap my head up to look at him, chunks of greasy hair falling in front of my eyes. "I don't like this any more than you do. So?" He holds his hand out to me. His tailcoat and polished shoes are cast behind us. His fitted white shirt sticks to sections of his skin that are slick with perspiration. "Together?"

Relief washes over me. I take his warm hand, the callouses on his palm tell a story of how hard he works. "Thank you, Quicken."

He returns a modest smile, nearly black eyes sparkling with something like admiration.

We step into the water, and as the cold liquid

sloshes against my ankles, I shriek and leap closer to him, tugging his arm until he's half bent over and chuckling. "Just take a deep breath. I've been to Aquartia before, delivering a gown for Mr. Tailor. Trust me when I say that it gets better beneath the surface."

I trust him, not only because my Soul Sight lets me, but because I know he'd never lie to me. Never misguide me. A true friend wouldn't.

I take a deep breath and force my rigid form to fall forward, parting the darkness of the foreboding lake. The cold water shocks me, and for a second, all I can do is wave my arms and kick my legs, desperate to not sink farther. But as I open my eyes and see the kingdom hewn from the lake floor, I want to go deeper, to study the architecture and statues of mermaids; carved scales sparkle like diamonds, like the walls of the Glaven palace itself.

Magic is too modest of a word to describe the impossibility of Aquartia. I don't think there is an accurate enough word in the entirety of the English language.

The water is cool, warming against my skin. Far beneath me, half obscured by a robust patch of rose-colored coral is Kisha. Her torn dress twists about her legs. She spreads her arms and thrusts forward, trailing after the rapidly shrinking forms of Jax and Sky.

Quicken waits beside me, his cheeks full of air. He nods toward our friends, his dreadlocks floating above his head like the wild tentacles of an octopus.

With a nod, Quicken takes my hand again, pulling me deeper and deeper into Aquartia. From above, the roof of the palace looks like a shell with multicolored veins spiraling downward, ridges rippling from the hard material, and dark brown pinpricks speckling the edges that shade the pock-marked, coral-like walls.

Arched windows are carved from the palace; pearlescent light shimmers from within, reflecting on the bubbles that part from the lips of rainbow-colored fish.

A fish swims by me, vibrant yellow eyes fixated on the undulating surface.

Music drifts from the palace. The calm, serene notes are smothered by the weight of the water.

I start to forget about the fear that paralyzed me moments ago, of monsters lurking in the dark tides, of creatures just waiting to reach out and tug me under, until a hard, swamp-green body brushes against my side. I squeal, gritting my teeth as a creature swims by me.

It turns to glare at me with spring-green eyes, as if *I* was the one in *its* way. The creature looks exactly like a horse, save for the unusual color of its skin and the fact that its mane appears to be made of seaweed. And that the back half of the creature isn't horse-like at all. A fishtail writhes in place of two legs.

I shoot Quicken a questioning glance. He points below us, where a pebble-lined walkway leads into the palace. I hesitantly take my eyes off the creature, following Quicken to the lake floor.

My lungs burn with the urgent need for air, and by the look on Kisha's face, I know I'm not the only one starting to get a bit panicked. I don't want my death to be something stupid like…*she didn't know when to go back up for air*. Let me go out doing something heroic at least. Or impressive: old and lined with wrinkles, having seen everything I've dreamed of, everything I've wanted to.

I land somewhat gracefully on the pebble path, the smooth stones are hardly noticeable beneath my feet. Sky and Jax are walking ahead; the navy blue of the water around us, paired with the slow, struggling movements of my friends, reminds me too much of the space movies I watched with my brother. Fantasy has always been my comfort. The endlessness of science fiction has always freaked me out.

We make our way to the gaping mouth of the palace; pearls as big as my head embellish the archway leading into an equally extravagant foyer. A wall of water, shimmering with purples and blues, seals the archway. As soon as Jax and Sky step through it, they're dry, enveloped by fresh air.

I part the wall of magic with my hand, watching in awe as I flex my fingers on the other side. I step through with Quicken, glad to finally expand my lungs. The air smells sweet, like salted caramel.

The foyer is massive…and completely dry. The water stops at the magical barrier, preventing any of the aquatic animals from passing through. I run my hands down my worn dress to find it completely dry.

The foyer sparkles with gold and silver trimming. The floor is made of veined coral, bumpy and uneven beneath our feet.

A woman with a short sky-blue dress swims by us—and I do mean swims. In the air. With a scaled tail protruding from her skirts.

"A mermaid," Quicken explains, nodding toward the woman. He points toward the horse-like creatures that swim within reach of the shadows; luminescent eyes glowing through the murk. "And those are kelpies." A smile tugs at his lips. "Welcome to Aquartia."

The mermaid does a double take, her thin lips spreading wide to reveal rows of short, pointed teeth. She hurries over to us, webbed hands thrown wide. "Welcome!" she calls. Her voice sounds warbled as if heard through an endless waterfall.

"You must be Princess Emilia Strazenfield and her court!"

I force down my fright at her appearance, her two-pupiled eyes watching me like a spider. "Were you expecting us?"

The mermaid nods, waves of pink hair flowing out behind her. "Yes, yes. We knew you'd be coming. We've been waiting for your arrival for a long time, ever since we first offered refuge to a traitor of King Aaron's court."

"King Aaron?" I ask, arching an eyebrow. The title seems wrong. Aaron shouldn't be a king of anything.

The mermaid gives me a pitying look. "So, he was right. You have lost your memory." She gestures with her hand absentmindedly, rolling her yellow irises to the domed ceiling. "In order for the Sword of Death, Aridam, to be wielded by another hand—the ruler of Nether must be killed. The throne and sword will automatically be passed to the one foolish—or perhaps brave—enough to succeed." She smiles sadly. "And Aaron did. I'm sure your court knows—of course they know. King Aaron of Nether, Beholder of Destruction, Bringer of Death, Leader of the Shrouds."

"The Shrouds?" I curse myself for my lack of knowledge. I tried to study, and learned a bit I could about banished Unnaturals, but clearly I didn't learn even the basics of our current situation.

"They're mages who've sworn an oath to the king of Nether. Half consumed by the Veiling." She shudders. "Come along. King Hanson has been waiting for you for years."

Chapter Twenty-Nine

King Hanson's scales gleam in the bioluminescent light of thin, blue fish. They swim in circles, trapped in a glass cage embedded in his study wall.

His waist sparkles with green scales, as they fade from tail to dark skin. He forwent a shirt, his stomach looks chiseled enough to sharpen blades with. He has long, black hair that's swept away from his face by a strand of pearls.

"Mesmerelda," Hanson addresses, nodding to the mermaid who escorted us. On the way, I couldn't help but gawk at the scenery: walls wide open to the diverse aquatic life surrounding us, nothing to keep the ten-foot-long fish from eating us save for the magical barrier. Mermaids swimming about, holding the hands of younger ones, who'd point and whisper about how strange we look. *The mermaids with the legs.* "Is this them?"

Mesmerelda curtsies. "Yes, Your Majesty. He was right." I want to meet this so-called *he* she speaks of; the traitor to the Bringer of Death.

Hanson swims around the table, hovering roughly half a foot off the floor. His narrowed green eyes inspect me. "You must be Princess Emilia Strazenfield. Survivor of Aridam. The one destined to end Aaron's reign."

I balk. "What?" I've only ever been Emila, the one who's going to *try* to save Glaven from Aridam's curse. Not end the rule of a king.

"It's written in the stars," Hanson says calmly. His hollow cheeks lead down to a stubbled chin. His eyes appear shrunken when I'm this close; he looks tired as if he's been awake for a century. "Or so Adriene says."

Is Adriene the '*he*' they've spoken of?

"I want to meet him," I say, forgoing being polite. I need to see the one person who's escaped Aaron. The one person...except for me.

Hanson raises a pair of thick, black eyebrows. "Mesmerelda? Take her down to the C Floor. Give her some time...alone...with Adriene."

Mesmerelda seems hesitant. She nibbles on her bottom lip, tentative eyes flitting from her king to me. "Are you...sure?"

Hanson shoots her a glare that sends her wiggling toward the doors. I follow behind her, casting Sky and Jax a nervous—yet determined—look. "You've got this?"

Sky nods stiffly, looking anywhere but at me. The tension between us pulls taut. "I know what we need to do. We'll talk to him. You go." His voice is cold, chilling my heart.

I have to trust them. They know what they're doing. They'll get the piece of Eve from King Hanson. And while they work their diplomatic magic, I'm going to speak to the only other survivor of Aaron's brutal reign. *Adriene.*

The C Floor is dark and musky, slithering with watery shadows. A faint blue light emanates from the rock walls. I glance back at the staircase, tempted to retreat to the gentle white light fading down the steps.

"This way," Mesmerelda calls in her watery voice.

I swallow down my fears, rubbing away the goosebumps peppering my arms, and follow her further down the dark tunnel. My lungs heave, desperate for a breath of fresh air as the rough walls narrow around us. I trip over a stone in the ground only to slam my toes into another. I yelp and Mesmerelda sighs.

"It's just a precaution to make sure he doesn't

escape. I forgot to warn you about those." She gestures to herself, hovering safely above them. "People like me tend to forget about them."

I grunt. "I can see why." We continue. I hop when she tells me to, narrowly missing breaking my ankles or snapping my toes off. The darkness is not my friend, though I can't recall a single time it has been.

"Here we are." Mesmerelda's throat tightens and her lips thin. She holds her hand out, palm up, toward a cell roughly carved into the wall. Rusty metal bars keep us divided from the prisoner.

"Why is he locked up?" I ask, stepping into the white light tumbling from the cell; a conglomeration of glowing flora frames the low ceiling. My question dies in the air when I see him, no longer hungry for the answer.

Adriene is balled up in the corner, head of disheveled white hair tucked in between his bone-thin arms. He's wearing a black jumpsuit that hangs loosely around his skeletal form.

I know something is wrong with him even before he raises his head. Before his dead black eyes meet mine. His face is gaunt and sickly, his cracked lips peel back in an all-too-knowing smile. "So the day has come."

I realize, as terror slides down my spine, that there's no white in his eyes. "What's—" I whisper, turning to face Mesmerelda, who seems stricken and upset by his presence.

"What's wrong with me, you mean?" Adriene adds. His voice is like dragging a razor across my skin; sharp and deadly, promising pain. He unfurls from his position on the floor; the creak of his bones echoes around the cavern. The ceiling is too low that he can't stand properly, hunched in half. The vertebrae of his spine protrudes from his back, and as he shambles forward, he barely has enough strength to keep his ankles from buckling.

He grabs onto the bars, pressing his face against them. His shark eyes search mine. And he starts to laugh. A maniacal sound. The sound of a million nightmares coming true.

"It's the Veiling, Your Highness," Mesmerelda explains, squeaking when Adriene throws his head back, cackling. "He's a Shroud, almost entirely consumed."

So, basically, he's insane.

"Let's go," I say, though some part of me wants to stay. To see what a Shroud is capable of. But all my alarms are ringing. It's worse than being around a vampire, at least then I know I'm being deceived. This fear is primal. A human fearing a human.

"King Hanson told me to leave you two alone. I think you should stay. Talk to him." Her features soften. "There's still a bit of him left, Your Highness.

Maybe, well… Maybe you're the only one who can get through to him."

"Why?"

She ducks her head. "Ask him."

I'm afraid to know the answer, but I stay as Mesmerelda floats down the cavernous hallway.

Adriene's smile returns, coy and curious. Still delirious. "Emilia," he sings, extending a bone-thin hand between the bars. I stumble back a step, but his fingers scrape my cheek, tugging on a strand of hair. "Emilia. Princess. Survivor. Savior." His lips pull back to reveal surprisingly human teeth; round and flat-edged. "*Bride*."

My teeth grind against each other and I rip my hair from his grasp, pressing my back against the slick walls. "I'm not a bride."

"But you are." A pink tongue flickers across his front teeth and a shadow passes over his face. "You're his bride."

"Whose?" Dread settles in my stomach, making me want to curl into a ball, to hide from the evil lurking in the world.

"Master's bride…" He seems to have a moment of clarity, his shark eyes sharpening, zeroing in on me as if for the first time. His smile falters and he almost looks sympathetic. "He's coming for you. He's coming to stop you and take you as his own."

I step closer to him. His breath is cold, winter-

258

kissed. "Why did Mesmerelda say that I was the only one who could get through to you?"

Adriene's fingers curl around the bars. "Because we are each other's shadows, princess. Both touched by the Veiling, both survivors of King Aaron." His knuckles caress my cheek; cold, almost dead. I can't be sure he's even a survivor. Sure, he's breathing… but is he truly alive?

"We are nothing alike," I hiss, disturbed and angry. But his words scratch my mind. My Soul Sight stays silent. *True. We are alike. In some way, perhaps.* "The Veiling hasn't touched me."

Adriene stares at me for a long while that I can't even be sure he understands what I said. "Maybe not now. But it's written in the stars. Master's seen it. You will turn to the Veiling, princess. You're destined to."

I want to scream at him to shut up, to stop lying. But I know better than anyone that he's not. He's speaking the truth. The Veiling will come for me, and I won't be able to deny it.

"*Who* are you?" I ask, immobilizing terror rooting me to the spot in front of his cell. A vision pulsates at the edge of my consciousness, bringing with it a dizzying headache. I grit my teeth, listening as Aaron's voice fills my head. '*Someone, keep an eye on Adriene*'. So Adriene truly is a Shroud who was once under Aaron's control. A Shroud powerful enough to cause the Dark King to fear him, to track him.

"There's no need to ask, princess," Adriene drawls, clicking his tongue. He tilts his head to the side, bone-white hair tumbling across his forehead. His beady eyes peek out from between strands, even more unsettling than if they were fully revealed.

Aaron may be the Bringer of Death, but this man is Death himself. This man didn't survive Aaron... He survived his twisted mind. But what is he doing here? Beneath a palace at the bottom of a lake? Trapped between bars, left to suffer a mortal fate... "What are you doing here?"

He draws back, grinning. His eyes glaze over as a shrill laugh parts his lips, bouncing across the slick cavern walls. Apparently, that's all the answer I'm going to get, so I do the only sane thing I can do:

I run.

Chapter Thirty

"So, you figured it out," Hanson states, floating alongside Jaxon and Sky, toward a staircase that winds up to the highest point of the palace. "Who we have trapped down there."

Jax gives me a questioning look, but I don't respond. Too shell-shocked and petrified to speak of Death incarnate lurking beneath the palace. If he's so powerful, why is he letting himself rot here? What is his end goal?

"Did he really seek refuge here?" I ask, my voice timid and unsure. As if treading on thin ice, the wrong word might pull me under.

Hanson twists his lips to the side, his eyelids shuttering in thought. "Yes, he did. He begged us to keep him here. At the time, he had a clearer mind. There's been speculation that he surrendered himself to us…to prevent himself from hurting others." Hanson looks down at the stairs, though they seem more of a formality since all the mermaids here just float above them. "We cannot be sure what he has planned. Maybe he and Aaron had a falling out. Or…maybe he's been waiting for you." He gives me a long look as something dawns on him. "What did he say to you, Princess Emilia? Ever since he's been here, all he talks about is you."

I don't feel inclined to share the truth, but lying to the man we need something from seems like the last blow the ice needs to crack. "He said Aaron is coming for me. That he's going to take me as his bride." Not a lie, perse, just a half, selective truth.

Hanson seems satisfied. "We've heard rumors brought down from traders going past Nether that King Aaron is rallying an army…of…*vampires*." He takes a shuddering breath. "If that's true, I fear all our kingdoms will have to band together to stop them, lest they destroy us all."

"Is that why you're helping us restore Eve?"

He turns a corner as the staircase moves with the mishappen, coral wall. "I suspect every kingdom is going to help you. A war is on the horizon, Your Highness. We need all our allies in the best shape they can be in, with nothing else to steal their attention besides taking down King Aaron." He mutters something under his breath about how a baker's son could turn into such a monster.

Jax and Sky shrink away from the king's words. I wonder what it's like for them, to be compared to their brother, to be looked at with a new pair of eyes once the relationship has been drawn.

We continue up the stairs in silence. Though my mind is bellowing with a cacophony of questions. *What if he's right? What if there is a war coming? What if…what if none of us survive it? Is this journey—securing Eve—even worth it, when our entire kingdom could be destroyed in little to no time?*

When, why, and where is he going to strike first…

The answer doesn't require much thought. Lightning may not strike twice, but Aaron sure will.

He's going to Glaven. Even as the words ring through my mind, I know they're true. He's going there to finish what he started. I don't know what the future holds, or what he's predicting to happen. And I may be falling into a carefully planned trap, just like at the Maribelle Inn, but I'm not going to leave my sister, my people, defenseless. If I'm the savior—as Adriene so bluntly called me—then I'm not going to stand by.

I'm going to save my people.

Or I'm going to die trying.

We step off the winding staircase, vertigo spinning my vision as I peer over the edge of the narrow strip of floor. Unsurprisingly, there's no railing. A flying mermaid wouldn't need that safety precaution.

Hanson crosses his hands in front of him, brow

furrowed as he silently passes a wall of identical blue doors.

He stops in front of a solitary brown door at the very end of the walkway, without a word, he twists the door knob and it swings inward. A salty gust of air darts from the room like a released spirit, entwining around our ankles before dispersing.

The room is dark, swathed in a navy glow. The walls ripple like water.

"We keep our piece of Eve in here, the safest room in the palace." He frowns as his eyes land on me.

"Why is it the safest?" I ask nervously, squinting into the dark.

"We've been visited by mages before, Your Highness. Some come offering gifts, others come for trade. One particular mage was gifted with the ability to warp minds, to curse objects and places." He sighs. "Adriene, it was. We met him way before the rise of Aaron and the fall of your father. When he was of sounder mind. When the Veiling had barely touched him. He did this favor for us, to protect Eve. Only those with good intentions toward the sword may find it."

"What happens if someone has bad intentions?" Kisha asks, her voice squeaky. She clears her throat, face flushing.

Hanson offers a breezy, nearly nonchalant smile.

"Then they lose their mind." He sighs, studying the door again. "There's something you should know: Adriene wasn't born, Your Highness. He was created, which makes him immortal." He looks shamefully at the pock-marked floor. "He was created from blood, magic, and sacrifices. He was created by a late Nether king. First as his right-hand man. Second as his executioner. Third as the heir to the throne. Though he's always wanted something bigger than being king." He shrugs his shoulders solemnly. "Regretfully, Adriene's life is but a mystery. Made up of rumors, tales, and delirious stories. We can only be sure of one thing: Adriene is dangerous. Too claimed by the Veiling to be of any good."

I almost feel bad for the immortal mage. The Shroud, rotting in a cell and unable to die.

His eyes flick through my mind. The moment when they cleared of fog. When I sensed a curious man through the Veiling.

"I recommend only one steps through," King Hanson says, pulling me from my thoughts.

"I'll do it." I step forward, knowing I should be afraid of whatever delusions await me. But I'm not. This is just one step on the long path to repairing my kingdom, to helping my friends. It's only right that I'm the one to do it. I shrug my satchel off my shoulder and hand it to Sky. We meet each other's eyes for a moment, lingering as the invisible string between us pulls taut. Something melancholy passes over his oceanic eyes and I draw my hand back. "Hang onto that." I nod to the satchel, where the fragment of Eve we received from King Jayden is resting, wrapped in a cloth.

Sky's hands tighten around the strap of the satchel, his shoulders slumped and his face clouded with an emotion resembling despair.

I don't know what to do to comfort him. Do I simply clear away the tension left after our fight? In the face of everything that's going to happen, an argument seems trivial. But I can't bring myself to break the growing distance between us, so I clench my fists and walk into the room.

The room is empty, save for a wooden chest sitting in the center. The pattern of moving water spreads hypnotizingly across the walls. It can't be this easy. I take a step toward the chest, and another, figuring the fragment of the sword is trapped within.

I crouch down and run my fingers across the bronze latch, the gold details inlaid along the edges. A headache teases at the corners of my mind. Not now. Now is not the time to be seeing Aaron, to be reliving that same day two years ago. Now is not the time to be wrung of my energy.

As my headache intensifies, transforming from a

background purr to a roaring migraine... I realize that it's not my usual headache, for where is my usual memory?

I pinch my eyes shut, determined to force the headache away. But as I open them, I'm no longer touching the chest... My hand is resting on the hairy back of a man-sized spider.

I shriek and fall backward, slamming onto my butt. I try to crawl away from the beast, whose red eyes drink me in. But its spindly legs scratch the floor, slamming down as fast and as powerful as an arrow loosed from a tight bow. The monster approaches; each strand of hair coating its tremendous body is as sharp and thick as a barb.

I risk a look over my shoulder, gauging the distance between me and the door. But as my eyes desperately scan the wall, I'm struck by the impossible absence of the door. The wall is but a wall, solid and moving in waves.

A scream is building in my chest, begging to be released. But I know that even if I do scream, no one is going to come, no one is going to even hear me.

The spider's jagged legs strike either side of me as it draws itself closer, face hovering only a foot over my own. Acrid breath tickles my skin. Its pure red eyes blink. White fangs as long as my forearm hang from a mouth as dark as shadows. Green rivulets trickle from the spider's tusk-sized fangs. A drop hits my collar, burning through countless layers of my skin. I use my arms to shuffle backward, toward the wall, biting my cheek to stop from bellowing in agony. The venom *hurts.*

I scan the room, searching for anything I can use against this monster. But, just as before, it's empty.

Where's the chest?

My hands hit the wall and I press my back against it. The wall is slick and wet beneath my fingers. Cool to the touch. I stand up, my legs shaky beneath me as the spider approaches. It stops a few feet away. A moment passes as we stare into each other's eyes, waiting for the other to react. Then, the spell of silence is broken when the monster rears back, brandishing its front legs like daggers. Its fangs move as a sharp *hissssssss* cuts through the room, sending a spike of fear down my spine.

The spider lunges forward. I duck simultaneously, slamming into the floor as its claws tear through the wall.

I slide under the spider's wriggling body, pressing myself as low and flat as I can get. If a single hair touches me, I'll be having nightmares for the rest of my life.

That is if I make it out of here alive.

I crouch on the other side of the spider. Its abdomen writhes as it struggles to free its legs from the wall. Chunks of coral litter the floor as it rears back, another nerve-tingling hiss parting the air as it finally manages to free itself.

My eyes flick from the spider to the twin holes it left in the wall. The water effect is undisturbed, gliding over the holes as if they aren't even there.

I swallow, my throat suddenly dry. *As if they aren't even there…*

The spider pivots toward me, anger slashing through its paralyzing gaze.

This is just a test, I have to remind myself. *None of it is real.* I suck in a breath of the horrible, constricting air. The harsh smell of the arachnid threatens to overwhelm my senses.

My fingers graze the skin papered over my collarbone, searching for a divot in my flesh. But there isn't one. My fingers find nothing but smooth skin and the supple arch of bone.

None of this is real.

As the spider moves toward me on spindly, multijointed legs, I reach my palm up. My hand quivers and I have to use my other hand to still it.

The spider came from the chest. The spider is *the chest.* But as the spider nears dangerously close to my outstretched hand, a fleeting *what if* echoes through my panicked mind. What if I'm wrong?

I pinch my eyes shut as the spider presses its forehead against my palm. I expected to be stabbed with a million barbed daggers but the texture resembles more of the fur of a puppy than the spikey hair of a venomous spider.

Then it purrs, vibrating under my palm. A blinding light pierces my eyelids and I snap my eyes open. Laying in my hand, wrapped in a silk cloth, is an intricate fragment of the spider-web thin sword. Small, almost imperceptible carvings run through the middle. Runes with slanting edges and harsh lines.

The sword radiates warmth, a promise of life. Tranquility washes over me, so I don't move even as Hanson and Sky's voices pitch through the room.

"She's been in there a long time," Sky argues.

Hanson's stern, authoritarian voice silences him, "She will take as long as she needs, Skylar Baker. Are you doubting your princess?"

Sky demurs, "Of course not."

"Then enact patience."

I glance up from the sword as its spell is suddenly broken, sliced by responsibilities. When I pass by the wall, I check, merely curious to see if there are any markings of the spider's failed attack. None. It looks the same, though as I step toward the door, a single, small, pebble-sized piece of coral on the floor beside me catches my attention. Out of place, yet still there.

I shiver, turning my back on the cursed room. Maybe some part of it was real, after all.

Chapter Thirty-One

$\mathscr{M}$esmerelda and Hanson's faces are both drawn with worry. Yet the king's precisely sculpted features also convey knowledge, as if he knows what I must do, and has known, long before even I.

I cannot continue with my friends to Olympus, the next stop on our mission to make Eve whole again. I need to return home. And, hopefully, I'll make it there before Aaron does. I need to warn my sister, to help prepare my kingdom for another assault.

We're standing in the foyer of the palace. My friends are beaconing to me, waiting patiently in front of the wall of magic; kelpies swim in the distance, luminescent skin glinting from the vibrant shine of each other's eyes.

"She cannot go on with you," Hanson declares, holding my eyes.

Silence threatens to suffocate me. I don't break away from the king's intense gaze, too scared of what I'd find on my friends' faces.

"What do you mean?" Sky is the first to ask.

I bite my lip, bucking up enough courage to finally look at him. His blue eyes glow with concern and anger. He has a right to be mad. I'm abandoning the very notion I fought for—what I was brought here for. But…maybe I wasn't brought here to just repair Eve. Maybe I was brought here to stop Aaron. Maybe, in the end, that'll save my kingdom long before Eve will.

"King Hanson is right," I say. My voice sounds distorted like I'm listening to it through a waterfall. It takes me a moment to gather my thoughts and realize it sounds that way because I'm on the verge of crying. "I can't continue with you to Olympus. King Hanson said that Aaron is rallying an army of vampires, preparing for war. We all know where he'll strike first."

I watch as their faces fall. Kisha's skin pales. She sucks in her bottom lip, piercing it with her front teeth. Jaxon doesn't meet my gaze, looking instead to the floor. His black hair swoops in front of his eyes, hiding whatever he's feeling right now.

Sky and Quicken are the only ones who look at me. Quicken gives me a reassuring nod. Sky presses his lips into a thin line, the gears in his head spinning.

"Are you sure?" Sky asks quietly.

I nod, my face grave. I feel as though I've aged a lifetime in mere minutes. "I need to be there. For my sister, our people…" I let the rest of what I was going to say die in the air. The impossibility of stopping Aaron, the power-hungry king who I was once engaged to, needs not be said. "You guys are more than capable of securing the rest of the fragments of Eve, and once you do, meet me back at the palace."

Sky opens his mouth to say something, but Jax cuts him off, "I'll come with you."

"What?" the group says in unison, all staring quizzically at the middle brother. But he's only staring at me. Determination lights a fire in his eyes, in his face, bringing a flush to his cheeks.

"I'll come with you and help the best I can."

"But what about the map? Our directions?" Sky asks, shooting his brother a meaningful glance.

"I charted our course on a piece of parchment that anyone can pick up. It's easy to read. I left the Solstice Map at the palace. I had a feeling I'd be returning to it sooner than the rest of you."

"Then it's settled," I say.

Silence blankets us. I can feel the ravine growing between me and everyone else. I'm on one side and they're on the other. Jax steps over the growing divide, bridging the ever-expanding gap. His presence beside me gives me a boost of courage. I'm not alone.

"I can have a carriage prepared in under an hour. Sadly, I can't supply you with a driver. Mermaids don't last long in arid environments." Hanson exchanges a look with Mesmerelda, who shakes her head, wide eyes panicked. "If you're going to challenge Aaron, Princess Emilia. It may be best that you go there with a weapon comparable to the one King Aaron is bringing with him." He frowns as if the words he's about to say taste bitter. "I'll have Adriene prepared to leave with you. Cuffed, of course."

"Adriene?" I squeak, unsure if I want such a dangerous immortal riding in the same carriage as me.

"Adriene?" Sky asks, stepping toward the king. Head tilted to the side and eyes narrowed. "You just said he wasn't to be trusted, that there's no good left in him. And you want him to accompany Emilia?"

Hanson glares at Sky. "Aaron fears Adriene, knowing what the immortal is capable of doing, and frankly she'll need as many allies as possible."

Sky lifts his chin, trying to squash the growing concern I can see spilling from his eyes. "Will he keep her safe?"

Hanson's green eyes flick between me and Sky. "She's the only thing he's spoken of for the past two years. I believe he's been waiting for her. Waiting for this very moment." He pauses, considering his words. "I have little reason to believe that he'd hurt her. Kindred spirits, perhaps."

Can he see the Veiling growing inside me too? Can he see the Veiling fated to overtake me in the future?

I swallow my rising bile. *I will* not *turn Dark*. What could make me throw my morals to the wind, to turn against everything I believe in?

Aaron, the future-seer, would know.

"Then it's settled," Sky says, throwing my words back at me. They sting, though he's right. What else is there to discuss?

"I'll go make the arrangements." Hanson rests his hand on my shoulder. "Take this time to say your goodbyes."

His melancholy voice makes it seem so final.

Maybe…it is.

The carriage rumbles away from the lake, from Aquartia, traveling in the opposite direction of my friends. The air is dry and humid, smelling of pollen and just blossomed flowers. It's always felt like spring in the blessed Solstice Realm.

My dress is ravaged by the journey, stained and

torn. And I smell as foul as the breath of the spider, which still haunts my senses.

Jaxon, baker's son turned cartographer, snaps the reins of the boars; tusks as long as my arm protrudes from puckish, brown lips. Hanson said they couldn't provide horses, but a few wild boars were given to them as a token from a passing traveler. Boars in trade for a boat of mermaid design. The king felt like he should accept the strange, unusual offering, knowing that someday they'd be of use.

Fate is a queen well-believed in this magical land.

The string between me and Sky draws thin as the second carriage hurries Southwest. I can still feel where his fingers grazed my cheek, the heat of his eyes lingering on my skin. Our goodbye will forever be seared into my mind.

For Kisha, it was a simple hug; a path of tears carving a similar trail down our cheeks. We both know that we might not see each other again, depending on how these next few days go. Depending on if Aaron really is coming and when. I may have enough time to help my sister prepare Glaven, praying to whatever God there may be that the rest of my friends can repair Eve and release our kingdom from that formidable curse, long before Aaron arrives. But a taunting tug of my gut is telling me, like a needle pointing North, that he's coming.

And he's coming quickly. That, no matter how fast we force the carriage to move, we may already be too late.

Quicken's goodbye was straightforward, so completely him. He told me that I'm doing the right thing and that he wishes us luck. With a warm squeeze of his hand, he was gone.

I sniffle, watching the landscape roll by. The sun is lowered now; the moon awakening, preparing to take its place in the sky. In a few hours, I fear it'll be completely dark. How will Jaxon drive in the dark? I glance out the window at the boars as they grunt and writhe against their restraints, eager to be free. After they've serviced us and we've made it safely to Glaven, I'll make sure they're returned to the wild.

"You can feel the Veiling, thick in the air, too. Can't you?" Adriene's voice is ethereal, his black eyes glaze over as he sticks his cuffed hands out of the window, feeling the wind between his fingers.

I watch him. Ever since he's stepped foot out of the shadows, into the light of day, color has returned to his sullen cheeks. Death wasn't meant to be kept in the dark.

"I don't know about that. I just…feel like he's coming." I keep my voice low, not wanting Jax to catch onto what we're talking about, to consider the possibility that I may have anything in common with the monster beside me. "I'm right, aren't I?"

He gives me a sly, cracked smile. Shark eyes sliding over my skin. "Why are you asking me?"

I rest my elbow on the ledge of the window and my chin in my hand. Why *am* I asking him? "You worked with Aaron, I figured you'd know."

I can feel his beady little gaze on my face, tracing the supple curve of my jaw. For a while, as we pass into the forest, branches marring the exterior of the carriage once again, he doesn't say anything. Then his voice is soft, nearly…*kind*. "You're right. The Dark Master always spoke of securing the one thing he lost."

Bile rises up my throat. "Me."

Silence swathes the carriage again. Him, watching me. And me staring off into the distance, at the underbrush that bursts with scared rabbits, the trees that sway when birds take off, the orange and yellow blossoms that protrude from the untrodden ground. I don't need him to confirm. Aaron wasn't going to leave me be, for that day two years ago, I said yes. I said yes to marrying him, and he hasn't forgotten it.

Chapter Thirty-Two

*N*ight shrouds us as we pull into the still-empty streets of Kase, traveling back the way we came. The string between me and my friends is tight, so tight that my chest constricts with the pain of leaving them, the pain of not knowing if I'm going to see them again.

"We should stop for the night and grab something to eat," I say, my stomach rumbling with the vague thought of food. I haven't eaten since this morning, when we first left Kase and the apothecary. Food, just like so much, lost importance in my life. Pushed aside with the need to save this realm, to save my sister and my friends, and the people that are undoubtedly mine.

Adriene nods, watching the town out of his window with eyes as wide as saucers. It's been years since he's seen something besides the dreary walls of his underwater cell. A pang of sympathy hits me, but I push it aside. Who am I to feel sympathy for Death?

Jaxon pulls over to the side of the eerily dark town. The wind picks up, cold and biting against our skin. I regret not bringing a coat, a foolish thing to do when going on a long journey in the midst of changing seasons.

Jaxon opens my door. His eyes scan Adriene before glancing away just as quickly. A shudder runs through his body as he steps aside to let me out. We walk beside each other, our hands hanging by our sides, fingers almost brushing. He lowers his head, his wind-swept hair is disheveled and stuck up in odd directions from driving. "Are you sure we can trust him? He creeps me out," he whispers, jutting his chin toward Adriene as he hops down from the carriage.

"He won't hurt me," I say, watching the Shroud. He's standing at his full height, half a foot taller than Jax. Ever since leaving Aquartia, I've noticed small changes in him. Ten minutes away from the lake his arms gained back definition, thin still but corded with clear muscle. His chest no longer folds around his ribs, hardening and tapering down into a modest waist and athletic legs. Where is the shriveled, half-man that I saw squatting in the Aquartia cell mere hours ago? Where is his bony wrists and hungry smile? Where are the bumps of his spine pushing against his thin, pale skin? Looking at him now, you'd never believe he was locked in a cell for two years, starved of sunlight, food, and water.

He catches me studying him. His cheeks are now full and tinted rose. His lips are thin, peeling back to reveal his white smile. His smile is both coy and malicious. I glance away.

Jaxon tilts his head back to search the shop signs waving on the rising wind. "That must be the inn." He points to a copper sign depicting a bed, a trail of hand-carved *zzzzzzs* drifting above it like chimney smoke.

We hurry down the sidewalk, dirt spiraling from the ground in tiny tornados. Jax reaches for the handle of the inn's door, which squeaks on rusty hinges. Warm light falls across the floor, dispelling the encroaching darkness of night.

He opens the door and we huddle inside, relishing the warmth of a nearby roaring fire and the smell of freshly baked bread and seared meat. My stomach rumbles even louder and I press my palm against it in an attempt to stop it, to quiet the hungry monster awakening.

The door leads into a small hallway, much like the apothecary; a staircase is across from us, leading to the second floor, and the hallway branches into two rooms. One is blocked by a closed door, and the other is an archway glowing with yellow candle-light.

A woman comes through the archway on the

right, a hummed melody dying on her tongue when she sees us. She has reddish brown hair wrapped in a scarf, a flour-spattered apron tied around her waist, and a simple, gray dress kissing the leather cuffs of her boots. She smiles, brown eyes twinkling with kindness. "Welcome, welcome. I thought I heard someone. Though the wind always plays with the doors and windows, so I wasn't positive." She beacons us forward, taking my hand and pulling us into the kitchen. Another woman is at work behind the counter. She's older than the first, with gray hair tied at the nape of her neck and gentle wrinkles lining her face.

"Mama, we have guests." The woman pulls out a chair at the small, four-person table situated only a few feet away from the tiny kitchen. "Please, take a seat. Are you hungry?"

"Starving," I answer rather quickly, sliding into the chair. Jax and Adriene take a seat on either side of me. I notice Adriene ducking his head, casting his eyes down toward the table, away from the innkeepers.

The younger woman removes a tray from the oven. A waft of herb-scented smoke fills the room and my mouth waters. She sets the tray on the counter as the older woman removes dough from a ceramic bowl, presses it down on the counter, and starts kneading it into the scattered flour.

The younger woman removes a chipped, white ceramic plate from the cupboard and fills it with whatever divine creation she pulled from the oven. She sets it in the center of the table, clasping her hands in front of her apron and donning an eager smile. "My name is Mercy, and that is my mama, Matilda. If you have any questions or concerns, please do reach out to us." She waves her hands at the steam rising from the top of the flaky, cheesy pastries. "Eat, eat. Then I'll show you to your rooms."

She doesn't need to tell me twice. I reach for the pastries, pulling one apart in my hands. Cheese strings dangle between the halves like a rope bridge, and bits of herbs add green to the flaky dough. Adriene and Jax hesitantly take one; adoration plain in their expressions, as if they're beholding gold instead of food.

The inn's bedrooms are small, almost closet-sized as if the design was to squeeze as many as possible into the humble abode. Which, let's be honest, it probably was.

I lean against the intricately carved headboard, wool blankets tucked around my feet and shoulders.

The moonlight paints the narrow aisle between my bed and the door silver. What I've learned from both of my journeys through Kase is that the houses are cheaply built. Insulation must only be a fantasy here, for the ever-chilling air kisses the room, infiltrating from between the thin walls and cracks in the window frame.

I can hear the gentle snoring of Jax in the room beside mine, and the footsteps of the innkeepers busying themselves in the kitchen below. I don't know what time it is, for time is only told by the placement of the sun and the moon in the sky, and I've forgotten, much like everything else, how to read the sky.

Sleep is not going to find me, no matter how heavy my eyelids grow and how desperately I want to close them. My mind is coming up with the most terrifying, probable visions of the future. Aaron, standing over me again. A sword dripping with my blood, instead of my father's. My kingdom turning to ash, being destroyed by Aaron's vampire army instead of Aridam's withering curse.

I wonder how Aaron came to create his vampire army. Did he sneak vampires out of the Banished Realm somehow? Or did he find those who stayed, despite the monarchs' exile?

I chew on my lip, knotting my hands in my greasy, unkempt hair. In the room to my left, someone begins to pace. Adriene.

I listen to his agitated footsteps, shuffling across the floorboards and periodically stopping. His breathing is labored, occasionally disturbed by a grunt or a sharp, sudden cry. I knit my brow, my heart thumping erratically in my chest. But this time, it's not because of my own worries. It's because of the familiar sound coming from Adriene's room; an anxiety attack that pulled him from slumber. I've suffered through countless bouts of my own, back in the Earthen Realm, wondering when another headache will fill me with, what I thought at the time, delusions.

During each bout, I wanted someone to be there for me, to calm me. To tell me everything would be okay, even if it was a lie. Sky was that person for me back at the Glaven palace, and in turn, I was that person for him. But he's not here, and I know for a fact that Adriene doesn't have a shoulder to cry on, a person to hug, to relinquish his worries to.

I slide from my bed, my footsteps quiet on the cold floor. I wrap a blanket around my shoulders and open the door to my room, stepping into the shadowy hallway. I still in front of Adriene's door, listening attentively. His bed squeaks as he sits down, then it squeaks again and his pacing continues. Occasionally I'd pick up on a muttered curse, a plea. I twist open the door.

Moonlight casts shadows through his feathery hair, across his pale face. He has his back to me, staring down at the silent street. I pull my blanket tighter around me, unsure of what to say. He solves that problem for me when he turns around to resume his pacing.

He's still wearing the black prison garb. The back of which is soaked through with sweat and his bone white hair is disheveled.

His black eyes stare at me blankly, though the rest of his face conforms with surprise and embarrassment. Thin paths carved by tears glint in the moonlight.

"What are you doing here?" He doesn't sound angry. He only sounds defeated.

I don't know what to say. Suddenly, I wonder if I made the wrong decision. If I should've left him alone to pace, to cry, to curse. But a flicker of wonder crosses his slender face, pulling me toward him. "I wanted to make sure you're okay."

His lips quiver, but still, he stares at me.

"I want to make sure that you'll *be* okay," I rephrase.

For a moment that is so quick I start to doubt that I even saw it, white rims his black eyes. "Would someone who is constantly battling against their own mind ever, truly, be okay?" The tone of his question sounds more like a blatant statement, but I note the hope in the deep timbre of his voice. He wants to know what I think. So, I tell him.

"Eventually," I whisper.

He swallows. "When would 'eventually' ever come for someone mad?"

He doesn't mean mad as in angry. He means mad as in crazy.

I've been called crazy too many times in my life. I understand how he feels, to a certain degree.

"I don't know," I answer truthfully.

He drops his chin in a dejected, despondent nod. "That's what I thought."

Silence washes over the room again: him, deep in agonizing thought. Me, conflicted about how I can help him. I know the trenches of anxiety, and I know the hopelessness of battling through it alone.

"Do you want to talk about it?"

His head snaps up and he narrows his eyes. Venom leaks into his voice. "You wouldn't understand."

I take a step back, stung. He may be right. "You said we're alike. Maybe I'll understand more than you give me credit for."

He stares at me again, with those unflinching, shark eyes. "I'm a monster. My mind is a cage. I think of ways to hurt people, to kill them, to torture them. Every room I walk into, every item I see, I envision killing someone with it. Do you relate to that?"

I take a shaky breath. No, certainly not. "I don't see you killing me, right now. Or the innkeepers down below. Or Jax."

He scoffs. "But that doesn't mean I didn't think of it."

Goosebumps pepper my skin. Why did I feel so certain that he wouldn't hurt me? "Is that why you turned yourself in to King Hanson? Why you let yourself be locked up for two years?"

His lips thin. "I know I'm a monster. But that doesn't mean I want to be."

There's the human part of him. The boy he was before the Veiling overtook him like a plague. Adriene is still fighting against himself, against the thoughts in his mind.

I suppose he was trapped long before the Aquartia cell. Though, sometimes, the cage of your mind is worse than one with four walls.

I step so close to him, I can feel his breath against my forehead. I take his hands in my own, carefully untying the ropes that bind his wrists. "I can see that."

Silence again as we stare at each other, as he challenges me with those unflinching, terrifying eyes of his, to take back my claim. To put the cuffs back around him. But what I said is true. I can see how much he struggles against the Veiling. I admire that. If—or when—the Veiling comes for me, I fear that I won't put up a fight.

Chapter Thirty-Three

*D*ays pass as the carriage bounds across the evolving terrain of the Solstice Realm. We don't stop, save for the occasional inn or bakery. Adriene and I haven't talked about the night at the Kase inn; about the hours we spent just standing in his room, waiting for the sun to rise, calming each other by presence alone.

Silence has been our friend these past few days, I swear my voice has gone dormant from the lack of use.

When the cozy, green hills of Glaven roll into view, I'm ready to scream in relief. I will physically implode if I have to go through another hour of tense silence. Nothing but the wind rushing by my ears to confirm that I'm not deaf.

The sweet smell of maple and flowers and the sound of creatures scurrying in the underbrush, all stand to remind me of where I belong. This kingdom, surrounded by cozy, ethereal magic, is my home.

I watch as the thatched houses come into view, waiting to see the friendly faces of the village people as they go about their daily routines. But there's something off in the air, in the way the villagers seem to hide behind drawn curtains and locked doors. Adriene sniffs the air, straightening in his seat and peering skeptically out the carriage window. The hair on the back of my neck stands on end. I can almost hear Adriene in my head, asking if *I can feel the Veiling, thick in the air*. I can. I can feel it like a mist against my skin.

Jax snaps the reins and the boars charge forward, thrashing their heads aggressively to either side, fueled by whatever evil is lurking nearby. Jax grunts, pulling back as the boars charge even faster; hooves stamping cracks and holes into the street.

The houses on either side of us look worse than they did when we left; roofs dipping as if a boulder is resting on top, crops dying, flowers sagging and petals floating to rest on the disturbed ground. The closer we get to the palace, the more noticeable the dissipation of Glaven's floral, country perfume becomes. The air is acrid, smelling of rot and decay.

Jax pulls the carriage into the courtyard, the stones of which are upheaved and uneven as if an earthquake shook this ground alone.

I push open the carriage doors, a sense of dread growing inside me, as I take in the desecrated flowerbed. The rose bushes, if not completely dug out of the ground, are chopped so low you'd have to squint to see anything at all. I don't realize I'm shaking until Jax's warm hands cup my arms, in a chivalrous attempt to steady me.

"They're here…" I whisper. An inaudible sound half-choked by my sobs. We're too late. Who else would dig out the roses? Who, but a king controlling an army of vampires?

"We don't know that," Jaxon whispers, though by the pallor of his face, and the gulp shortly following, I'd say he doesn't believe himself either.

I look back at the carriage behind us; sleek black paint marred by the passing of tree branches on our journey here. I'm tempted to run away from the danger, to get help from King Jayden or King Hanson. To tell them the war has already begun. But my sister is in that palace, at the mercy of a vengeful king and an army of blood-drinkers. I came here to protect her; I'm not going to turn back now.

"You both should leave," I say, thrusting my hand toward the carriage, where the boars are snorting and digging their hooves into the rubble.

Jax shakes his head, looking at me as if I'm wearing a scarf of human intestines. "No. If Aaron really is in there, it's best if I stay. He's my brother. Maybe I can deal with him."

I turn to Adriene, whose face doesn't betray even an ounce of his emotions. His shark eyes hold mine and a devilish smirk plays with his lips, pulling them up until his sharp canines glint from sunlight. "King Hanson gave me to you as a weapon, Emilia. Lest you forget?"

"You may be a weapon, but you're still a person." He flinches as if I slapped him. "Are you sure?"

He steps up next to me, his shark eyes twinkling. "I'm positive."

I can sense Jax's presence beside me as well, even though I'm staring straight at the crystalline doors of the Glaven palace. Normally, I'd be able to see what's inside, at least vague outlines. But there seems to be a smoke curling from within the palace, fogging the walls and windows. I don't know how many vampires await us, or what condition my sister is in. There's only one way to find out.

With the boys flanking my sides, I take a steadying breath, trying to quell the rapid animal released inside me, and step up to the door. The handle is warm beneath my touch, and as I tug the door open, I'm hit in the face with the most retched, gag-inducing odor as if the spider is breathing over me again; an acrid, ghastly scent. Reminiscent of death itself, of decay, of blood.

Copper and iron burn my nose, the underlying

hint of rose petals makes it so much worse.

When I finally bare my senses, I'm expecting to find a conglomeration of stone-faced monsters, all watching me with their unsettling, deceitful eyes. But the foyer, and as much as I can see, is empty.

I step into the palace, my Soul Sight blaring in my mind. *Lies, lies, lies. Deceit.*

My nose tingles with the cloying smell of blood again, though now it's stronger. I glance down at the marble, my pulse hitching and my heart dropping into my stomach. Bile climbs up my throat, and I have to swallow to keep it down.

A trail of blood leads to the staircase, streaked and trampled in. Whoever was following behind the victim stepped in their blood, leaving shoeprints alongside.

"Oh God," I gasp, covering my mouth. I've never seen something so ghastly. So inhuman. Who bled this much? The amount of blood they lost leaves me to question if they're still breathing. *Please, please don't let it be my sister.*

As we venture closer to the staircase, and the flat landing before it twists upward to the rectangular balcony, our answer is given.

"No," I mumble. My throat is ravaged and hoarse, closed by fright. As if fear is an allergy.

With her head limp against the wall, one hand clutching a wound above her stomach, is Trelia. Her brown eyes, once so full of life and laughter, stare blankly at the stairs. A sign, telling us where to go next. As if Trelia was little more than a pawn.

I drop beside her, checking her neck for a pulse. A worthless attempt, since its spread open like the maw of a great beast. There's a trail of blood down her skin, some parts dried. It must have only been an hour or two since they killed her. Her arm is still wrapped in a sling of sorts from when it was crushed.

I cup her cheek, bringing her face up to meet mine. The slit in her neck oozes more blood down her white apron. I press a kiss against her forehead, cold and clammy against my lips. If only I got here quicker. If only I realized what they were going to do sooner. I could've saved her…somehow. At least, I would've tried.

"Trelia," I whisper, sliding my fingertips over her eyes and closing them to the world forever. Jax pulls me back to my feet, but not before I make out the small, identical pair of holes punched into her wrists, up along her arms, some along her neck. *Food*. She was more than just a sign left here for us to follow, she was a meal for Aaron's soldiers.

My breathing is harsh, my vision going red and watery. I wipe my eyes, biting my lip until I taste blood across my tongue. *Trelia, I will avenge you*. I will avenge all those whose lives have been wrecked by Aaron.

Although I'm not a mage and I'm not armed, I will find a way to bring this king to his knees. To make his blood spill at my feet.

I pull my arm from Jax's grip, facing the final flight of stairs on my own. I know I'm walking into a trap, that there will be murderous vampires waiting for me at the top, but this time I'm prepared. This time, I'm not going to freeze or run away. This time, the prey inside me is replaced with a predator. A rabbit with a wolf.

We ascend the steps, careful to not step on the specks of blood soaked into the carpet. Dripped from the fangs of a quenched vampire.

The balcony, just like the foyer, is empty. Quiet. *Too* quiet. Not a bird sings outside, not a single creature dares to move.

My Soul Sight still screams of deception, of danger, as I step onto the second floor. I swallow, watching as the *drip-drip-drip* pattern of blood leads to Soph's office, slipping under the door like a trail of ants.

A trail of blood. How macabre.

"I—" Jax starts, pupils dilated in fear as he stares at the daunting door. His heart is so loud, I can hear it. I don't know why mine is so calm…beating in regular intervals. I silence him with a finger to my lips. Aaron will see us coming, of course. He sees everything. But there's no need to alert everyone in the palace to our current position. I don't know if there's a single person left that's on our side, let alone Soph.

Though, wouldn't I feel it if she was dead? That spoken about bond between sisters… Wouldn't I know if my baby sister wasn't alive? *She has to be.* She cannot leave me, not like this.

We follow the crimson trail: Jax solemnly. Me, resigned, prepared, determined. Adriene, gleefully. He's been waiting years to come face to face with his master again.

We stop before Soph's study. I strain to hear anything on the other side: a sign of life, a gasp of pain, a single footstep. *Nothing.* It's as silent as a tomb.

I exchange a look with Adriene, raising my eyebrows in a silent question. *Are you ready?* His shark eyes sparkle, and I fear what's going through his head. What kind of murderous, dangerous things is he imagining? The worst part is that it brings him so much happiness, twisting his lips into an unsettling, macabre grin. He's a monster, undoubtfully. Though he's a monster helping us. A monster channeling his monstrous deeds to benefit us, so how bad could he possibly be? A silly question. A monster is still a monster.

I open the door and take a step into her study.

Sitting in the chair, with a spider-web thin blade pressed against her throat, is Soph. Aaron, with his familiar sandy-brown hair and that face I've seen haunting me for two years, stands over her. Soph's blue eyes widen in fear, and, before I can reach her, Aaron drags the blade across her throat. A gurgling sound emits from her as her flesh flays, as blood spurts across her desk. She slumps forward, her chest writhing as she struggles to breath, as her blood flees her body like a faucet left on. Then, she stills.

My heart stops, at least it feels like that. I don't wipe away the tears that cascade down my cheeks. I don't stop the scream that tears from my throat. I fall to my knees. Her blood drips onto the carpet, spreading across her desk and over the edges.

My chest aches, my heart shredding from within me. If this isn't death, I don't know what is.

"Emilia," Aaron purrs. That pompous voice drills into my head as he steps around the desk. His feet are clad in iron boots. He elegantly sheaths the dagger, slick with my sister's blood. "It's great to see you again, my love."

I want to rip that dagger from his waist and cut his head off with it. For my father, for Trelia, and for my sister. If this is the Veiling Adriene warned me about, then I welcome it. For my family will be avenged.

He squats down in front of me, and I finally steal

enough enraged courage to look him in the eyes. His face is smooth, free of stubble. His sandy hair falls across his face in trifled waves. A drop of blood stains his cheek. And his eyes... Black, completely. Not a single shine of the hope that Adriene still clings to. The Aaron I fell in love with is gone. Whatever beast has stolen his skin will be slayed. By my hand, and my hand alone.

"You still have that fire," he purrs, flashing a set of humanly flat teeth. They seem wrong paired with his demon eyes. He extends his hand to me, waiting rather patiently for me to take it. I don't. I'd have to burn whatever skin he touches. "Come now, my love. It's time to go home."

I curl my lips in disgust. "I am home."

He tilts his head, those shark eyes studying me. Tracing the curves of my face, the intensity in my set jaw. He'll have to drag my corpse out of here if he wants me to come with him, for I'd have to be a fool to walk beside him of my own will.

Then, he notices the people accompanying me. His smile widens as he stands, towering a few inches over his younger brother. "Jaxon... I forgot I would be seeing you." He turns to look at Adriene. "And you... It's good to have you back, Adriene. I've been watching you, wondering why you allowed yourself to rot in that infernal kingdom." His lips pull back to reveal a skeleton's smile; wide and impossible. "It's good to have you back, my friend."

Chapter Thirty-Four

*T*raitor. He's a *traitor*. And I began to trust him, to see the human in him. To think I could be so foolish. To think my Soul Sight could be so broken, not even sensing the deceit before my very eyes. I was glamoured by his lies, by his claims that we're similar. I guess I wanted to believe I could trust him, help him. How stupid I was.

I thrash away from Aaron, crashing into someone behind me. They pull me to my feet, their hands wrapped tightly around my arms. Definitely going to find a band of purple fingerprints later—if I'm still alive, that is.

"Get your hands off of me," I growl, glaring at the person behind me. My mouth pops open in shock; those sly, cunning red-flecked eyes, rimmed with blotchy skin. *Garamond.* "You…" I don't say anything else—I can't say anything else. How did so many traitors wander by me, and interact with me, all while knowing that they'd be hurting me in the future? How could he stand by and help the man who killed our beloved Sophia? "I trusted you… with *her*." My throat closes, tears blurring my vision, hot on my cheeks.

He reels back as if I struck him…a wish I'm in no position to grant. But his fingers dig deeper into my arms. His bottom lip quivers at the mention of Sophia.

"You're coming with us," Aaron says, eyes roaming over the slouched body of my baby sister. His face remains expressionless. I turn my head to the side, refusing to look at her corpse again. I can still hear the sound of her throat splitting open, of her struggling for her last breaths. I fear that I'll always hear them; when I lay awake at night, when I see something that reminds me of her, when I'm forced to lead a kingdom I never wanted to. I scoff, knowing I'd never rule Glaven. Either I'm Aaron's petty, prisoner-bride. Or I'm dead. If there's another option, I pray that it's revealed to me.

"I'll never go with you. Anywhere," I snarl, spit flying from my mouth and spraying Aaron in the face; a small victory.

He smiles; an uncanny smile, promising pain. He nods toward another one of the vampires in the room; a pale face, one I won't even give the honor of describing or naming.

I struggle against Garamond's ever-tightening grip, releasing a string of obscenities at Aaron.

Garamond. Adriene. I've cursed them all to Hell, one day I'll make sure they get there.

"Fine, then I'll make this easier for you, my dear," Aaron coyly adds, gesturing to his vampire solider. The solider shoves Jaxon in front of Aaron; he stumbles, frightened like a deer caught in a trap. Wolves descend. Aaron produces the bloody dagger, pointing the tip toward Jax. "Come with us willingly, without a fight, or he dies."

Jax meets my eyes, straightening his posture. His eyes, though wide with fear, are blanketed in resignation. He subtly shakes his head.

But I can't let Jax die. I've lost Soph already. I can't lose another friend.

I set my jaw, my steely eyes sliding over to meet Aaron's. My voice trembles as I say, "Fine. I'll go with you, just promise me that Jaxon won't come to any harm."

Aaron smirks. Garamond pulls my arms behind my back, tying a rope around my wrists. He doesn't flinch as I whimper, as the rope threatens to cut off my circulation, chafing against the thin skin protecting my veins.

"Perfect. Now dear, shall we go?" It's not a question. Of course it's not a question. A woman steps forward from the throng of vampires, concealed in an elaborately embellished navy cloak. Everything is hidden, save for the wispy tendrils of blonde hair that fall across her chest. She removes a stone from her tunic pocket, the familiar, wispy blue tendrils of magic pulse from the etched rune. "Take her to the palace."

The woman lets the stone skid across the floor, quiet words, practically whistled, catch in the air.

So that's how Aaron and his army got here so fast. He has a Runespeaker working for him.

Blinding white light starts to overcome my vision, fading the edges of my sight; a headache throbs through my skull. Though I don't need to imagine the Dark king standing before me, for he is really here.

Just as the last specks of color start to fade away, enveloped by the fast, encroaching magic, I lock eyes with Jax. His mouth falls open, his eyes widening, color draining quickly from his skin. I want to step forward, to help him, to find out what went wrong.

Crimson seeps through his chest as Aaron thrusts the blade of his dagger through Jaxon's heart. Again and again. A scream claws its way up my throat. He *promised*. He promised that Jax wouldn't come to harm if I went willingly.

Hot magic licks across my skin, burning every inch of me. I can't move, can't speak, can't do anything.

Jaxon is dead.

I open my eyes groggily. Cool stone kisses the slick sweat of my back. A stone ceiling spins above me and I wince, waiting for everything to stop moving before sitting up.

The air smells of sulfur, mold, and the earth after a storm. I glance around, my shredded purple dress is hugging my body, sticking to my cold sweat. My hair is flattened against my scalp with grease and I smell worse than the room I'm sitting in. My wrists aren't bound anymore.

The room is small. The floor is made of uneven, mis-matched stones. As if this cell was made at the last minute, a conglomeration of leftover materials. A patchwork prison.

Rusted metal bars are in place of a wall in front of me, standing on the other side with her hood down and her back to me is Aaron's Runespeaker. Her fingers are tapping against her thigh in a nervous manner.

I lean against the wall, struggling to stand. My legs feel like jelly, like they're going to give out on me any minute now, sending me crashing back to the cold, damp floor. Everything about me is sore.

In the center of the walls on either side of me are

roughly constructed brackets, a torch with a dying flame flickers in each, casting pale light around the dingy cell.

I suck in a ragged breath of air, filling my lungs. My throat burns from the chill of this winter-kissed dungeon. I only assume it's a dungeon, for where else would Aaron keep his prisoners?

The hallway outside of the cell is dark, similarly dim torches line the wall every five feet, leaving shadows to reach toward the Runespeaker like skeletal fingers.

I rest with my back flush against the wall.

The cell is bare, save for an iron bedframe and a mold-spotted mattress. A dark green, wool blanket is neatly folded in the center of the mattress, like they were expecting my arrival. Well, of course they were.

He saw it all play out, long before it even began.

"Where is he?" I croak out, glaring defiantly at the Dark mage. She flinches, tensing with her hand around the hilt of a crystalline dagger at her side. She doesn't turn to face me, nor does she say a word. Almost as if she's afraid of what I'll do. Silly, considering I'm locked behind these infernal iron bars. "Where is your king? Where is Aaron?" My words drip with venom, hate, repulsion, despite how weak I sound. How ravaged and raw my throat feels.

Minutes pass; the Runespeaker seems to ignore me, though her shoulders don't relax, nor do her fingers move from the hilt of her dagger.

"Are you going to answer me? Or did your king command you to be silent?" I demand, pushing off the wall and staggering toward the front of the cell. I grip the bars, feeling the rough rust beneath my fingers. The smell of sulfur increases.

The hallway stretches endlessly in both directions. An underground tunnel enveloped in weak torchlight and shadows, cast away from the rays of the sun or the glow of the moon. Without the sky, there's no telling what time it is, or how many days pass by while Aaron's prisoners rot down here.

"*Pathetic*," I hiss between my teeth. "How pathetic do you have to be not to even look at me? Your master killed my sister, my friend," I swallow down a sob, scrunching my nose. "He killed all I had left of a family. And here you stand, a slave to his every command. Without even the decency to *look* at me." I spit at the mage's feet.

She sighs, turning a fraction toward me, her face still shielded by the cloak. But that voice... I'd recognize it anywhere. "I'm not pathetic, Em. I'm ashamed." Her words tremble, as if she has the capability to feel emotion, to care about *me* after so much misleading.

I reel back, struck by utter disbelief. "No…" I try to form a coherent sentence, but my attempts come out half-choked, half-sputtered. "No. How—why?"

I remember—only a day ago—when I first had a vision of Aaron confessing his power to me. He mentioned that he couldn't see everything, how some things would end, and that he had assistance.

It makes sense now. Everything has been a lie. The two years I was living in the Earthen Realm were a lie.

I was never free of him and I fear that I will never be.

Garamond was sent to watch over Soph, to keep tabs on the kingdom Aaron vanquished years before. And I…was sent my best friend.

She tilts her chin up, and the hood of her cloak falls back to reveal her petite face. Her blonde hair falls in ringlets down her chest. But I'd recognize her anywhere. How foolish of me to feel guilt over leaving her.

"Samantha…"

Her face is pinched, her cheeks tinged pink. Her eyes glisten with unshed tears.

I take a shaky step away from the bars, my foot landing in a puddle of indistinguishable liquid that pools in the place of a missing stone.

"Was it all fake then?" I need to know the

answer. Was our entire friendship, all the sleepovers we spent gossiping over boys at school, braiding each other's hair, flipping through Ricky's graduation yearbook and laughing at his senior photo...fake?

Samantha's eyes flash with hurt, her lips twisting into a pout. "Of course not, Em. At first it was. King Aaron sent me to watch over you until the day came that you returned..." When she's speaking, I catch a glimpse of her perfectly straight teeth. So, her signature themed braces were a lie too. A clever trick to blend in.

"*King Aaron*," I hiss. "Do you even know what he's done? Do you know who that girl was he *slaughtered*?"

Samantha's mouth opens, but I don't let her get a word in edge-wise.

"That was my little sister." I fall to my knees, tears streaming from my eyes. I'm sure I look like little more than a wounded animal stuck in a trap, but I couldn't care less. "The last person I shared my blood with. *Gone*." My voice cracks and I press the heels of my hands into my eyes, my head splitting open with an all too familiar headache.

Footsteps echo down the dungeon hallway and Samantha's face falls. "Your Majesty," she says, dropping into a low curtsy.

I stand up, my knees wobbling, my vision

blurring with both sorrow and rage. How *dare* he show his face after killing two of the people who meant the most to me.

Aaron stops in front of Samantha, a pleasant, audacious smile curling his lips. "You may rise."

She straightens reverently, as if he's a god to grovel at the feet of. Her eyes shine.

I scoff, pulling her from her deferential trance. Her face flames with humiliation when she meets my scornful, judging gaze.

Aaron doesn't turn to address me. Instead, he tilts his head down to talk to Samantha. "Bring my bride to her respectful rooms, won't you? And make sure she's fitted and…washed…for tonight's dinner."

Samantha nods. "As you wish, Your Majesty."

Aaron's black eyes finally slide over to me. His lip curls with disgust when he takes in my diminished state; my dress is little more than rags held together by clumps of string, my skin is covered in dirt and my hair shines with grease. Normally, if spotted under such distasteful conditions, I'd burst into a flame of mortification. But now I tilt my chin high, challenging him. He can mock me, judge me, but he'll never win my worship.

I bite my tongue, forcing a question back down my throat. I don't want to initiate a conversation with him, to even acknowledge him as a person. He's merely a figment of displeasure.

But he catches onto my slip up. "Spit it out."

I don't know why I do anything he demands of me. "How could you kill your own brother?" The question leaves an empty hole in my chest, in the hollow where my heart used to beat. Now it's replaced by fragments, broken as quickly and efficiently as glass.

Aaron arcs an eyebrow, as if the question amuses him. His answer is delivered unflinchingly. "The same way I killed your father." He steps closer to my cell, tilting his head to the side. Analyzing me with the studious gaze of a zookeeper, and I the rare breed. "You'd be wise to remember this, my dear. Blood means nothing in the face of power."

Then he walks back down the hallway. Each footstep a blow as sharp as a knife.

Chapter Thirty-Five

unlight filters through a series of even, square windows that line the border of the elegant bedroom. A canopy bed with sparkly pink drapes and dusty-rose-colored blankets rests directly in the center of the room, a circular rug beneath. On the perimeter of the room is a birch desk, my satchel waiting patiently for me to reclaim it, a hand-carved wooden chair, a white settee, and a low birch bookshelf. A few tomes already line the shelves, caked in dust.

I wonder who lived here before, if anyone did at all. The room gives the impression of a show room, designed to make you fall in love with the possibilities, but, just like everything else I'm discovering, it's fake.

I pick up my satchel, digging through it, desperate to discover if Aaron or his vampire lackeys took anything from it. I set the ink pot and quill on the desk, hugging my journal to my chest. It still smells of Glaven; blossoms, honey, *springtime* eternal.

I place the journal carefully on the desk and glare at Samantha, her presence makes me uncomfortable.

"You can leave. It's not like I'm going to run away," I growl, not daring to turn my back on her again.

She's standing just inside the doorway, hand on the hilt of her dagger, expression sheepish as if she shouldn't be here, but can't find it in herself to leave. She ducks her head. "If that is what you wish, Emilia."

I bristle as she turns to leave, calling over her shoulder that she'll be back to collect me for dinner. The windowless door closes behind her, trapping me in a cell much finer than the one in the dungeon. A cell is a cell, though, even with luxuries and cushions, and windows too high up to crawl out of.

I lean against the carved post of the bedframe; the light wood twists and spirals, oak leaves are intricately carved into flat segments of the post, bordering thin, lacey vines. I look up through the windows, enjoying the bright sunshine.

I sit down at the desk and pick up the quill, dunking it in the ink pot. I flip to the first new page in my journal. In rough, heavy-handed scripture, I pen one simple word. My new task to complete. The only thing that'll prevent my mind from spinning, from questioning how I could've stopped

Aaron, how I could have saved Soph and Jax.

Even thinking of their names makes my chest ache. Tears splotch the ink and paper.

o *Revenge.*

If only it's as simple and easy as writing it, as reading the word over and over again. Revenge will take time, patience, and an opportunity.

If an opportunity presents itself to bring Aaron to his knees, I won't hesitant. I won't let my sister's, my friend's, names disappear; their deaths become meaningless.

My journal is spread open in front of me, my quill is tight in my hand, and I begin to dream of a time when this is all over, when I'm back with my friends. When Aaron and Aridam is a thing of the past.

For some reason, when I try to imagine it, I hit a barrier, a block in my mind preventing me. Goosebumps speckle my skin and I rub them away. Maybe it's a sign that nothing good is in store for me. That my future was sealed the instant I returned to Glaven.

There's a knock on my door, and I stir, my face splotched with tears and ink. I push my journal away, slamming it shut. And try to compose myself to the best of my ability, and with the limited time Samantha gives me before just barging in. I rub the sleep from my eyes and straighten my ruined skirt, raising my chin in defiance. Sure, the king commanded that I ready myself for presentation. Though he should've expected me to do anything but that.

Samantha's face is poised, as expressionless as stone. With her hand on her dagger and her blonde hair swept behind her, she nods toward the doorway, her voice cold and distant, "Come now, Emilia. King Aaron is awaiting you in the dining hall."

I don't move, contemplating if I even have a choice in what happens to me. Not anymore, I determine. I lost that right the moment I fell into Aaron's trap. The sunlight drifting down from the windows is golden, fading away to the coming night. It gives a bit of color to my skin as I pass under the rays, warming the chill that seems constant.

I pass Samantha without as much as a word, a look. She's nothing more than a guard, a servant of the Dark king. She's no longer my friend, my dear Samantha whom I felt so guilty for leaving behind. To think I once cared for such a monster.

She walks behind me, occasionally barking a

direction on where to turn, in which I comply—how else am I going to survive this prison? Compliance feels worse than torture. As if, with every turn, I'm losing a part of myself.

The hallways are tiled with a dark, textured stone. Lava rock, I believe. The walls are equally as dark and strangely slick. As if this entire palace was carved from a mountain.

Torches line the walls in brackets resembling metal hands. Light flickers across the walls, the floor, and my feet as I pass by.

The archway at the end of the tunnel is flooded with sunlight. My breath hitches, wondering if it could possibly be open to the outside. I quicken my footsteps, ever so slightly, desperate to feel the wind on my skin again. To feel the grass beneath my feet.

But the dining hall is enclosed, a ceiling of glass watching tall pines sway outside, the sun sinking lower. The sky is streaked with pink and orange, and my eyes water. Is this the only beauty I'll ever see again? The sky, fading into darkness.

I bring my gaze back down to the dining hall, which is long, with a table stretched in the middle. It's dark and polished to a shine, knife marks mar the surface where simple white, ceramic plates are donned. At the farthest head of the table sits Aaron, a black fur cloak spilling onto the floor, a crown resembling the bones of fingers donning his head of styled hair. His black eyes watch me, taking in my still disheveled appearance, and he scowls. A small victory.

Then I take in the rest of his servants at the table…the only spot left open is the opposite spot to Aaron. I swallow as I take the seat. Samantha pushes my chair in; the legs of which scrape against the ground, creating an ear-splitting shriek.

Adriene sits directly to my left, studying me with his shark eyes.

I clench my fists in my lap, digging my nails into my palms, avoiding his gaze. He abandoned me. I thought we had each other's backs. I thought… I bite my cheek. Trusting Adriene was yet another bad decision, a mistake marring my past.

"My love, thank you for joining us this evening," Aaron calls, his voice booming around the hall, ringing with power. He spreads his hands to either side, a cocky smile tugging at his lips—as if he's won. *Won me.* "This evening is particularly special. We have everyone of importance here. My right hand has returned." He dips his chin toward Adriene, who bows his head. "And my queen." He gestures toward me this time and my stomach curls. I feel sick. "Shall we dine in celebration? A dance will be held afterward. A dance to welcome this next chapter of our lives." He lifts his wine glass toward the ceiling; the red liquid sloshes against the rim, a drop spilling onto his plate.

The rest of his Shrouds follow, lifting wine into the air. They don't say anything, which is more unsettling than if they did.

Then they settle into mindless chatter with each other when butlers drift into the room on silent feet, setting silver-domed platters in a row on the center of the table. They lift the domes off and I gawk at the spread.

This isn't food.

On the platter closest to me is a pile of bugs, drowned in a potent sauce. A beetle crawls across the top, trying to escape the mass murder of its friends.

I gag, my face paling.

I can't help peering over the pile of bugs to see what else there is to eat. My stomach bottoms out and my vision blurs. Repulsion is too weak of a word to describe what I feel as the people on either side of the table reach forward with their forks, skewering eyes on the ends and pushing them onto their plates before eagerly going back for seconds.

Eyes…with the muscles still attached.

Adriene plops one onto his plate and I get a closer look; to my relief, they don't appear human. The pale iris is green, the pupil a long slit in the center. I don't know what kind of creature they came from.

I scoot back in my chair, still disturbed.

The eyes of defenseless creatures...scooped out without consideration of leaving them blinded, mauled. These people aren't just monsters... They're psychopaths. Murderers. Devils incarnate.

Aaron chuckles, raising his hand into the air and tilting back his head. The severed rat tail wiggles as he drops it into his mouth. "Don't like the spread, my dear?"

I shove out of my chair, looking aghast at the behemoths on either side of me.

Adriene watches me with distant, detached eyes as if eating parts of brutally mutilated animals is perfectly normal.

I know there's nothing I can say that'll get through to them, so I swallow down my rising bile and sit back down. My appetite is lost now, not like I had much of one, to begin with.

I stare down at my plate, waiting for this to be over. The sounds of them smacking their lips, biting into the soft texture of the eyeballs, and slurping down rat tails like spaghetti, drills into my brain. Playing alongside the sound of my sister choking to death, the sound of her blood dripping off her desk and staining the carpet. The sound of Aaron's blade sliding through Jaxon's heart. Tears flood my eyes, dripping onto my empty plate. I don't even care if they notice, if they judge me. I feel numb, like I'm dying inside, losing myself.

"It's not too late," someone whispers, so quiet, it can't be heard over the chaotic din from the other side of the table. But I hear it. My head snaps up to stare at Adriene, who's attentively not looking at me. He's chewing on a bug—the beetle's little legs squirm from the corners of his mouth, trying to escape the jaws of Death.

For a brief moment, I think I'm going crazy—that no one said anything after all until he speaks again. His lips part so little that to anyone else it'd seem he was just chewing.

"Aaron saw two paths this can go."

I drop my gaze back to my plate, refusing to give away our conversation.

"The ball tonight will determine which path you choose," he whispers, swallowing the beetle. He stabs another on his plate, bringing it to his lips. "Aaron can't see how everything will end, that's why he needed to send spies to the Earthen Realm and your palace. He doesn't know how this is going to go. But…if you take the opportunity presented to you, you'll be free of him."

"Free? Really?" I whisper to my plate, rubbing my hand under my eyes to wipe away my drying tears.

Adriene swallows again. "That's all I can say. Just watch for the opportunity."

I nod, conversation dwindles and the sound of chairs scraping back floods the dining hall that's pitched in moonlight now.

"To the Eastern Ballroom, shall we?" Aaron asks, leading his pack of ghouls down the hallway. I trail behind, close to Adriene's side. Maybe he didn't abandon me after all. Maybe he was just surviving the only way he knew how.

Adriene and I are in the back of the pack, looking straight ahead at the backs of Aaron's soldiers, flickering in torchlight.

His fingers brush mine, and I know he's returning the favor. The night I comforted him at the inn... He's now comforting me, through the only way he can. A discrete touch in the darkness.

Take the opportunity. Keep your eyes open. I raise my chin higher. *I can be free.*

Chapter Thirty-Six

The Eastern ballroom is a wide cavern—chandeliers made from the bones of dead animals hang from the stalagmite-covered ceiling. Water drips from the stalagmites, rippling in puddles littering the cave floor. Torches line the walls, evenly spaced from each other. Torchlight flickers across the carved, uneven walls and across the parade of Aaron's men.

There's a quartet in the center of the room, violins are perched against chins and cellos are supported by arms, ready to be played.

The musicians' eyes have color. They don't look like the rest of Aaron's Shrouds with emotionless shark eyes. Maybe the Veiling didn't touch them. I glance over at Samantha, who's hovering near the entryway to the ballroom. She's staring at one of the chandeliers, her mouth set in a stern, resigned line. Her eyes aren't black either. But isn't she a Dark mage? I turn away. Samantha doesn't deserve any more of my consideration.

Adriene moves away from me, taking the arm of a woman, brandished in metal armor. The quartet begins to play a slow, methodical melody that brings a chill down my spine.

"My love, will you give me this dance?" Aaron asks, sidling up next to me, his arm poised for me to take it.

I don't want to, but by the way his shark eyes glint, I know it's not a question. I don't have a choice. I loop my arm around his, the music surges, rising into a heart-thudding crescendo, as he pulls me onto the dance floor.

Bodies mingle around us, heads thrown back in gaunt laughter. The way these monsters dance is almost practiced, as if they've danced every day of their lives. How many balls does the Dark king host?

I catch sight of Adriene as he twirls with the woman. He's elegant on the dance floor. The mass of his body has returned, filling out the sharp angles of his jawbones, of his wrists and ankles. He looks normal now—as normal as Death can look, in immortal human form.

He catches my eyes and something sparks in the swirling black of his. *Look for the opportunity*, I can almost hear him whisper.

So, I return my attention to Aaron. His touch against my skin, against the thin material of my ravaged dress, is enough to make my stomach turn.

If I pay attention, if I take advantage of the opportunity that presents itself, as I promised the memory of my sister, Jaxon, and Trelia that I would, then I'll be free. He won't ever touch me again.

Samantha pushes off her post near the door, weaving through the twirling mass of bodies. In the light from the chandeliers and torches, the dagger at her waist—the one she's rested her hand on every time I've seen her—glints. She's so close now, so close I can hear the sound of the blade sliding from the sheath. The blade glints with a thin trickle of torchlight. She pushes past a couple dancing; they grumble about her rudeness but she doesn't stop. Her hazel eyes are locked on me. Instinctually, I know what I have to do. I know what opportunity Adriene talked about.

The room seems to pause; the couples stop mid-step, as eyes land on me and Aaron with feverish curiosity. As if they've awaited this moment their entire lives.

Aaron saw it coming. He's waiting to see which choice I make.

Samantha withdraws the dagger completely. She stops beside me, resting the blade casually in her palm and vanquishing the hilt to me. It's thin and elegant, just as I was told Aridam was. Spider-web designs make up the hilt and the blade is jagged as if the rest of it was broken away.

My heart stutters and my mouth opens and closes like a fish gasping for air. "Is that—"

"A fragment of Aridam? Yes, it is, my love," Aaron answers breezily, as if presenting the one person who longs to kill him the most with the cursed blade that doomed her kingdom is a smart idea.

"But I was told it broke."

"It did. But not all of it shattered."

The room is deathly silent, deathly still. More of a tomb than a ballroom.

I lift my chin, searching for Adriene over Aaron's shoulder. It's odd, the stillness. People waiting to see what choice I make. But what choice is there to make? Either decline the blade, or take it? And do what with it?

I spot Adriene, who's snaked through the crowd and now stands on the outer ring, watching me with such an intensity that my skin pricks. He is Death and he is waiting for me to play my hand.

Samantha moves the blade closer to me, directing her gaze elsewhere.

I take it, my hand shaking as I grasp the hilt, as I lift it in the space between me and Aaron.

His shark eyes linger on my face, tracing the curves and hollows, the tear stains and caked dirt. "You have a choice, my love." His voice rings through the cavern and the quartet dart their bows across their strings, the tempo rapidly increasing before dying out with a nail-biting shriek. "You can either take the blade, keep it, and rule side-by-side with me." He reaches out, caressing my cheek with a singular, cold knuckle. "Or you can take the blade, vanquish me, and take on the curse bestowed upon the rulers of Nether."

"So I either become your queen, and keep my sanity, or I…"

"Lose yourself to the Veiling, and become the lone Queen Emilia of Nether," Aaron explains. He appears patient for someone whose fate hangs precariously in the small space between Aridam and his heart.

Either I am a prisoner, wrought with my morals and my grief, destined to live a life beside a man whom I could never love again. Or I am a queen, without morals, without grief, without a care for anything but spreading the Veiling. If I kill him, as I long to do, then I become him.

I become the one person I hate the most.

I meet Adriene's eyes again, searching for an answer. A spark of wisdom. Something that'll direct me. Do I really have to make this decision on my own?

Time seems to slow as I stare at the blade in my hand. I can see my warped reflection in it; my disheveled brown hair, hanging around my shoulders in greasy clumps. My face windblown with dirt, clean streaks carved by my tears. I blink, unsure. But what did I promise Soph and Jax? I promised them that if an opportunity presented itself, I would take it. I would wreck my revenge upon Aaron.

So I shall.

I raise the blade, my grief, my rage, powering my hand as I thrust it toward his chest. His face falls when he realizes what choice I've made, what path I'm going to take, but he's too close to move away.

The blade cuts through his skin, his muscles, tearing into his heart. Red blooms from the wound, like the petals of a macabre flower, spreading outward, staining his shirt. Blood spots my fingertips as I shove the dagger through him, up to the hilt. He sputters, life draining from him, paling his face.

The crowd gasps before falling back into the unsettling quiet.

Aaron stumbles back a step, hand clutching at his fatal wound. My fingers itch for the dagger, to pull it out before thrusting it in again. Over and over until he's gone. Until he screams for mercy and I get to choose not to show him any. But his death isn't as satisfying as I wanted.

For he just falls to his knees, his mouth forming an inaudible word as blood seeps from the corners, staining a path down to his chin. Then he's gone, falling forward, his skull cracking against the stone and a puddle of blood quickly spreading from beneath him.

I don't move as the blood nears, as it forms around my feet. And I don't move as it floods over my shoes, inching up my legs, across my skin, slicking my dress and dying it crimson. It slithers like a living, tangible creature toward my face; creeping over the ridge of my chin and spreading open my lips. Sulfur and iron bathe my tongue. I shake my head, clawing at my face to get it to go away, shaken from my stupor. It pushes down my throat, blocking air from reaching my lungs and I start to choke on the thick current of blood.

Adriene watches me struggle, his fingers itching at his sides, though his face doesn't convey any emotion.

I'm dying now. At least, that's what it feels like. Being suffocated, choked, and drowned, by tangible evil. This must be the Veiling, passed on through the rulers of Nether. Crimson drips onto the floor around my feet, into the thin puddle that still stains the stone. My head snaps forward; pressure burns my veins, and my muscles, as if bugs are crawling under my skin, tearing my ligaments and stitching them back together. I attempt to scream, but it comes out a hollow moan. I spit onto the ground, desperately trying to get rid of this awful, acrid taste.

Samantha steps into Aaron's blood, watching me scratch myself, claw at my face and my arms, so feverishly it looks like I'm trying to rip my skin off.

She drops into a curtesy and the rest of the conglomeration follows suit. It takes me a minute to realize who they're bowing to—for their king is dead. Until it dawns on me that they're bowing to me.

Now I'm the queen, and the blood soaking the ballroom floor...is his.

After

 stare at myself in the mirror. My hair is neatly combed and braided down my back, my skin is pale and clean, and the dress falling from my shoulders in silky-black waves is covered with intricate sparkles embroidered in spirals. A stitched-on moon curves above my breast, along with a series of tiny, detailed stars. The dress is slit above my left thigh, revealing my moon-kissed skin to the unearthly glow of torches.

It's been two weeks since I slayed the Dark king, since Aaron's blood pooled around my feet. And, for those two weeks, I haven't emerged from my private room even once. I can feel the Veiling growing within me, festering until my thoughts turn to violence, to murder, to causing mayhem. The guilt that used to wash over me at the mere thought of my little sister and of Jaxon has long since diminished. I can still hear the sound of the blade ending their life, but now the sound sends a gentle tingle of satisfaction down my spine. I know I should be terrified…for this is not who I am. But as I lean closer to the gilded bronze mirror, watching my hazy reflection, I see the blackness of my eyes. I can't remember the color they once were. Nor do I care very much. Precious little Princess Em is gone.

I am Emilia Strazenfield, Queen of Nether and Bringer of Death.

I run my hand over the soft fabric of my dress, feeling every stitch and bead under my fingertips. With the Veiling coursing through my veins comes an unexpected surge of my senses. I can smell the blood seeping from the mauled creatures floors beneath my room. I can hear their pitiful calls for help. I can hear the dark chuckles of my people as a blade cuts through the air. I can almost taste the mutilation, the satisfying, victorious taste of power.

A smile stretches my lips and I turn to the door of my room, securing a black fur cloak that rests on the end of my canopy bed around my shoulders. The cloak is still flecked with Aaron's dried blood. I like the feel of it under my fingertips, so I never found it in me to wash it away. Let me wear a part of the past king. Let me feel his presence with me, watching me as I rule the land that was once his.

I open the door and step into the drafty hallway. Torchlight flickers across the cloak, catching on every stiff strand of fur. A servant wanders by me, a broom in hand. He does a double take, vivid fear in his brown eyes. He drops into a stiff, slightly awkward bow, pinching the handle of the broom beneath his arm. I nod my dismissal and he quickly scurries away.

I turn back to the hallway, following the scent of cooking food. My footsteps ring about the arid caverns. Stalagmites drip stale water, matting sections of my cloak.

I stop in front of an archway on a floor beneath mine and peer inside. It's a kitchen; stoves are lit and counters are vibrant with vegetables and insects, every color of the rainbow represented on each platter.

The chef spots me; he's a tall, fat man with a long, brown beard. His eyes aren't dark. Instead, they're a jovial blue. I stare into his eyes for a while; blue eyes. Who did I know who had blue eyes? Who of significance? I scrunch my brow, trying to figure it out. It'll drive me mad not to remember.

Though, I suppose it's too late for that.

I watch as the chef grabs a handful of wiggling insects: beetles, worms, and butterflies. He raises the knife to chop them into pieces, but I stop him. He looks at me in shock, but understanding soon dawns on him. He offers me the handle of the knife. "Did you want to do the honors, Your Majesty?"

I glare at him, picking the butterfly up by a purple wing. It has dark purple tendrils that trail behind it. "No, you fool. Don't kill the butterflies."

He raises an eyebrow, mouth turning into a little 'o'. "May I ask why, Your Majesty?"

I snarl at him, cupping the butterfly in my hand. Its wings are gentle against my fingers, almost tickling, as it tries to escape. I've always feared butterflies—*that* I remember. But now...seeing it so helpless, so fragile... "Let the butterflies live. Send them to the alchemist—unharmed."

"The alchemist?" The chef looks at the staff around him, blanching. "We don't have an alchemist, Your Majesty."

"No alchemist?" Of course they don't have an alchemist. This kingdom doesn't have a single person of use. "Then who do we have craft elixirs?"

"Well, we've been going to Adriene, Your Majesty," the chef stammers, dropping his gaze to the butterfly in my clutches.

"Adriene." His name rolls smoothly off my tongue. I haven't seen him since the night I killed Aaron, since the night I became his queen. Maybe now is the right time for a visit. "And where can I find him?"

"Down in the dungeons. That's where his room is," the chef answers, gesturing toward the staircase on the other side of the wall—the one that'll take me down onto the next floor of the palace—with the tip of his knife.

"Perfect. Send all the butterflies down to him. Immediately," I demand, turning with a last sharp, controlling look. He quakes under my gaze. I exit the kitchen and begin my descent toward the dungeons. The metallic stench of blood gets stronger with each step. The creatures' brutal cries get louder. I step off the final set of stairs and into the dingy hallway where I spent my first few hours imprisoned.

I pass my cell with a scornful glare and head down to the door at the end of the hall. It's dark, carved from the wood of a dying, grayish tree. Etched into it is the depiction of a person shrouded in a cloak and hood, a scythe clutched in his hands. Has this always been Adriene's room? I knock on the door—though I really don't need to—and Adriene opens it almost immediately. He startles when he realizes it's me.

His white hair is disheveled and his shark eyes are blurry with sleep. I peek behind him to a desk scattered with papers. An oil lamp is flickering, almost burnt out. His room is small; an iron-framed bed rests against the left wall, and on the right is a short, packed bookshelf. Bits of paper poke out from the books as if he's annotated every single page.

"I have a request of you," I say, returning my attention to him.

His lips quirk up in a daring smirk. "And what

does the Dark queen want of me?"

I push him aside and step into his room. I open my hands, showing him the scared, desperate butterfly. "Can you turn these into servants of my crown?"

He gives me a skeptical look. "Butterflies?"

"Yes. Can you do it or not?" I snap.

Adriene takes the butterfly from my hands and examines it. "What are you going to use them for?"

"Spies, of course. Versatile, discrete. I'll be able to keep an eye on everything happening outside of the kingdom without traveling there myself. Since I don't share Aaron's particular gift, I'll need more spies than even he planted. Besides, there's still a war coming, Adriene. You and I can both sense it," I explain.

He considers my words, eyeing the butterfly as it attempts to flutter from his palm. "I think I can come up with some kind of elixir that'll make them obedient, loyal even." He purses his lips and his eyes flick from the butterfly up to me. "Though it'll take time. I'm a bit rusty at alchemy."

"You did spend two years rotting away in a cell, Adriene," I respond, stepping around him to the door. "Why'd you do that anyway?"

He turns to face me, white rimming his eyes momentarily. "Because I knew that if you were the only one destined to take down Aaron, then you'd need guidance. I waited," he steps toward me, "for you, my queen."

"A foolish choice," I hiss between my teeth as his fingers raise to caress my cheek. "You sacrificed two years of your life. Foolish, indeed."

"Two years is meaningless to an immortal," he answers. His touch is cold, corpse-like.

I step away from his touch, back toward the door. The hisses and moans of the tortured creatures are loud as if it's coming from the room mere feet away. The stench of their sweat, urine, and blood is intoxicating. The scent of power is intoxicating, should I amend. I shiver with ecstasy, their pain compelling me. Appalling, I'm aware. Em would've broken down and cried, and I know I should break down and cry, curl up in a ball, and weep for the poor, defenseless animals. But I don't... I feel their pain as if it's my own, and I revel in it. Does Adriene feed off the pain around him, just as I seem to? Or is it a trait particular to those holding the crown? In little time, I'm sure I'll find out. Another shiver courses through my body and I roll my neck, a rather feline, somewhat monstrous purr parts my lips.

Adriene steps toward me again, tilting his head as he inspects my eyes. His face is pale in the murky lighting. "Careful, your Veiling is showing, Emilia."

I bare my teeth in a genial, slightly morbid grin. "Let it."

To be continued…

~Acknowledgments~

Thank you so much for picking up *Return of Eve*, and delving into Emilia's adventure. If you enjoyed it, I'd appreciate it if you left a review on any platform of your choosing. And, if you're excited about the second book, you can follow me on any of my social media platforms to be the first to know when it's being released.

I want to give a massive thank you to my family and loved ones, who've done nothing but encourage me, help me, and fuel me with the determination to follow my dreams. I am endlessly grateful for every single one of you.

~About the Author~

Daphne Paige has always loved writing; watching and learning from her mother, who's also a writer. With the majority of her time spent writing, the breaks between stories makes her remember she has an actual life away from her characters. During those breaks, she loves to play video games, hangout with her various pets, and watch classic black and white films with her family. Daphne lives in Oregon helping her family with their popcorn business.